POSEUR

The Good,
the Fab
and the Ugly

POSEUR

The Good,
the Fab
and the Ugly

a novel by
Rachel Maude

Illustrations by Rachel Maude

Do-it-yourself patterns by Compai

poppy

LITTLE, BROWN AND COMPANY
New York   Boston

Poppy

Little, Brown and Company
Hachette Book Group USA
237 Park Avenue, New York, NY 10017
Visit our Web site at www.lb-teens.com

First Edition: October 2008

The Poppy name and logo are trademarks of Hachette Book Group USA

ISBN 978-0-316-06584-9

10 9 8 7 6 5 4 3 2 1

CWO

Printed in the United States of America

Book design by Tracy Shaw

For Gabe and Jess

The Girl: Charlotte Beverwil
The Getup: Crimson satin sheath by Narcisco Rodriguez, diamond briolette necklace by Chopard, and black patent slingbacks with matching black patent bow clutch by Christian Louboutin.

The Girl: Janie Farrish
The Getup: Backless gunmetal silk gown by Dries Van Noten, stacked diamond cuffs by Van Cleef & Arpels, silver mirrored leather peep-toe pumps by Chloe Eloise Ricoperto, and silver/gold tone lizard clutch by Bottega Veneta.

The Girl: Petra Greene
The Getup: Organic tulle toga by Behnaz Sarafpour, diamante platform sandals by Stella McCartney, and narcissus flower coronet by Nature.

The Girl: Melissa Moon
The Getup: Oh No She Didn't.

"Thank you! Thank you so *much!*" Melissa Moon cried to her adoring audience. Except she hadn't quite reached the microphone, so from *their* point of view she was mute as a puppet — a brightly glossed mouth flapping a series of silent O's punctuated by the unexpectedly loud ". . . *uch!*" Melissa refused to fret. Of course, they'd *assume* she'd expressed her thanks, and hadn't, for example, told them they were "Too ugly! Too ugly to *touch!*" This was the Academy Awards, after all, and her audience knew as well as she did: No Ugly People Allowed.

Well . . . at least not in the first two rows.

Melissa hugged the small gold man-trophy to her chest, wedging him deep into her jutting shelf of cleavage, while directly behind her, her esteemed colleagues gathered into a giddy half-moon. POSEUR, their new fashion label, had just won the Oscar for Best New Fashion Label — a category invented just for them. For the occasion, esteemed colleague number one, Janie Farrish, wore a stunning bias-cut gown in gunmetal satin, perfectly complimenting her elastic height and willowy limbs (and successfully disguising her somewhat wimpy personality). The petite and porcelain Charlotte Beverwil chose a strapless floor-length sheath in deepest crimson, a color as fiery and dramatic as she was (behind her cool and placid demeanor, that is). And Petra Greene, the reluctant Goddess of the group, donned an ethereal, one-shouldered toga dress in shimmering champagne tulle, her honey-hued locks crowned by a fragrant coronet of white narcissus, the flower symbolizing vanity (which Petra was anything but). Not that anybody noticed the flowers, the satin, or the crimson. Tonight, all eyes were on Melissa, who — for reasons she could not recall — had appeared in her underwear. She toyed with feeling embarrassed, and then brushed off the impulse. After all, she *had* worn her Agent Provocateur leopard-print stretch chiffon pushup bra with the matching low-rise bikini. And really . . .

Could you get more red carpet than that?

"This is just too amazing!" She gushed (into the mic this time) while the other three girls dutifully retreated from the limelight. As director of public relations, Melissa handled *all* POSEUR communication — including (she'd hissingly reminded them as they mounted the polished ivory stage stairs) Oscar speeches. "When I was a little girl" — she cleared her throat, assuming a serious tone — "growing up in the dog-eat-dog streets of South Central Los Angeles, I would not have dared to dream that I would one day wind up here, behind this podium, accepting this . . ." She held the small-yet-weighty Oscar aloft, and her dark almond eyes, which flaunted real fox-fur eyelashes, batted away her sparkling tears. "This incredible award!"

The star-studded audience churned into an exuberant round of applause, and diamonds, like sea spray, glittered on their wrists: clearly they were moved by her tale of woe. So many obstacles. Such struggle! Of course, Melissa was more *born* in South Central than she actually *grew up* there (she'd boasted one uber-exclusive Bel Air address or another since the age of three). But, seriously. Why bore them with technicalities?

"My hope," she breathed, clenching her paraffin-pampered fist, "is that our success with POSEUR serves to inspire young girls all over the world. No matter who you are, or where you come from — if you *believe* in yourself, if you *work hard* — you can rise above your circumstances, and . . ."

But before she could say *become a star,* her attention diverted to the opposite end of the pavilion, where two great doors had just swung open, thudding dramatically against the adjacent wall. With a swell of creaking hinges and rustling fabric, the illustrious members of her audience craned around in their deep red velvet upholstered seats, murmuring loudly. There, on the crest of the long, unfurled red carpet, a mysterious figure emerged from the gaping theater entrance. Melissa shielded her eyes and tried to make out his or her identity, but the blinding white glare of the spotlights rendered this effort futile.

"Um, *excuse* me," she huffed, continuing to squint behind the visor of her hand. "I *happen* to be in the middle of a history-making Oscar speech?"

She glanced commiseratively to her audience, inviting them to share her incredulity, and found the rows of velvet seats empty. Her audience had disappeared! With a startled gasp, she whirled around. Janie, Charlotte, and Petra remained huddled together, smiling and clutching their awards, but Melissa could tell at once: *something was wrong.* Their clothes hung without movement, and their eyes stared, unblinking, and dull as stone.

"*Why* are y'all just standing there like a bunch of manne-quins?" As if to answer, Charlotte's arm creakingly dislodged at the shoulder, and clattered — pure plastic — to the floor. A sound like a moth wing fluttered inside Melissa's ear and, fighting off a paralyzing twist of dread, she turned around again. The faceless intruder loomed only a few feet away, shadowy hands gripping the corners of a large sack, the gaping sack-mouth moving toward her like a toothless shark. In a spasm of self-defense, Melissa threw her Oscar with all her might, realizing only too late what she had done. As the sack's mouth closed around her prize, she choked out a noise of regret. Warm breath filled her ear like a soupy fog, and a cool voice whispered:

"Trick or treat . . ."

Melissa startled awake with a long and terrified scream. She looked around, palm pressed to her wildly bucking heart, and took a moment to orient herself. She was in an absurdly opulent bedroom, in a palatial cliffside house, in exclusive Bel Air, California: nothing out of the ordinary here, right?

Exhaling her relief, she collapsed against some of the sixteen rose-and-cream-silk boudoir pillows piled high against her ornate, cream-and-gold Louis XVI headboard, and patiently waited for her father to come console her. She strained to hear the distant rumble of his footsteps, the low drone of his concerned voice, but the only sound to break the Saturday 2 a.m. quiet came from

Emilio Poochie. Her somewhat asthmatic cream-and-tan Pomeranian lay sprawled at the foot of her bed, snoring like a micromachine truck.

This was seriously not okay.

Whipping aside her hibiscus pink silk Frette sheets, she padded a quick path across her hand-knotted ivory Indian silk rug, cracked open her solid oak bedroom door, positioned her Strawberry Rosebud Salve-slathered mouth inside the two-inch gap of space, and (oh yes she did) she screamed again. Eleven seconds later, her half-asleep dad appeared at her door, wavering above his half-dead Bugs Bunny slippers, and fumbling for the hall switch.

"What happened?" Seedy Moon's distinct nasal voice, one of the most renowned in rap music today, cracked thickly with sleep. He found the switch and winced into the light. "You okay?"

"It's nothing, Daddy," Melissa reassured him from the bed, having perfectly rearranged herself into a position of dreamy repose. Her down-stuffed rose-bouquet duvet muffled her words. "I didn't mean to wake you."

Seedy's eyebrows tied into a knot of suspicion, and his dark eyes slid about her high-ceilinged, birdcage-shaped room. "Cafeteria Lady in here?" he asked, referring to Melissa's boyfriend of four months, Marco Duvall. Upon first meeting Melissa's father, Marco made the grave mistake of wearing a hairnet, hoping to impress Seedy as a fellow reformed thug — maybe earn his respect. Sadly for him, the only thing earned was his not-so-thuggish nickname.

"No, Cafeteria La . . . *Marco* is *not* here," Melissa scoffed. "And just 'cause he snuck in my room that *one* time . . ."

"One time is one time too many," Seedy cut her off, whipping aside the sliding mirror door of his daughter's wall-to-wall closet. He frowned, prodding the dark hanging clothes with his bunny-clad foot.

"Daddy, would you *stop?*" Melissa reached to drag the still-slumbering Emilio Poochie into her lap. She hugged him close, diminishing her voice to a plaintive squeak. "I had a real bad dream."

"You did?" Seedy plopped on the edge of her featherbed-topped mattress and she instantly relaxed into a smile; the tug of her father's weight on the end of her bed never failed to comfort her. Seedy smiled, too, squeezing the blanketed lump that was her foot. "What about?"

"Well . . ." She rubbed the furry point of Emilio's ear between her forefinger and thumb. "It started with I won the Oscar . . ."

"Oh no . . ." Seedy laughed. "*That* dream again?"

"Okay, would you please *listen?*" She scowled, waiting a punitive beat before she resumed. She recounted the whole dream-turned-nightmare, taking care to omit nothing, not even the most seemingly insignificant detail (well, except that bit about the underwear). "And after that" — she widened her almond-shaped brown eyes for dramatic effect — "I woke up screaming."

"Huh." Her compact-yet-muscular father squeezed his interlocked fingers, free of their customary jewel-encrusted rings, between his soft gray sweatpant-clad knees, and frowned. "Seems pretty obvious to me. I mean, we're getting into October now, right? It's a spooky time . . . Halloween around the corner . . ."

"Daddy!" Melissa grimaced with disapproval. "Halloween hasn't been 'spooky' since, like, the Middle Ages. And besides, that is the *obvious* interpretation. You got to get *beneath* all that. Crack the surface!"

"Okay, okay, lemme think." He closed his eyes, pushing his fingers deep into the sockets. After a moment, he removed his fingers and blinked.

"I got nothing."

Melissa smacked her overstuffed down comforter, launching a light-as-breath feather into the air. "It's about the person who broke into my contest. *Obvie!*"

By contest, of course, she was referring to the raffle POSEUR had organized for their now infamous label launch (also known as the "Tag — You're It!" party) one week ago, last Saturday. They'd been having major trouble picking out the perfect name for their new label, but (a few cat fights and one silent treatment later) Charlotte Beverwil proposed a simple solution: instead of naming it themselves, why not leave it up to their guests? It was, as Miss Frenchie-pants Charlotte herself might say, *un bon idée.* They mailed pink-and-black-lacquered invitations with small white tags attached, as well as instructions for the invitee to fill out the tag with the label idea of their choice. As their guests arrived to their swank-a-dank venue (the Prada Store on Rodeo), they dropped their completed tags into a clear globe-shaped safe (Melissa had chosen the globe to best convey her modest goal: to take over the world).

But "safe" their tags most definitely were not. Someone had busted the globe wide open — someone had *tagged* the *tags* — and scrawled one word, POSEUR, across each one.

"Until I find out who is responsible," Melissa ranted to her father, "how am I supposed to get a decent night's sleep? Ever since the launch, that crook's been all up in my *sub*conscious. Invading my dreams! It's like she, he — *whoever* — has broken into my *head*."

"Alright, alright, now hold up a minute." Seedy fixed his daughter with his sternest you-better-calm-yourself stare. "Do you remember why, despite everything that happened, you decided, *contrary to expectation,* to go ahead and name your label POSEUR?"

"Because," Melissa sighed. "It's a message."

"You remember that message?" Seedy asked. His daughter only shrugged, gently squeezing Emilio Poochie's padded foot; hard, moon-shaped nails, painstakingly manicured in Chanel's Blue Satin, protracted from the fuzzy ends of his toes. Her father believed naming the label POSEUR took away the word's negative power (he called it "appropriating the language of the oppressor"). Still, despite her best efforts, she couldn't *quite* let it go. "POSEUR" was maybe the worst thing someone could call you ever; it meant you weren't who you were; it meant "you" was just an act. And (this is what *really* nagged) who among them *was* the POSEUR? If the perpetrator of this heinous crime meant to implicate all four of them, then he or she would have written POSEURS instead of PO-SEUR . . . right? Who among them was the target?

Was it her?

"The message *is,*" Seedy continued to lecture, happily under the impression she was hanging on his every word, "*insults won't keep me down.* And as long as that message was heard — which *you know it was* — who cares about a little thing like 'who did it,' right? 'Who did it' is just secondary, unnecessary, *supererogatory* information!"

"Right," Melissa dutifully replied. "I guess."

Seedy kissed his daughter on the side of her Phytodefrisant-scented head and got to his feet, rolling his shaved head around his neck so it crackled. But as he shuffled toward the door, he heard her turn under her ironed sheets, releasing an extended, tragic sigh. *Oh man.* He winced.

Did she have *to sound so sad?*

"All that said," he surrendered, and waited for his daughter to turn under her blankets and blink at him from her downy pink pillow. "If it's real important to you . . . I could make some calls, you know. Try to figure this whole thing out."

"Oh, Daddy!" she gasped, causing the ever-dozing Emilio to squinch his eyes open and flatten his ears. "Thank you! Thank you so much!"

The Girl: Janie Farrish
The Getup: Vintage navy-blue welt-pocket pants by
Dickies, studded pink hipster belt from Jet Rag, and
ladybug girl tank by babyGap.

Janie directed her cranky old black Volvo sedan, which she shared with her sixteen-year-old twin brother, Jake, toward their private high school's entry, Winston Gate, which wasn't so much a gate as a breezy peach-stucco Spanish Colonial archway, and tapped the gas, soliciting one of the many mysterious noises in the Volvo's eclectic junk-heap repertoire: a frenetic clicking.

"Steady there, ol' Bess," Jake jokingly cooed, running a soothing hand along the car's weathered black dashboard. "It's gonna be *all right.*"

"Okay, *why* are you insane?" Janie bit the insides of her cheeks to keep from laughing, resuming what her mother liked to call "that simply *terrible, sullen* expression." She shook her silky straight, brown, bobbed hair away from her lash-shadowed, soft gray eyes. "I mean, ol' Bess? It's a *car,* Jake. Not a cow."

"What's so cowy about ol' Bess?" Jake asked, widening his dark brown eyes as if he were totally wounded. "Bess is a *beautiful* name," he insisted, offering the dash a final, loving pat. "Isn't it, Bessie girl?"

To their mutual shock, the stressed-to-the-max Volvo responded, not with a clicking noise, but with an actual, angry sounding *meeuuurrrrroooo*. One mutually stunned moment later, Jake and Janie turned to face each other, locked eyes, and promptly dissolved into laughter.

"It mooed!" Jake clenched his fists, his dark eyes bright with the miraculousness of it all. "It friggin' *mooed*!"

"Omigod," Janie squeakingly gasped, her earlier restraint a distant memory. "It's too perfect!"

With a final, offended *huff,* the abused Volvo crested the top of the drive, and Winston Prep's campus, with its Spanish-tile rooftops, spiraling staircases, terracotta courtyards, and tiered fountains, glinted dauntingly into view. Janie eased on the brake, allowing the Volvo to coast downhill, so by the time they rolled into the student parking lot, it percolated contentedly as a coffee-pot, barely audible above the outside racket. Teeming snarls of students in their Monday bests laughed and shrieked, hollering greetings above the heavy slam of luxury car trunks and doors, the buzzing thump of state-of-the-art speakers, and the staccato *pang-pang-pang!* of Marco Duvall's league-regulation basketball — just a final few hoops before the bell, *a'ight*? Jake and Janie grew quiet, their former exuberance squelched by a painful, if familiar, self-consciousness. According to an unspoken rule (at Winston, there were many) this particular lot, "the Showroom," was reserved for the most popular students. As Jake and Janie puttered toward lesser, underground parking — aka "the Cave" — they couldn't resist a wistful backward glance at a particular parking space, currently unoccupied, under the dappled shade of a Winston willow.

Hard to believe, but as early as the week before last, that spot had belonged to them.

"I hate myself," Jake muttered, and squeezed his dark brown eyes shut, blocking the spectacle of his squandered past. Due to some epically drunk behavior at his sister's Prada fashion thing the weekend before last, he'd somehow cheated on his supremely hot, now ex-girlfriend, Charlotte Beverwil, with a whatever eighth grader named Nikki Pepperoni (or something). The kiss was meaningless, as accidental as tripping — not that Charlotte cared. She'd dumped his ass like diarrhea.

"Don't hate yourself," Janie sighed as she cranked the wheel, winding the car into now the *third* level of this dank, subterranean wasteland. *I'll do the hating for both of us.* Okay, *not* that she hated her brother (she could never *hate* him), but could she seriously pretend she wasn't a *little* annoyed he'd so royally screwed things up? Breaking up with Charlotte meant so much more than just "breaking up with Charlotte"; it meant breaking up with *an entire Winston lifestyle*. Goodbye long lunches at Kate Mantellini, and lounging poolside at Charlotte's sprawling Hollywood Hills estate; goodbye romantic rides down Sunset Boulevard in her mint-condition cream-colored 1969 Jaguar, and prestigious West Wall seats at Town Meetings; goodbye to Cartier clocks ticking! But of all her brother's revoked privileges, Janie found his Showroom parking spot the most difficult to suck up and accept. After all, however indirectly, that parking place had belonged to *her*.

They crammed into the elevator with a handful of fellow

Nomanlanders, and one rumpled, coffee-reeking Winston faculty member, and pressed the glow-white button with the five-point star. Thirteen eternal seconds and one *bing!* later, they spilled into the terra-cotta-paved courtyard, blinking mole-ishly into the bleach white California glare. Jake and Janie were both on Accutane, a strong acne medication with bizarre side effects, for instance, trouble adjusting to changes in light. Janie re-squinted at their old parking space, now occupied by a glinting fire-engine red 911 Porsche, and sighed. That particular Porsche belonged to Evan Beverwil, Charlotte's brutally handsome older brother, who Janie had disdainfully rechristened "Alan," a term coined by her non Winston–attending best friend, Amelia Hernandez. "I mean, *Phantom Planet?*" she'd scoffed, referring to a sort of trendy band to which Amelia's own band, the up-and-coming Creatures of Habit, had been recently compared in *LA Weekly*. "Those guys are total ALANS." Off Janie's blank look, she'd impatiently clarified: "All Looks And No Substance?"

Janie secretly disagreed with her best friend's harsh take on Phantom Planet (they were good, okay?), but in the case of Evan Beverwil, she decided, the term totally applied.

Except . . . she got to thinking, having advantageously positioned herself at the Showroom's bustling periphery, the edge of her painted-black thumbnail firmly lodged between her teeth. *What if I'm wrong?* Evan leaned against his buffed Porsche fender, his almost-too-hot surfer-boy body aglow in the morning light, and frowned deeply into a beat-up paperback edition of *The Bell*

Jar, one of Janie's absolute favorite books. *Alans didn't read books by suicidal feminist poets, did they?* She sighed, liberating her mutilated thumbnail as he dipped his godly chin, ran his hand through his longish dirty blond hair and absently licked his middle finger. He pushed the moistened digit to the lower right-hand corner of the page, so that it (along with Janie's poor, baffled heart) arced up and flipped.

"Ironic," Jake remarked, and she blushed, paranoid he'd somehow divined her innermost thoughts. As the blush subsided, she realized his comment didn't refer to Evan, but to his car — or, more specifically, the classic Porsche emblem on the end of its glossy, sloping red hood. Against a shield backdrop, a silhouetted stallion kicked into the air, its sprightly mane like a flame.

"How is that ironic?" she asked.

"You know" — Jake shrugged with a tiny, defeated grin — "just that it's a horse. And not a cow."

"Oh," Janie forced a laugh. "Yeah . . . how embarrassing for him."

And then, as if to charitably save them from their lame joke, which only thinly masked their paralyzing envy, the bell rang.

The Girl: Charlotte Beverwil
The Getup: White fringed tweed strapless dress and black skinny-bow belt by Chanel, black suede ankle boots by Christian Louboutin, and aquamarine-white-and-black block print silk scarf by Lanvin.

Charlotte Beverwil pinched her aquamarine silk scarf at both ends, snapped it open, and guided its fluttering, floating descent to the assembly hall's cool, brushed concrete floor. For this Monday's school assembly, known to Winstonians as "Town Meeting," she'd worn her brand-new fringed white tweed dress — emphasis on the *white* — and planned to keep it *pristine* (emphasis on the *priss*). Her two best friends, Kate Joliet and Laila Pikser, chattered on either side of her, brainstorming sexy Halloween costumes, their bright eyes all but bolted to identical MAC compacts. Charlotte planted her ballet-butt on the square of designer silk, her long legs folded and modestly angled to one side, and propped her posture-perfect back against the West Wall. At the cool yet rough touch of brick, a pleasurable shiver of triumph ran up and down her spine. A West Wall seat not only broadcasted popularity, but also popularity of the very best (in Charlotte's humble opinion) type. West Wallers exuded elegance, culture, sophistication; they were classically beautiful, they were beautifully bored; and among these refined urbanites it was she, five-feet-two-inch-tall Charlotte Beverwil, who reigned supreme.

(Okay, technically Adelaide Dallas reigned supreme. But *only* because she was a senior.)

Two hundred and fifty plus students, grades seven through twelve, were already seated on the brushed concrete floor, buzzing like worker bees on a slab of honeycomb. Charlotte fluttered her starry black eyelashes and scanned the expanding swarm, her chlorine-green eyes alert for signs of her latest little project: Jules Maxwell-Langeais. Illegitimate son to French playboy racecar driver Marcel-Antoine Langeais and eccentric British socialite Minnie Maxwell, founder of luxury candle and fragrance chain "Minnie Maxwell, London," Jules's arrival to Winston had been the hot topic of Showroom gossip for weeks. Sadly, Charlotte had been far too wrapped up in Jake Farrish to pay attention.

Good thing *that* was over.

Okay, not that it *was* over. Not completely. Jake had been the first boy to weasel his way into her heart since Daniel Todd, the Australian fashion photographer to whom she'd lost her sacred virginity in Paris last spring. She'd feared her return to L.A. might tear them apart, but passionate Daniel had calmed her anxiety, dismissing their rupture as "mere geography." He promised to call, to write . . . or else throw his camera into the sea and never take photographs again (their *adieus* had been thrillingly tortured). But to Charlotte's anguished disbelief, he never contacted her again. As for throwing his camera into the Atlantic, well . . . a recent photospread in French *Vogue* suggested otherwise. Unless the subject of his shoot — a vacant eyed, pucker-mouthed, floaty-looking model

Kinga Fish! (very rare)

Janie Farrish

named Kinga — was *actually* a rare species of fish, Charlotte could safely assume Daniel Todd's Nikon D300 was *not* underwater.

As painful as the Daniel episode had been, the Jake Farrish fallout was a million times worse. She actually had to *see* him, five *excruciating* days a week, with his obnoxiously caressable dark brown hair, and his heartbreakingly familiar laugh. *Uccchh!* That he *dared* to laugh *at all*! Did he *not* realize he had cheated on her and they were living in a post-laughter world? Unless, of course, you counted the fact that she, the revered and ravishing daughter of Hollywood Royalty, had ever *deigned* to date him, the lowly and (until *very* recently) pimpled, pony-tailed spawn of Valley Village Peasantage. Even in a post-laughter world, *that* remained hilarious.

She attempted to recover in the usual ways — spa days at Pore House, shopping sprees at Ted Pelligan, fizzy peach cocktails at Chateau Marmont — but then she'd spot Jake in line at the food truck (that he *dared* to have an appetite!), and a week's worth of pampering — down the drain. By the time Monday rolled around, there was only one sensible, mature way to proceed . . .

Revenge.

She could give him a taste of his own medicine, she decided. Let him stew in his own rancid juices. As her bosom friend and neighbor, Don John, advised in his cheerful Texas twang: "nothing goes down harder than a good, old-fashioned Jealousy Julep. No sugar, straight up . . . and honey, make sure that cup is *chilled*."

"*Enfin,*" she gasped in French, springing her back from the West Wall. Having fixed her chlorine-green eyes on her target, she clutched Kate's bony knee with one hand, and shot the other into the air. "Jules!" she sang, fluttering her pearlescent fingertips. "Jules, over here!"

"Oh my God." Kate lowered her powder puff in shock and smoothed the immaculate fingerwaves in her platinum pixie cut behind her Jo Malone orange blossom-scented ear. "You *know* him?"

"Not yet," Charlotte trilled, as Jules, with a confused-yet-pleased expression on his face, carved a path through the floor-seated crowd, heading toward her while tying his wavy-ish black hair into a neat ponytail at the nape of his deeply tanned neck. Charlotte decided he was the spitting image of Orlando Bloom in *Pirates of the Caribbean* — *if* you could ignore the Eurotrash-tight

Rock & Republic jeans. She smiled. With his transcontinental accent, moneyed lineage, acid-green Ferrari, and guy-in-a-Folgers-ad stubble, Jules exuded everything Jake did not. And nothing rankles an ex more than moving on to his or her direct opposite. It's like saying: all those things I found oh-so-attractive about you? *Turns out I was lying.*

"Charlotte!" Laila cheeped in high alarm. A swooping wave of copper hair concealed her right blue eye, leaving the other to bug out for the both of them. "He's a *senior.*"

"*Mon dieu,* you have to be kidding." Charlotte beamed through her dear friend's complete idiocy. "Wasn't the guy you hooked up with at Villa, like, twenty-three?"

"Yeah, but he didn't go to this school!"

"Um . . . congratulations." Charlotte crumpled her porcelain brow. "You made zero dollars and no sense."

"Seriously, Lie." Kate clapped her compact shut, dropped it into her Tory Burch floral-print ballet tote, and sighed. "Don't be a leotard."

Charlotte giggled, rewarding her friend with a quick kiss on her freshly powdered cheek. "Listen" — she lingered, whispering into her tiny silver Me&Ro hoops — "do me *une petit faveur* and tell Janie Farrish she should sit with us."

"What?" Kate wrenched away with abject disbelief, her NARS lip-lacquered mouth agog. *"Why?"*

"Just do it," she hissed, before quickly tilting her face, fixing the

full light of her attention on Jules; he had arrived, finally, in the grand tradition of most Winston boys . . .

At her feet.

"Okay, everyone!" Glen Morrison gently leaned his buttercup-yellow guitar against the North Wall, tucked his wiry gray bangs behind his ears, and surveyed the boisterous student audience at his Jesus-sandaled feet. In addition to chairing Winston's estimable Social Studies Department and founding their bongo-therapy elective, Glen also found the energy to conduct the bi-weekly Town Meeting. As the babbling horde continued to ignore him, he clasped his hands and chuckled, shaking his shaggy head — the absolute image of parental indulgence. But behind his mild-mannered smile and crinkly brown eyes, there was a glow, a near-imperceptible pinpoint of hellfire.

Unless they shut up soon, he'd seriously lose his mind.

"We have a *lot* to take care of today, people! So please, settle down and take it down a notch, or two . . . or *three*." The hot light in his eye dimmed at the same rate the volume decreased. At long last: peace. "Thank you!" he exhaled. "Welcome to the first Town Meeting of October. As you know, October culminates with one of Winston's oldest and most anticipated events of the year: The Happy Hallow-Winston Carnival!"

The student body erupted into a round of whoops and hollers, and Glen straightened his posture, beaming. (He didn't mind outbursts of enthusiasm when he was directly responsible.) The Hallow-Winston Carnival served as a "fun way" to raise funds for ongoing Winston improvements: last year the board agreed to establish Doggie Day Care (Melissa Moon being their most impassioned and vocal advocate), and this year they hoped to install state-of-the-art cedar wood saunas for the respective boys' and girls' locker rooms. Not to say the piffling two-thousand-something dollars raised from an annual sale of pumpkin cookies, carnival rides, and raffle tickets could possibly cover one of their extravagant construction projects. But they could pretend, right? The Monday following the festival, Bronwyn Spencer would stand up at Town Meeting and say, *thanks to everyone's participation, our saunas are a go!* She'd clap her hands like a bored flamenco dancer while the good people of Winston hollered and cheered, congratulating each other for a *job well done.*

The following day their parents would mail in their checks.

But back to the present. While Glen blathered on about carnivals past and pending, Evan Beverwil seized his moment. Abandoning his seat at the Back Wall, he boldly clambered forward into the great uncharted masses. He tapped a few unsuspecting shoulders, muttering his polite excuse-me's, but all they could do was turn around and stare, identical masks of confusion on their faces. Peering eyes followed his journey into the crowd with wonder and vague concern. What was he doing? Who in their right minds left a coveted seat along the wall to sit here, with *them,* in No Man's Land?

He was like one of those poor whales that become disoriented and, like, beach themselves.

Oblivious to the silent tumult he'd caused, Evan planted his manly palm on a square vacancy of floor and settled into his new seat. Jake Farrish held his breath, the color draining from his boyish face, and forced a sideways glance. Evan trained his blue-green eyes on Glen, of course, but of his purpose Jake had little doubt: the day of reckoning had arrived. Jake had broken his little sister's heart, and Evan was here to kick some ass.

"Halloween may be about terror," Glen pontificated. "But it's also about *togetherness.* About ghosts . . . but also about spirit. *School* spirit!"

He braced for a second round of applause, but was met with a wall of silence. Jake watched Evan's strong tanned fingers drum the brushed concrete floor.

"Alright," Glen surrendered. "More on that later. Our special studies director, Miss Paletsky, has a few quick announcements . . . Miss Paletsky?"

As their cute (but in desperate need of a makeover) twenty-eight-year-old teacher shyly approached the mic, Evan flexed his mighty hand, releasing a series of menacing crackles and snaps. Jake clamped his eyes shut. He wasn't seriously supposed to just sit here and, like, *take* this, was he?

"Listen dude," he muttered under his breath. "Do you wanna

say something? Or did you just come here to show off your knuckle-cracking skills?"

Evan faced him with a blank stare.

"Because if it's the latter, man, I give you a ten. Okay?"

Evan scratched the sandy, golden stubble at his jaw, waiting out a wave of mild applause as Miss Paletsky bobbed into a little bow, heading back to her seat. He cleared his throat, frowning at the rubbery toe of his navy flip-flop. "Um" — his blue-green eyes flicked up to meet Jake's — "is it true Janie's into that book, um . . . *The Bug Jar,* or whatever?"

"What?" Jake crumpled with relief. Then again, he really wasn't in the mood to talk about Janie. She'd totally abandoned him to sit at the West Wall, which practically declared to the whole world that, yes, *she'd taken sides:* Charlotte was right and he, Jake, was wrong. In other words, she'd *publicly denounced* him — and for what? The cheap and ephemeral thrill of vicarious popularity? Could anyone be so pathetic?

Never mind he'd done the exact same thing to her last month.

And now, to make matters a million times worse, here was Evan Beverwil, politely inquiring into her reading habits. The dude could probably justify scalping Jake with a math compass, and yet he'd elected to just *sit* here, like, "being nice." Jake's relief subsided, making room for a slew of unsettling questions. Had his social status so dramatically nose-dived as to disqualify him from even the *smallest* act of vengeance? Or, perhaps, was Evan's present indifference an act of revenge in and of itself, as if to say: "Dude, I *hardly* need to punish you. Just *being* you is punishment enough."

"I guess she likes that book, okay," Jake begrudgingly replied at last. "Why?"

Evan shrugged, looking briefly pensive. "It's just, I was wondering if there was another book she liked? Because that one is kind of, like, weird."

"I don't get it." Jake's eyebrows collided. "You only read books my sister likes?"

"Uh . . ." Evan's pool-blue eyes stared, fixed on nothing, the black pupils afloat like tiny bobbing tops. "It's for an assignment," he replied, blinking at last.

"*Holler,* people!" Glen obligingly stepped aside as a white-glitter-tanked Melissa Moon leaned into the microphone, whipping her audience into insta-frenzy. She raised her toasted-almond brown arm and swiveled her platinum belly-chained hips, grooving to the beat of their applause. "Thank you. Just wanted y'all to know that our mystery label winner has yet to step forward and claim his or her prize. So, if any of y'all know *anything* . . ."

"You know what book she *really* likes?" Jake blurted under his breath, deciding to reward Evan's insultingly nice behavior with the most intensely vagina book he could think of, something that would make the feministy *Bell Jar* read like an issue of *Sports Illustrated*. He repressed a triumphant smile. *Are You There God? It's Me, Margaret.* In fourth grade, he'd picked it up, mistaking it for a companion piece to *Super Fudge* (both books are by Judy Blume, okay?), and got about ten pages in when the word *period* blazed from the page, and blinded him like a nuclear flash.

"Cool," Evan replied, scrawling the title on the back of his hand with a black razor-point pen. Jake rolled his eyes. No *way* was he going to read that shit. He'd have to be in love with Janie to get halfway through it. "Thanks," Evan murmured, click-closing his pen. "I appreciate it."

"No problem," Jake muttered, bumping Evan's fist. The student body dissolved into another round of applause.

Town Meeting was officially dismissed.

Just as it's near impossible to spot the one missing bead on a Swarovski crystal-beaded Christian Lacroix couture gown, student absences at Town Meeting typically passed by undetected. The most focused glance, for example, would not reveal the non-appearance of seventh grader Teddy Raisin (home in bed, glued to *General Hospital,* and stealthily tapping a thermometer to a light-bulb) or junior Bronwyn Spencer (locked in a bathroom stall, wailing into her cell, because anything less than an A in Chem and she could kiss her chances at Princeton — not to mention life — goodbye), or sophomore Tyler Brock (deep in the musty depths of the gym-equipment closet, plundering Coach Hollander's cherished stash of Haribo gummy bears). And then, of course, there was eighth grader Nikki Pellegrini, home sick in bed, because unlike oblivious little Teddy Raisin, *she* didn't have to *watch* soap operas for *her* daily dose of drama . . .

All *she* had to do was wake up.

The weekend before last, she'd kissed the love of her life, Jake Farrish, which *should* have been heaven, except he had a girlfriend, and that girlfriend happened to be Charlotte Beverwil, which meant heaven really had nothing to do with her situation. To put it simply:

She was in hell.

Charlotte was one of, if not *the* most, popular girls at Winston Prep — the kind of girl other girls looked to for inspiration: a style icon, a muse, a *tastemaker*. When she reinterpreted a pink leather crystal-studded Louis Vuitton dog collar as a bracelet, one in seven Winston Girls imitated the same look by the following week. When she dismissed Wayfarers (the retro-eighties sunglasses favored by sulky Starbucks-toting starlets) as "Way*overs*," she practically precipitated a schoolwide "Ban on Ray-Ban."

Charlotte decided what was in. Charlotte decided what was out. And (as poor Nikki was soon to discover) her influence hardly stopped at accessories.

Nikki logged on to her MySpace account to assess the ongoing collateral damage. As of yesterday, she'd suffered a few deleted friendships, a bitchy comment or two. But they'd proved mere foreshocks to the massive quake to come. In less than thirteen hours, a total of one hundred and ninety-four friends had dropped from her four hundred and fifty-one-person network. Far worse, someone had hacked into her account and *edited her actual profile.* Goodbye, Nikki Pellegrini, fourteen years old, from Hancock Park, California. She was now "Icki Prostitutti," general interests: "macking on your boyfriend," "spreading herpes," and "being a big-ass bitch."

No doubt about it, Nikki realized, baby-pink fingernails trembling above her Apple wireless Mighty Mouse. *I'm out.*

Unable to wrest her cornflower-blue gaze from the laptop screen, she'd reached for her pearl-pink Nokia flip-phone, and clumsily uprooted it, charger and all, from its Winnie the Pooh outlet. She had to contact Jake. Not just because she'd kissed him, but because *he'd kissed her too.*

Which meant they were in this together.

To: Jake Farrish
From: Nikki Pellegrini
Are you ok? ☺

She went outside and paced the gentle slopes of the private tree-lined lawn, eyes fixed to her phone, waiting for him to respond. The hours passed: shadows grew longer; sprinklers spattered and hissed; and then, terrifyingly, a black Bugatti sports car *verroomed* over the curb, barreling down the brick-paved drive toward their six-car garage. She gasped and staggered backward, her flimsy pink floral knee-length skirt aflutter in its wake, as the

Bugatti came to a screeching halt. The gleaming doors opened, unfolding into the air like insect wings, and revealed, at long last, the dreaded driver.

"You are trying to kill me?" Her father squawked, clutching the glistening gray curls on his Banana Tropic–tanned cave of a chest. With his scrawny neck, beaked nose, and shock of white hair, seventy-one-year-old Giovanni Pellegrini brought to mind a newly hatched chicken, a resemblance not lost on Lucia, his twenty-seven-year-old Brazilian girlfriend, who liked to call him "Clucky." He emerged from the ticking car, took one swipe at the lapel of his deep purple silk Valentino suit, and locked Nikki into his dark-circled gaze. "You are trying to give me an attack?!"

"No." Nikki cowered, hoping to appease his tyrannical heart. He ignored her, turning instead to address Lucia, who remained inside the gleaming black car, staring into the rearview mirror.

"Oh, Looocia!" he sang. "Perhaps you did not know my daughter has murdered me? Lucia, I am speaking to you from beyond the grave!"

Lucia picked the inside corner of her bored, mascara-encrusted eye. As founder and CEO of the legendary Italian lingerie line La Mela, Mr. Pellegrini thrived on a diet of non-stop attention, but if you desired *his* attention, it was better to pretend he didn't exist. Simpler said than done — not one of his previous wives *or* girlfriends (including Nikki's own mother, God rest her soul) managed to do it. Until, of course, reptile-hearted Lucia, who had the skill down pat.

The curvy black-rooted blonde exited the car — her dark eyes and spidery lashes now concealed by enormous black Fendi sunglasses — and headed slowly, tick-tock, to the main house.

"Never have I known such a sow!" Mr. Pellegrini cried to her retreating, Versace-clad, apathetic ass. Lucia didn't so much as twitch. She planned to ignore him all the way to the altar.

Unable to cope with her father's ridiculous antics on top of her far more serious stresses, Nikki fled to the secluded orange-tree grove along the west wall of their estate. Within the dense, citrus-scented shade, she listened to the noisy bustle at the main entrance: the jangle of jewelry and dog leashes, the rise and fall of her father's Italian-accented voice, the icy click of Lucia's stilettos, the door's resounding slam. Nikki sighed, twisting her hands. It was already dusk. The world was spinning, whether she wanted it to or not, and bringing her closer to all she dreaded most.

Monday morning.

"Nicoletta!" A weary old voice leaked into the twilight, croaking like a bog creature. "What are you doing out there? Digging like a gypsy in the leaves. You make me *pazzesco.*"

"Sorry, Nonna," Nikki addressed the last in a long row of windows on the estate's ground floor. "I didn't mean to disturb you."

"What is wrong?" Her grandmother coughed behind the antique lace curtains. "Are you *sique?*"

"No," Nikki squeaked. *If only I were sick,* she thought. *I wouldn't have to go to school.*

Wait a second.

"I-I mean *yes*," she stammered, cringing with guilt. She never, *ever* lied. "I . . . I threw up."

"*Il mio povero bambino!*" her grandmother cried. (Nikki wondered if nothing thrilled her grandmother so much as illness.) "Let me see you, *cara*. Come inside!"

She obliged, finding her Nonna exactly where she always found her: in bed, propped into place by plump virgin-white lace-trimmed pillows. Her four poodles — Belinda, Bambi, Fausto, and Spot — were curled into motionless balls, pinned like fur buttons on the four corners of her mattress. "What happened?" She lifted a thin, pale hand, beckoning her closer. "Why are you *sique?*"

Nikki perched on the mattress's outermost edge (she was only half-convinced old age wasn't contagious) and stared into her wrinkled cotton lap. "I have a sore throat," she ventured, amazed how easy it was to lie once you got started. "And, um, my stomach hurts."

"Terrible, terrible . . ." Her grandmother reached for a forbidden pack of Capri cigarettes. "Perhaps you went to another party last night like the one last weekend?" She stuck a cigarette in her mouth, squinting.

"No." Nikki flushed, still embarrassed by the memory. To her grandmother's concern, and her father's outrage, she'd come home drunk. Mr. Pellegini had threatened to send her to a nunnery, but her grandmother had intervened. "When I was her age I was pregnant . . . *with you*. If *I* learn from my mistake, *so* will Nicoletta."

"I promised I'd never do that again," Nikki reminded her, staring at the plush beige carpet.

"I know, *cara,*" her grandmother consoled her with a gravelly laugh. "I only ask to get your mind on other things. Because you are so *sique.*"

"I *am,*" Nikki emphasized, sounding more defensive than she would have liked. She sighed, looking at her lap.

"What is it?" Nikki the First exhaled, careful to direct the smoke away from her precious granddaughter's face. She smiled, settling back into her pillows. "Tell me."

"It's just . . ." She hesitated. "Something happened at that party. Something I didn't tell you." She confessed the final words in a whisper. "Something bad."

"Something bad? *You?*" Her grandmother laughed, bringing on a second fit of coughing. Clutching her heart, she reached for a glass of water. "Go on," she gasped after a sip. "Please, continue."

Nikki examined her grandmother's face. The wrinkled mouth, the rice-paper skin, the floating halo of downy white hair: *she is so . . . old,* Nikki surmised, resolving to change the subject. But then she looked into her eyes. They were a lively shade of blue, and bright — almost as if fourteen-year-old Nonna was *in* there, *watching* — merrily observing life from behind a ninety-two year-old's mask.

"Nonna." Nikki cleared her throat, summoning every ounce of her courage. "Do you, um . . . remember your first kiss?"

"Ach!" She collapsed against her pillows, and for a terrified

second, Nikki thought the question killed her. "I try to remember," she roused herself. "I must have been, what. Five years old? Six?"

"Not *that* kind of kiss," Nikki clarified. "I mean like a *real* kiss. Like the way adults do it."

"Adults!" Her grandmother rasped with laughter. "Adults do not kiss, *cara*. Only children."

"You don't understand," Nikki sighed, shaking her head. But her grandmother only smiled, patting her white knit blanket until she found her granddaughter's hand.

"So you kissed someone at this party?"

"Yes," Nikki confirmed in a whisper.

"This is what you call your *bad thing*. Why is this bad?"

"He . . . he has a girlfriend," Nikki stammered, once again unable to meet her eyes. "*Had* a girlfriend. They broke up because of me. And now she, like, *hates* me, and everyone *else* hates me, too, which isn't even fair because, it's not like I *meant* to do it! I just . . . Oh, Nonna. *I just like him so much.* I swear I've never, ever felt this way. Not about anyone *ever*." Her grandmother squeezed her hand, and Nikki's emotions rose in her throat. "It's like I *love* him," she choked. "And he won't even text me back!"

"Forget about this boy," her grandmother sniffed, mashing her fuming cigarette into a flowered, porcelain dish. "Men can rot in the ditches. Concentrate on the girl. Try to earn her forgiveness."

"Okay," Nikki blotted fresh tears with the backs of her wrists. "But . . . *how*?"

"You will think of something." She chuckled softly. Her eyes fluttered shut, and her chin sunk into the hollow at her throat. "I am sorry," she apologized, cracking her eyes open. "All of a sudden I am tired."

"Okay." Nikki nodded, sliding from the edge of her mattress, then hesitated. "I lied to you about being sick," she confessed in a rush. Her grandmother bobbed her nonexistent eyebrows and smiled.

"Yes . . . you are a bad liar, Nicoletta. You need to learn to *fake* being sick — like me," she remarked with another gravelly laugh. Gazing at her prescription bottle–cluttered night table, she sighed. "I am a professional."

Perhaps it was punishment for her lie, or perhaps reward for confessing it; in any event, Nikki woke up that Monday with the worst sore throat of her life. While three hundred plus Winstonians roused themselves to attend that morning's Town Meeting, Nikki stayed home. She sipped hot tea and lemon, reread her favorite Sailor Moon manga, and tried her best to recuperate, to gather her strength.

She knew she'd need every ounce of it to return to school.

The Girl: Petra Greene
The Getup: Sapphire blue and parrot green Ella Moss chemise, United States of Apparel black cotton-stretch leggings, and turquoise Havianna flip-flops.

On Rodeo Drive, beautiful sixteen-year-old girls are a dime a dozen, but a beautiful sixteen-year-old girl bending over a gigantic metal trash bin and rummaging through garbage like a beggar — *that* was worth noticing. Petra gritted her teeth and scowled, ignoring the beeping horns of passing luxury cars, the averted eyes of appalled pedestrians, the stupid catcalls: "Come on baby. Don't throw yourself away!" Weren't any of these materialistic bastards even the tiniest bit *concerned*? Wouldn't someone like to know how she ended up in such desperate circumstances?

She woke that Tuesday to the sound of her phone. Judging by the cool, bedroom dark, it was early — five in the morning, tops — which meant whoever was calling had to be a nut job, most likely a member of her family (most nut jobs were), which meant one thing: do *not* pick up. With a dramatic groan, she executed her reliable Human Taco Defense: 1) stuff face into pillow, 2) wrap pillow around ears, 3) pin pillow in place with arm, and 4) enjoy. Within seconds she was fast asleep.

But then her phone rang again.

Kicking aside her tangled sheets, she embarked on the angry pursuit of her Nokia, a task you *might* compare to finding a needle in a haystack, except that gave haystacks way too much credit. When it came to concealing the whereabouts of tiny objects, Petra's bed had haystack's butt kicked. In addition to the rumpled green-and-purple-paisley patchwork bedspread, her lofted futon boasted a lopsided mound of dirty laundry, a toppled pile of clean laundry, her crocheted hemp hobo, a scatter of loose change, two mechanical pencils, and a random peppering of grayish-pink eraser boogers. (There was also a half-eaten brownie encased in tinfoil, but she would not learn of its existence for another two weeks, when her sheets hacked it up like an old metallic hairball.) Despite the increasing chaos of her room, Petra refused to allow Imelda, the Greenes' cheerful Guatemalan housekeeper, to clean it up. When her exasperated mother claimed she *didn't hire Imelda to sit around and do nothing* (Imelda was almost always within earshot, bent over an ironing board, or crouched by a dryer door), Petra would retort: "I can clean up after myself!" And she *could*.

In theory.

She found her phone at last, bleating like a lost lamb in the narrow crevice between her futon and bedroom wall. *"Hello?"*

"Finally!" crowed the bright voice on the other line.

Petra sighed with mind-altering exasperation, belly-flopping across her mattress. "Hey, Melissa."

"Alright, listen up. Emilio Poochie, down! I was talking to my dad, right? And he was saying all we have to do is bring him *one* vandalized tag and he'd take it to his guy in K-town to have the handwriting *professionally analyzed.* Apparently, the man can tell your *shoe* size from, like, the way you cross your *T*s!"

At the goatish staccato of her friend's laughter, Petra winced, rolling onto her back. "Melissa," she yawned, blinking her bleary eyes at the ceiling. She'd have to choose her next words carefully. "What?"

"What do you mean *what?*" Melissa sputtered in disbelief. "Do you *not* recall that ridiculous launch party we hosted?"

"Of course, but . . ."

"Remember the contest we held to name our new label, only to have some raggedy-ass riffraff rifle through our raffle?"

Petra furrowed her pretty brow. "Okay, was that even English?"

"We need to *revisit the scene of the crime,*" Melissa pressed on. "All we need to do is find *one* tag and then . . . *Emilio,* I swear to . . . In the *back!* In the back, *now!*"

"Melissa" — Petra covered her aching eyes with one hand — "we left those tags in the gutter, remember?"

"So?" her comrade in fashion bristled.

"So . . . do you really think they're going to be just, like, *sitting* there? Exactly where we left them?"

"No," Melissa chortled at the sheer absurdity of that statement. "I mean, they're probably blowing down the street or something."

Petra's perfect jaw dropped. "They've been blowing around for *over a week.* They're probably halfway to *Borneo* by now."

"Okay," Melissa announced. "I am outside your house."

"What?"

"I know, right? Janie and Charlotte are *so* out of the way, but you're right on my way to school. *Oooo . . . !"*

Petra grimaced as her ear filled with what had to be a thudding hip-hop base, but through the cell sounded like a tortured black fly. "This song is so old-school!" Melissa sang.

She grimaced again, holding the phone from her ear, and crawled across the futon, pushing aside her hand-painted Balinese wood-beaded curtain. She peered outside, scanning the quiet Beverly Hills residential street, where, through luscious green hedges and imposing wrought-iron gates, she could *just make out* an all-too-familiar platinum Lexus convertible, parked illegally at the curb. The female driver, unidentifiable at this distance, bopped about in the breezy front seat, one long, bronzed arm extended. Light refracted from her wrist as her hand flapped around: first up and down, then side to side. Petra frowned.

Was she . . . spanking the wheel?

" . . . an' if I hit da switch, I can make the *aaaaass* drop!" her tinny voice crooned in perfect time to Mystery Driver's enthusiastic wheel-spanks. Petra shook her tangled honey-blond head.

It had to be her.

"Okay," Petra intruded into her friend's buoyant rap rhapsody. She released the curtain so that the swinging strands of beads clattered. "I actually don't think I feel up to . . ."

Melissa yelled over the music. *"What?"*

Petra cleared her throat and raised her voice. "Um . . . *I'm kind of not at my house right now?"*

"Halfway *home* and my pager still *blow-*in' *up.*" Melissa cackled with delight. "Oh no. Step back, y'all! *The man has a pager.*"

"Melissa . . ." Petra pressed two fingers to her throbbing temple. "Did you hear what I said?"

"Yeah, yeah, yeah, I heard you," she admitted, melting the volume on Ice Cube and cracking her gum. Petra breathed a low sigh of relief, cast one wistful glance at her organic Kapok pillow, and crawled toward it on her hands and knees. Closing her throbbing eyes, she collapsed like a parched desert wanderer.

"Petra," she heard Melissa whisper in her ear.

"Mmrph . . ."

"If you do not get your ass outta your house in two minutes, I will lean on this horn and blast you out of it." Petra's wide-set tea-green eyes popped open. "And then I'll make it my life's mission to hijack your sorry ass to *Borneo,* where you will spend the rest of your *life* looking for those vandalized tags because they are *not* in Borneo. *They are on Rodeo Drive, where we left them.* I feel it in my gut, and my gut *does not lie* — unlike certain Kumbaya-my-Lord blond chicks I may or may not mention!"

As Petra fumbled for an explanation, an abrupt Lexus car horn exploded across the stately Beverly Hills quiet. "Okay-okay-okay-okay!" she cried into the phone. The horn fell silent among the panicked twitter of a thousand treetop sparrows, not to mention the melancholy yowl of Job, her neighbor's basset hound, and a maddening *yip-yip-yip-yip-yip-yip-yip* she could only assume belonged to the notorious E. Poochie.

"I'll be down in a sec," she surrendered, miserably.

"*Down* in a *sec*, 'cause she *know* I don't *play*," Melissa rapped in sweet reply, returning Ice Cube to his original booming volume. Just before she hung up, Petra heard his thick baritone finish the verse:

"I got to say it was a good day."

Not that she was an expert on the subtle nuances of Ice Cube. Still, Petra had a strong feeling his idea of a good day had nothing to do with Melissa Moon's. She couldn't imagine, for example, a four-minute-and-twenty-second rap song devoted to the pleasures of digging through trash bins behind Jamba Juice, even if that Jamba Juice *was* in Beverly Hills.

"Any luck?" Melissa called from the street corner where she'd spent the last twelve minutes investigating the gutter. So far she'd found a gum wrapper. Grasping the top of the trash bin, Petra heaved herself up and over the edge, landing with gymnastic grace onto the littered asphalt.

"Nada," she answered, brushing her hands and pointedly ignoring the scandalized look of a Botoxed dinosaur in Taryn Rose flats walking her snow white Bichon Frise.

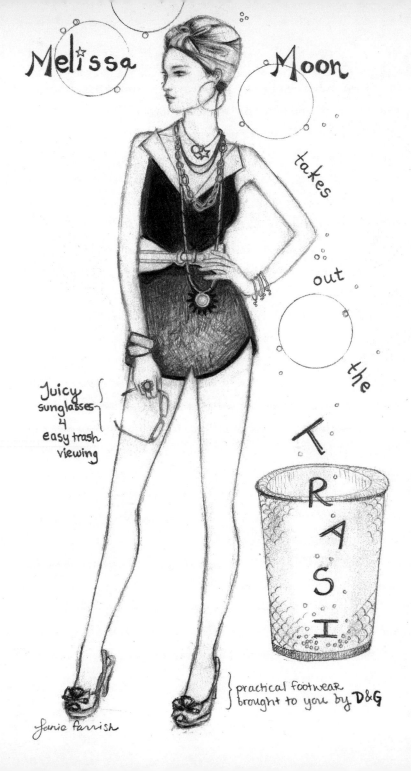

"Hey, baby!" A balding Mercedes driver buzzed down his tinted window and howled. "You like it dirty?"

"You *better* get your cheap-ass, pre-owned, C-Class Mercedes out of my face!" Melissa whirled, dark eyes flashing. Balding Driver grimaced (how did she know it was pre-owned?), and stepped on the gas. "Okay," she breathed, returning her attention to Petra. "There's just one more gutter we haven't checked."

"Melissa . . ." Petra reached into her crocheted hemp hobo, extracting the sole thing she held responsible for getting her into this mess to begin with: her purple Nokia. "School starts in fifteen minutes. If we don't leave now, we're going to be late."

"Since when do you care about being late?"

"Since when do you *not* care?" Petra pointed out, joining her at the curb. Melissa was wearing what she imagined Naomi Campbell might wear during a routine bout of community service: a belted, black silk romper, her "practical" blue and orange silk Dolce & Gabanna wedge pumps, and a poppy orange Prada turban (fashion's answer to the hard hat). Despite herself, Petra smiled. Leave it to Melissa to turn the gutter into a runway.

"Come on," Melissa begged, misinterpreting her bemused look. "Just five more minutes?"

"Fine," she agreed with a dramatic groan. "But after five minutes we . . ." She gasped, clapping her hand to her mouth.

"What?" Melissa sprung to attention, scampering to her side. She excitedly clapped her hands. "Did you find something?"

But Petra looked stricken, not overjoyed. Swallowing a twinge of disappointment, Melissa followed the line of her companion's tea-green gaze to a glittering pink granite medical office building, where just outside the revolving gilded doors, a man in his mid-forties and a very young brunette (practically *their* age!) were engaged in a totally disgusting, all-tongues-out kiss.

"Ew-uh." Melissa cringed. "It is *way* too early for this shizzle. I'm going to tell them to get a room," she laughed, taking a small step forward.

"Don't!" Petra grabbed her hand, urgently yanking her backward. She squeezed Melissa's long fingers, numb to the bite of her oversized topaz cocktail ring.

"Ow." Melissa rebelled against her friend's death-grip. "What's *with* you?"

The middle-aged man pushed through the office doors, disappearing behind a double-flash of glass, and the beaming brunette strutted down the sidewalk, hipbones first. She pulled her phone out of her red purse, dropped it back again, and — with a swish of her mirror-smooth hair — rounded the corner.

"Do you know her or something?" Melissa frowned.

"No," Petra offered, facing her friend with a feeble smile. She shrugged. "I just . . . I liked her purse."

"Really." Melissa dubiously scowled, still rubbing her hand. "Come on. We're going to be late."

Petra followed her to the platinum Lexus convertible, but not without a surreptitious backward glance. She knew that office building. She knew, for instance, the revolving doors sounded two hollow clicks at the end of each revolution. She knew an immense bouquet of lilies waited at the end of the hall. She knew the bright *bing* of the elevator doors, the little red velvet-upholstered bench inside, the silent vertical ride to the fourth floor, and the black lacquered office door with the gold adhesive letters, so immaculately placed.

Which was all to say, she *didn't* know that girl. But she *did* know the man. At least, she'd thought she known him. Until now.

Dr. Robert Greene. The most sought-after plastic surgeon in Beverly Hills. Her father.

The Girl: Miss Paletsky
The Getup: Charcoal trouser pants, white Ann Taylor
Loft polyester-silk blouse with "fashion flounce"
necktie, plastic blue bead necklace, skeleton
earrings, Via Spiga leather pumps in "neutral."
Everything from Loehmann's!

"Yes, I understand you require decision," Miss Paletsky, Winston Prep's special studies adviser, explained in her patient, Russian-accented English. "But do you ch'ave to ch'ave *right now?*"

She winced, holding the light beige plastic office phone from her ear as Yuri, the stocky, perspiring owner of the Copy & Print store on Fairfax, erupted on the other end. Of *course* he needed her to answer this minute! This was proposal of marriage, not pro-posal of . . . of *toilet paper.* So *why* does she treat him like toilet paper? Maybe she does not know her temporary worker's Visa is about to run out? She knows! So what does she want — a miracle? Either she marries him now, or *poka!* She is shipped back to Russia like a dog!

Miss Paletsky sighed, gazing around her small, festively deco-rated office. In another mood, she might have asked Yuri if *all* marriage proposals included allusions to toilet paper and dogs. But she wasn't in another mood — the mood to joke, to make light of what was no longer a laughing matter. It *was* true what he'd said. If she wanted to stay in America, marriage was her only option, and, as of that Tuesday morning, Yuri Grigorovich was her only offer.

Never mind she could barely look at him — let alone touch him.

"Normal behavior for a wife!" he'd reminded her that morning, calling down from their apartment building's asphalt-papered roof. He sunbathed daily in a stained white wife-beater and black garter socks, a damp washcloth on his steaming, bald head, and a pink bottle of Water Babies spluttering in his fist. "Life is not Cinderella!"

Uch . . . She'd had to spend all of her bus ride to work repressing the memory.

A soft knocking pulled her attention to her dark green office door, where her latest decoration — a black-hatted cardboard witch — vibrated a bit on her yellow papier mâché broomstick. She returned the plastic receiver to her ear, smashing a clip-on dangling skeleton earring against her neck.

"Yuri," she attempted to interrupt his crazed rant, "someone is at door." Cupping the mouthpiece with her hand, she boldly raised her voice. "*Yuri.* I talk to you later, yes?"

Before he could respond, she hung up.

Sweeping the crumb-ridden remnants of her morning Lemon-burst muffin into the wire-mesh trashcan under her desk, she flicked an automatic glance to the dark gray computer screen, examined her warped reflection, and sighed. "Come in!"

What she wouldn't have given to go back in time, examine her face in a real mirror, check her teeth for poppy seeds . . .

maybe apply a little Strawberry Lip Smackers. Because, contrary to her expectations, the door had opened not to reveal Glen Morrison — who would need to discuss upcoming HalloWinston Carnival logistics — but the most devastatingly attractive man she had ever seen. A slick blue-and-pearl-white Adidas tracksuit clung enticingly to his compact frame, and a glittering collection of gold chains drew attention to his gleamingly muscular chest. At her somewhat dazed nod, he glided into her office, walking in this way that was powerful, yet wounded — like a jungle cat with a slight limp.

"I'm Christopher Duane Moon," he oozed in a voice like warm molasses, extending his strong brown hand. He flashed a blinding mega-watts smile. "Melissa Moon's dad?"

She clasped his palm, and shook (all the way to the base of her spine). *This* was Melissa's father? But he looked so young! Even if he was, say . . . thirty-three, a good five years older than she was, he was *still* young for a parent, especially a *Winston* parent. When Melissa was born he must have been, what . . . seventeen?

"I'm Lena," she introduced herself, putting an end to her manic calculations.

"I was wondering if we could talk," Christopher continued. "Is this a good time?"

"Oh yes!" She exhaled and nodded, inviting him to sit. He plopped on her green velveteen couch, sinking deep into the needle-point squirrel cushions, his knees expanded at a distractingly obtuse angle.

"It's about my daughter," he began. "I've been a little concerned."

"We adore Melissa." Miss Paletsky clasped her hands so they sat like a peeled potato in her lap. "She is one our most . . . *energetic* students."

"Yeah, but she is *obsessed* with finding out who vandalized this contest of hers. . . ." He ran his ruby-bejeweled, and (she couldn't help but notice) wedding ring–free hand around his perfectly shaved head. "I try to be a good father, Lena. A provider. Someone who sets things up for their kids, you know — so they can have access to a future they deserve."

Miss Paletsky fiddled with the oversized blue plastic beads at her flushed neck. Never had she been so moved by a parent's concern. He was so invested. So sincere.

And he'd *so* just said her name!

"But ever since this contest," he observed, innocent to the effect he had on his trembling listener, "my daughter's been looking *backward* not forward. I know it's hypocritical, but . . . I just don't think it's healthy."

"How is that hypocritical?"

"Well, you know," he replied with a knowing chuckle. He leaned back into the pliant velveteen cushions, cradling his head in the hammock of his hands. "I kind of built my whole career on looking backward, right? Grudges, history, revenge — those are the building blocks of my business."

"I . . . I'm sorry." Miss Paletsky shook her head. As far as she could tell, he was either a history professor, a bounty hunter, or a Winston eighth grade girl. "What is it that you do, exactly?"

"For real?" Seedy sat to attention, and broadly grinned. "Christopher Duane, aka Seedy Moon?" He awaited recognition, but she responded with only a blank, befuddled look. "Lord of the Blings," he persisted. "The *Kimchi Killa?* Oh *man,*" he flopped back against the cushions. "Don't you listen to hip-hop?"

Miss Paletsky shook her head. "No," she admitted. "My music tastes are more, well . . . classical."

"Oh yeah?" He brightened in an unexpected show of interest. "You don't happen to know where I could find a classical pianist, do you?"

"*I'm* a pianist!" she blurted, unable to restrain her excitement. If she'd needed a sign, then this was it. She imagined meeting him at his recording studio, musician to musician — they would be professional at first, but gradually consumed by a simmering sexual tension. She would win him over with the Beethoven. No! *Prokofiev.* But wait, she was getting ahead of herself. All she *really* wanted was a small opportunity to get to know him outside her office, adult to adult . . . and after she'd applied some Lip Smackers.

"You're a pianist," Seedy repeated, amazed at his luck. "You're not free this Saturday morning, are you?"

A perfectly timed burst of sun shimmered through the willow leaves at her window and sparkled like champagne. "I'm free." She beamed.

"Would you be down to come by my house and play for us?

Vivien — sorry, that's my fiancée. She thinks it's important for us to hold some kind of audition first, so . . ."

"I . . . I'm sorry," Miss Paletsky stammered, attempting to hide her disappointment. *Of course, he had a fiancée!* She chastized herself. *Life is not Cinderella.* "What is this for, please?"

"Oh yeah." Seedy covered his eyes and briskly shook his head. "Didn't I say? It's for my engagement party. It's not until December, but we're trying to get everything set early, you know."

"Mm!" Miss Paletsky replied, plastering her face with her best flight-attendant smile. All at once the sparkling sunlight reminded her less of champagne than of a sudden blow to the head. "It is good to prepare," she murmured, thinking of the festivities involved for her potential engagement to Yuri. Probably Yuri's mother would throw a chicken bone at her head and call it a day.

"I know what you're thinking," Seedy invaded her thoughts with a knowing smile. "What's a rap artist playing classical music at his engagement party for, right? Well, believe me, this is all Vee, not me. Woman calls *all* the shots."

"Well, I look forward to it," Miss Paletsky the Russian Robot Flight Attendant assured him, ushering him toward the door. "And in the meantime I will think up some solutions for your daughter."

"Hey, that's great," a somewhat confused Seedy replied, obligingly exiting her office and stepping into the breezy corridor. He turned around with another dazzling smile. "Talk about killing two birds with one stone, right?"

"Exactly," she agreed, and politely waved before retreating into her office and closing the door. She slumped into her swivel desk chair, staring with bewilderment at the gray computer screen, which revealed the cruel state of her plastic clip-on skeleton earring: tangled in her hair like a trapped, semi-crazed bug. Had it *really* looked like that for their *entire* conversation?

Of course it had.

Willing herself to focus, Miss Paletsky slid open her top desk drawer and extracted a floppy, pocket-sized book: her English Idiom Dictionary. She thumbed the onionskin-thin pages until she found the desired entry.

When you kill two birds with one stone, you resolve two difficulties or matters with a single action.

She sighed, tracing and retracing the phrase with her finger. After a moment, the phone rang, jarring her from her trance. *Ch'ello.* It was Yuri. He wanted her to know just *one more thing.* She stopped him mid-sentence, stunning him into a rare silence. All it took was a single word. It fell from her mouth like a stone.

"Yes."

"Alright, that's twelve fifty," Melissa announced, her coffee-black eyes eschewing that lame-ass classroom wall clock for her *far* more glamorous diamond-and-stainless-steel, pink crocodile-strap Gucci watch. Raising her pint-sized silver Tiffany gavel, she rapped her desk four times — one tap for each girl. There was languid Petra, lying on her stomach by the blue plastic recycling bin; delicate Charlotte, perched like a pedigreed cat on the sun-drenched windowsill; and, of course, plainie Janie, the only member boring enough to sit at a desk. At least Melissa had the savvy to pick the teacher's desk, advantageously positioned at the front of the class and gleaming with a solid sense of its own importance — just as she did.

"It is with great regret that I begin this POSEUR meeting with some upsetting news." She sighed, resting her gavel next to her pristine white sparkle notebook. "Petra and I went to Rodeo Drive this morning, and despite a thorough and optimistic investigation, our best efforts have proved . . . futile."

"Oh, *quelle tragédie!*" Charlotte sighed, swooning against the windowpane. Seriously, she couldn't care less who the culprit was. "Can we puh-*lease* change the subject?"

"Change the *subject?*" Melissa clutched her poppy-orange Prada turban in shock. "I'm sorry, but justice has *got* to be served."

"But justice *has* been served," Janie countered. At Melissa's flashing attention, she ran a nervous finger under and around the green rubber band on her wrist. "I mean, in a way . . ."

"We *did* get our label name out of this," Petra leaped to her assistance.

"Exactement," Charlotte sang, having smoothed the A-line skirt of her green and gold floral Blugirl dress. She returned to Melissa with her haughtiest glare. "Frankly, Melly, I find this little grudge of yours . . . how do I put this?" Her porcelain forehead scrunched in thought. *"Boring.* I mean, you might remember I was *cheated on* at that party, but have I given it a second thought? No. I moved on."

"That's so inspiring," Melissa cooed, sweetly batting her Shu Uemura curler-curled lashes. "But before we quote-unquote *move on,*" she tightened her tone, "can I ask you just *one* question? 'PO-SEUR.' That's a *French* word, right?"

Charlotte gasped with laughter. "What are you suggesting? That it was *moi?*"

Melissa folded her arms across her daunting cleavage, lowered her chin, and pointedly cocked an expertly tweezed eyebrow. "Well?"

"Melissa." As a longtime pot addict, Petra felt it was in her authority to say: "You're being paranoid."

"Oh, am I?" Melissa scoffed, recollecting Petra's behavior that morning: the startled gasp, the brutal hand-grab . . . *the compliment of that woman's purse?* Petra was animal-rights *obsessed,* and that was a Nancy Gonzales shiny croc tote. You know: *croc* as in *croc-o-dile?* The whole thing had been without-a-doubt *weird,* she thought, savagely redirecting her eyebrow for Petra's benefit.

"Listen." Janie cringingly eased her way into the building tension. "We all need to just chill. I mean, if you think about it, we all want the same thing. Melissa wants to find the vandalizer, and the rest of us want to *design* something."

"How is that the same thing?" Melissa snapped.

"Remember in Town Meeting you said the contest winner should 'step forward and claim their prize'? Well, if it was *me* who did it," she hypothesized, studiously avoiding Melissa's accusing crazy eye. "Not that it *was* me, but *if it was* . . . I'd be way more likely to come forward if I *knew* what the prize actually was, you know?"

"And you're saying the prize should be one of our designs," Petra clarified.

"Yeah, but something super cool," Janie rejoined. "It's easy to resist a prize in theory. But when it's right there, like, *dangling* in front of your face . . ."

"Dangly!" Charlotte brightly chimed, clapping her well-manicured hands.

Melissa sighed, frowned into her white glitter notebook, and made a quick note. "Janie" — she looked up at last, smiling — "I like the cut of your jiggy."

"Yeah, Janie," Charlotte agreed, not without an edge of competitiveness. "What did you have in mind?"

"Oh." She blushed in her seat, turning her yellow Puma–clad foot toward her ankle. "I . . . I really didn't get that far."

"Well, I have an idea!" Charlotte virtually spilled from the windowsill, approaching the teacher's desk in light dancing steps. "Melissa, do you mind?" She unfolded a small square of antique yellow paper and smiled, facing the so-called class. "I prepared a little speech," she began. "Or as I like to call it . . . 'The Prettysburg Address.'"

"Oh my God." Melissa rolled her eyes, then joined Petra on the floor.

"So," Charlotte glanced once at her pristine paper and dropped it on the desk. "Kate and Laila and I were talking about what we were going to do for Halloween, and Jules — *so cute* — was confused, because Halloween's done a little differently in Europe. Anyway, I started telling him about all my favorite Halloweens growing up. Like when I was eight, and I was Marie Antoinette, and Daddy hired a beautiful horse-drawn carriage to take us all trick-or-treating —"

"Charlotte," Melissa interrupted, glancing at her watch.

"Okay, fine." She rolled her pool-green eyes. "Short version. Remember when we were kids, and we went around with those horrid little pumpkin buckets?"

"Not me," Melissa cackled. "I had a Ralph Lauren pillowcase, *hey-ya!*"

"Precisely my point," Charlotte pertly replied. "Pumpkins,

pillowcases — all that makes perfect sense . . . for a *child*. But Halloween is increasingly a holiday for adults, and *hello* — we have outgrown the plastic bucket. So, assuming we want to celebrate *in style* . . . what *is* there to turn to?"

"A new designer tote by POSEUR!" Melissa lit up.

"But," Janie timidly intruded, "isn't it a bad idea to design a bag that functions only once a year?"

"That's why we make sure the design is versatile," Charlotte arched a delicate eyebrow. "All we have to do is create something with non-season-specific appeal. That way, after Halloween, people will still want to use it."

"Okay." Janie nodded. "So then, the Halloween thing is just . . ."

"A marketing gimmick!" Melissa busted out, and her eyes actually glinted. Of all the *M* words in the English language, *marketing* had to be her favorite.

Well, that and Melissa.

"Just a little idea that popped into my head. I even came up with a slogan." Charlotte tipped her rosy mouth into a winning smile. "The Trick-or-Treater: a Piece of Candy Couture."

"Brought to you by POSEUR," Melissa added as Charlotte bobbed into a mock curtsy.

"So, we like?"

"Halloween is a cheap excuse for girls with low self-esteem to parade around like total sluts," Petra sighed, still thinking about *that woman*. "But yeah." She attempted a smile. "I like it."

"Well, I for one la-la-*love* it," Melissa crooned.

"I want to marry and elope to Belize with it," Janie added. Melissa laughed, rapping the wall with her Tiffany hammer.

"We're on!"

"Okay." Janie scribbled a note to herself on her sketchpad. "If you guys want to bring written descriptions of your designs by Friday night, I'm pretty sure I can have the drawings by Monday."

"And I'll manage the buzz!"

"And I'll make sure it's environmentally friendly."

"And I'll sew it!"

"All we have to do is vote on which Trick-or-Treater we should make!" Melissa concluded with an enthusiastic smile. Charlotte, Petra, and Janie flashed one right back at her. And why wouldn't they? Wasn't each of them equally sure *her* design would be the best?

It was, as they say, *in the bag.*

The Girl: Janie Farrish
The Getup: To be determined. (Hopefully . . .)

"I can't believe this." A shower-fresh Janie Farrish stood in her mother's best white terry-cloth bath towel and gaped at the few pathetic articles left hanging in her closet. She stamped her damp bare foot. "I have nothing to wear!"

"I can't believe she wants to meet you at a *fancy hotel,*" Amelia Hernandez snorted, tucking a wing of raven-black hair behind her chunky white plastic hoop. "Could she *be* more *predic?*"

"Are you kidding?" Janie faced her best friend, stunned. "It's the *Vicero*y."

"Um, exactly." Amelia pointed to the foot of Janie's unmade single bed and smirked. "And you just said 'the Viceroy' like my grandmother says 'the Vatican.'"

"I did not." Janie batted aside her black polyester-satin, star-shaped pillow, and plunked down. A shaft of afternoon sun filtered through her bedroom window, delicately gilding the chaotic sprawl of jeans and dresses on her creaky hardwood floor. Why, oh *why* had she so stupidly agreed to meet Charlotte for drinks when everything she owned made her look like Child Welfare Barbie?

"It's a cool hotel," she sighed, eyeing her crumpled rejects with refreshed scorn. "That's all I'm saying."

Shimmying toward Janie on her skinny jean–clad knees,

Amelia spun open a bottle of nail polish — NARS in Midnight Express — and wiped the drooling brush on the bottle's glassy mouth. She looked up. "Hand."

Janie dutifully surrendered her fingers. "You know what I don't get?" she pondered. "*Why* she even invited me."

"Maybe she wants to have an affair," Amelia deadpanned, widening her black liquid eyeliner–lined eyes. Janie made a face — *so not funny* — and Amelia sputtered a laugh, the wet wand of dark blue polish trembling in her hand.

"*Meelyuh,*" Janie gasped, whipping away her fingertips to examine her half-painted pinkie. "You're messing it up!"

"Oh, so sorry, Meece Hanie," Amelia apologized. "Pleece . . . I do bedder now."

"Shut up," Janie laughed. "Anyway," she continued, returning her hand, "you can't blame me for being curious. This is Charlotte *Beverwil* we're talking about."

"Um . . . Beverwi-wi-*what*?" Amelia plugged a bottle of nail-polish remover with a cotton ball and shook. "I go to *LACHSA,* remember? An entirely different school? Charlotte Beverwil means nothing to me."

"Well, she means nothing to me, too," Janie reminded her, but with considerably less conviction. Charlotte *did* mean something — although *what* remained unclear — beginning with Monday's Town Meeting and culminating at twelve o'clock earlier that day, with Charlotte's invitation to join her and her emaciated friends for lunch at the "upscale yet casual" Beverly Hills eatery, Kate Mantellini.

And even though Janie had complained to Amelia a million times about how vacuous, how superficial, how just plain *boring* they all were . . . she'd leaped at the chance. Reduced to ordering a pathetic side of steamed spinach, the cheapest thing on the menu, while the rest of them ordered delectably fresh chopped salads, heaps upon heaps of skinny fries, and *citron pressées* in slender, sugar-rimmed glasses — all of it scandalously ignored — she'd sat in dumb silence as they debated the virtues of heels versus flats, carbs versus fats, and, climactically, tweezers versus wax. *How vacuous,* she'd thought. *How superficial.* And yet. She hadn't exactly been bored. Okay, not even close. She'd savored their conversation just as she'd savored her sad lump of spinach: leaf by deliciously overpriced leaf.

Only now, in the presence of Amelia, the person who knew her best, did she feel the tiniest twinge of shame.

"Hey." Amelia pursed her brick red lips, blowing on Janie's dark blue–polished left hand. She looked up and smiled. "Maybe she wants to talk to you about Evan."

"Why would she want to do that?" Janie frowned.

"I don't know." Amelia's brown eyes sparkled. "Maybe she wants to, like, *sniff you out.*" She affected a dramatic semi-British accent. "*Does* the girl from the Valley love my brother for *him* . . . or for his *fortune.*"

"Omigod, ew!" Janie's face crumpled in disgust. "I do not *love* him."

Amelia grinned into her lap. "Okay."

"I *don't*," Janie squawked, regretting ever having told Amelia *anything* about Evan Beverwil.

The night of the label launch, at a loss for options, Janie had asked Evan if maybe he could give her a ride to Amelia's show, "in Silverlake," she began, "which is only, like, eighteen freeway exits away?" Before that night, she'd talked to him a grand total of three times, each conversation more cringingly awkward than the last. Still, she preferred nervous stammering (hers) and inscrutable pauses (his) to an out-and-out fight, which is exactly what happened in his Porsche on their way back from Spaceland. He'd pretty much treated her like a hypercritical, uptight bitch, which okay, *maybe* she had been, but *only* because he'd dismissed guys who wear eyeliner as "gay," which is a totally lame, closed-minded, and, to borrow one of Charlotte's words, *provincial* thing to say! *Ugh.* The memory *still* riled her, to the point that she almost forgot what happened next, once Evan pulled over to the side of the road, "to cool off." Reluctant to remain alone in that parked tomb of chrome and oiled Italian leather, she'd joined him outside by the chain-link fence. It was there, overlooking the La Brea Tar Pits, a famous dinosaur bone-filled swamp, that they . . . whatever. "Made up." It was there, accompanied by the embarrassingly flatulent sound of stinking tar, that Evan confessed, in so many words, that she looked "pretty." She'd returned the compliment with a baffled silence, which began at that moment at the fence, and two weeks later, still continued, outlasting all of Evan's inscrutable pauses combined.

"Amelia," she sniffed now, gazing imperiously downward from the rumpled foot of her bed. "Evan and I had *one* conversation. We haven't even *talked* since that night."

"Oh, Evan and I!" Amelia teased, protruding her lower lip into an exaggerated pout. She sighed a wistful sigh. "We haven't even *talked.*"

"*Ucchh.*" Janie gave up, glaring in frustration at the white bedroom wall. And then, to their mutual surprise, her gray eyes smarted.

"Oh, *Janie.*" Amelia couldn't resist an amused little laugh. "Come *on* . . . I was just joking. Obviously, you don't like him. I mean . . . he's a dumb, like, *surfer.*"

"I *know,*" she agreed, still staring at the wall. Her glassy eyes may have been a surprise, but the pang of protectiveness she'd felt for Evan after the word dumb (he wasn't . . . *dumb*), was both surprising *and* inexcusable. She had to recover from this. Now.

"How's Paul?" She exhaled, melting into a smile. *Yay.* All it took was his name in her mouth and Evan, like, evaporated, like bad breath after a mint — an achingly perfect-looking mint she also happened to love. True, with the exception of a few barbed insults, he'd all but ignored her at Amelia's show. But Janie couldn't help herself. She liked her mints mean.

"Paul's, you know . . . *Paul.*" Amelia shrugged. To Janie's continual amazement, Amelia refused to regard Paul Elliott Miller, god of Janie's idolatry, as anything more than her talented, if annoying, lead guitarist.

"He dyed his hair Electric Banana," she offered, dabbing Janie's cuticle with a Q-tip.

"Really?" Janie squealed. Because couldn't you just see it? Bright yellow hair would not only emphasize the blue in his mismatched eyeliner smeared blue-green and green-brown eyes, but also reveal the sunny quality he hid behind his brooding, punk-rock demeanor. Sigh . . .

Electric Banana was the best.

"Yeah." Amelia rolled her eyes. "But then he went swimming and it turned this really weird blue and he freaked out like a girl."

If only I'd had the chance to console him, Janie thought with a painful twist of hope. She would have told him Weird Blue not only emphasized the burnt umber in his eyes, but also revealed the bottomless well of sadness he worked so hard to conceal from the outside world. Sigh . . .

Weird Blue was the best.

"So now he's going to dye it again." Amelia rolled her eyes again. "I swear, if he spent as much time at band practice as he did primping, we'd be, like, legendary by now. And *speaking* of primping," she sighed, eager to change the subject.

"Don't," Janie whimpered, still clutching her white towel around her lanky frame. "Please, don't say it."

Amelia dropped the nail polish into her purse and smirked. "What *are* you going to wear?"

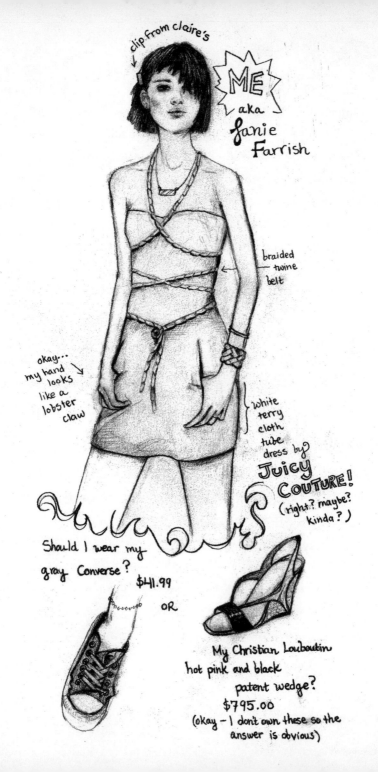

The Girl: Janie Farrish
The Getup: White terry tube dress by Juicy Couture
(that is, if anyone asks . . .)

She hurried down the hotel's lamp-lit cobblestone drive, along a long, lumbering line of gleaming luxury cars, and breathed a sigh of gratitude: *thank God I had the foresight to park the Volvo down the street.* With a quick, cringing smile at the humorless doorman, whom she half-expected to take her down by Taser, she swept through the ivy-draped glass entrance, beelined for the nearest gilded mirror, and smoothed the plush contours of her white terry dress around her narrow hips and skinny waist, examining her lanky, flat-chested frame from every possible perspective. The dress was less than two hours old — the product of a panicked whirl of scissors, needles, and thread — but she had to make sure it didn't look it. Sucking in her empty and fluttering stomach, she re-cinched the belt — an extra-long length of cotton twine, obligingly braided by Amelia — and slowly exhaled. She had to admit, the dress looked good, as good here as it had at home. *Better* even. She met her reflection with a co-conspiratorial smile. After all . . .

Who would have thought she'd make her grand appearance at the Viceroy in her mother's best bath towel?

She crossed through the moodily lit, pulsing hotel bar, where a burbling crowd of Hollywood types sucked down cocktails — the men in tailored suit jackets, distressed jeans, and candy-colored sneakers, the women in sheer cotton blouses over minuscule trouser shorts and four-inch designer heels. Janie observed them from the corners of her lash-shadowed gray eyes, squared her thin shoulders, and tilted her chin to a haughty degree. Was she pulling it off? Did she look like she belonged?

"No!" A platinum-haired girl in an equally platinum silk halter gasped as her spilled martini dribbled over the edge of the bar.

Janie slipped from the room and into the lantern-lit terrace, where Charlotte had suggested they meet. As instructed, she cut a path around the pool toward the white-and-black-tented cabana near the hedge. As she ducked behind a curtain and into the secluded lounge, her heart wobbled. Charlotte was there, as promised, but so was her entire family, all four of them languidly arranged around a crisply dressed table, like an Annie Leibowitz spread in *Vanity Fair*.

There was Evan.

Janie tried to smile.

"Janie!" Charlotte clasped her hands, and commenced her eager introductions: there was "Daddy," aka the Academy Award–winning actor, director, and producer Bud Beverwil; "Mother," aka the statuesque, chlorine-eyed ex-model Georgina Malta-Beverwil . . . "And you already know Evan," she added with an obligatory roll of her pool-green eyes. He glanced up, closing his latest paperback around his thumb.

"Whattup."

"We've heard a lot about you, Janie," Bud Beverwil boomed from his white wing chair. "From Charlotte and Evan both."

Janie glanced at Evan — that he had anything to say about her, let alone "a lot" was a mystery. Ignoring her inquisitive stare, Evan returned to his book and grimaced.

"Yes, it's a pleasure," Georgina smiled, her pool-green eyes aflicker. A sheer black silk Pringle of Scotland top gathered into delicate ruches at her pale collarbone. "But we'll leave you three alone. Charlotte" — she turned to her daughter, offering her cool cheek for a kiss — "you know where we'll be."

Janie watched the glamorous older couple glide away from the tent, their nearly matching wide-legged white linen pants flapping like sails about their tall, lean legs. An intoxicating fog of gardenia musk drifted in their wake, and it was all she could do not to close her eyes and surrender to it, like Dorothy in the poppy field.

While Janie lamely ogled her parents, Charlotte stabbed her icy drink with a stiff black straw and narrowed her eyes at her underdressed brother. As the aloof and beautiful daughter of two distinguished celebrities, she tried to dress the part (she was wearing a breezy, floor-length Moroccan tunic dress in swirling saffrons and indigo blues, and gold sandals that fastened around the toe with tiny, jeweled straps), but, as usual, her efforts were ruined by her beach sloth of a brother. In his little blue surf pants and flip-flops, Evan looked about as famous as a Celebrity Cruise bartender.

"Evan," she sighed. "You and your pull-ups can go now."

Golden-haired Evan remained in his seat and scowled. "They're *board shorts*."

"Yeah, board as in *we're bored*," Charlotte sighed, fluttering her ink black eyelashes. "Of you."

To Janie's surprise he glanced her way, a flash of wounded pride on his otherwise self-assured, handsome face, his blue-green eyes beseeching (there was no mistaking the question): *do you really think I'm boring?* Janie looked at the paved ground and blushed. Of *course* she didn't think he was boring (that he should even care!), but she wasn't exactly in a position to *say* so, either. Didn't he get that? Didn't he understand the *position* she was in?

Charlotte observed her brother storm across the terrace, and sighed. "Thank God." She returned her green-eyed attention to Janie. "I *really* need to talk to you."

"You do?" Janie perched on the edge of Evan's vacated white wing chair.

"I have something huge to confess." She lowered her voice, leaning forward. Her tumultuous ebony curls, which she'd tied into a low, side ponytail, tumbled over her left shoulder and bounced along her collarbone. "I haven't told *anyone*."

"Really?" Janie trilled. Of course, flattered as she was to be taken into Charlotte's confidence, she couldn't repress a small flicker of suspicion. If she hadn't told anyone, why in the world tell *her*?

"You look a little tense," Charlotte observed. "You like moji-tos, don't you?"

"They're pretty good," Janie ventured, guessing Mojitos were a high-end brand of chips, perhaps the gourmet cousin of Doritos, Fritos, and Cheetos. Charlotte reached across the table, clutched a slender frosted glass, and pushed it into Janie's hand. "What is it?" She blinked, sniffing the mysterious contents, a refreshing combination of what looked like crushed ice, lawn clippings, and pee.

"It's a mojito," Charlotte replied slowly, knitting her delicate eyebrows. Her glossy pink lips twitched with mirth. "What did you think a mojito was?"

"No, it . . . it's just . . ." Janie stammered, the back of her knees pricking with sweat. Unlike the majority of her Winston peers, she had yet to procure a fake ID, and she couldn't bear the humiliation of explaining as much to Charlotte, who most likely received hers at birth, along with her baby ID bracelet.

"Janie," Charlotte sighed, "is this going to be a problem? Because there's still time to change it to a Sunny-D."

"It's not that," she insisted. "It's just, um . . . I'm on this medication."

"Oh right." Charlotte leaned back into her wing chair with a delicate frown. "That's the same medication Jake's taking, right?"

"Accutane," Janie conceded with a hot blush, instantly regretting she'd brought it up. At times, admitting to taking acne medication was more embarrassing than having the acne to begin with.

"I'm on a very small dose," she stressed. "But still . . . I'm not supposed to drink."

"I know all about it." Charlotte offered her a wry smile. "Here." She wrested the mojito glass from Janie's nervous grasp and returned it to the table with a hollow *plunk*. "I wouldn't want you to do anything stupid."

Janie tried to laugh and failed. Charlotte's acid comment was in reference to Jake, after all, who blamed and continued to blame Accutane for his out-of-control drunkenness at their launch party — a bout of bad behavior that included, as they were all too aware, tongue-banging a random eighth grader. Only now, in the wake of Charlotte's wry aside, did Janie realize they'd never openly discussed it. Not directly, anyway.

Is *that* why Charlotte asked her here?

"How is he, anyway?" Charlotte popped open an exquisite black beaded clutch.

"He's good," she lied. Jake had been pretty much nonstop miserable for the past several days — Janie once caught him crying into his bowl of Cheetah Chomps — but she didn't think he'd appreciate it if she told Charlotte. "He hasn't even *talked* to that girl Nikki since that night," she offered. "If it makes you feel any better."

"Janie, 'feeling better' implies I feel bad." Charlotte tilted her head, affecting the confused expression of a professionally adorable dog. She snapped open a polished rectangular silver case, revealing a tidy packed row of cigarettes. "And I *don't* feel bad, I mean . . . isn't that obvious?"

"Yeah," Janie shrugged, confused. It was true. Charlotte *didn't* appear to feel the least bit badly, and Janie couldn't understand it. If it had been *her* boyfriend . . .

She stopped the thought right there. Already the hypothetical was too absurd.

"No offense but . . ." Charlotte extracted a gold-tipped Gauloise, and pinched it between two long fingers. "Your brother didn't exactly challenge me. And in a way, I don't know . . . I was, like, *relieved* when he cheated on me. I wanted a good reason to break up with him, and he *gave* me one."

Janie played with her twisted twine belt, averting eye contact. She wanted to be polite, but at the same time she wanted to be loyal. "I'm glad it worked out for the best," she declared, tying her belt into a knot.

"Yeah," Charlotte sighed. "It did. I mean, it'd be so inconvenient if we were still together when . . ." She drifted off and smiled, stabbing her swamp-green brew with her stiff black straw.

"When what?"

Charlotte lowered her voice to a whisper. "I may have met someone else."

Against her better judgment, Janie reached for the stranded mojito and took a sip. She realized she was supposed to ask Charlotte to whom she owed her pangs of *amour,* but she couldn't. She *wouldn't.* She was on a slippery slope: the more she knew, the more she'd have to tell Jake, and the more she told Jake, the more upset he'd be. Not a day went by that he didn't regret that stupid kiss, and she genuinely felt bad for him. If he found out about this, he wouldn't just cry into his Cheetah Chomps — he'd drown in them.

Time to change the subject.

"Mmm . . ." She returned the drink to the table. "Minty."

"I'm in love with Jules!" Charlotte exploded, clapping her hands, and Janie blinked, horrified. *Seriously.* Was "minty," like, Beverwil code for "spill the beans"?

"That's great," she replied dully. *Now she knew.*

"Janie." Charlotte pouted. "You don't sound happy for me."

"What? *No.*" In fact, she was weirded out. She'd always assumed Charlotte's feelings for her brother, if completely annoying, had at least been geniune. But, if that was the case, how was she so, like, *over* it? When Ted Hughes cheated on and abandoned Sylvia Plath, the tortured author of *The Bell Jar,* did she get all *la-di-da* about some Aqua de Gio-marinated foreign exchange student? No. She stuck her head in an oven and baked herself to death. *Not* that Janie was suggesting Charlotte do *that*, but . . . couldn't she at *least,* like, eat too many cookies and *cry* for a while? "I am *so* happy for you," she affirmed with a feeble smile.

"Eeeee!" Charlotte beamed, tilted forward, and touched her lightly on the knee. "I *knew* we were friends."

Friends. It was the first time the word had actually left her mouth, and Janie had to admit, it didn't sit right. Weren't friendships, especially friendships between former mortal enemies, supposed to develop gradually, like, over time? It took no less than four *years* of traded lunches, borrowed bathing suits, marathon phone calls, and saved bus seats — not to mention sixteen fights followed by sixteen make-up sleepovers — for her and Amelia to get their act together, bite the bullet, and commit to an exclusive best-friendship. But Charlotte hadn't taken four years — she hadn't even taken four *minutes*. Their friendship didn't blossom so much as just . . . *appear*. Like one of those big fluffy white mushrooms on her front lawn.

And weren't those kinds of mushrooms poisonous?

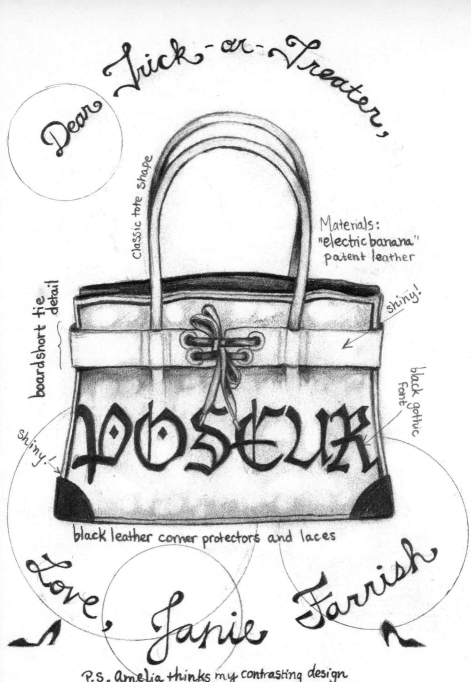

Dear Trick-or-Treater,

Classic tote shape

Materials:
"electric banana"
patent leather

shiny!

boardshort tie detail

black gothic font

Shiny!

POOSEUR

black leather corner protectors and laces

Love, Janie Farrish

P.S. Amelia thinks my contrasting design elements point to my "subliminal conflict" between Paul and Evan! Seriously, is she completely insane?!

The Girl: Petra Green
The Getup: Auto mechanic cutoffs by Dickies, cotton slippers from Chinatown, Ikat headwrap from Urban Outfitters.

While *some* people enjoyed themselves at the Viceroy Hotel, Petra was stuck at home. She stared at the sheet of paper on her cluttered desk and sighed. Along the margin, in neat, block script, she'd written POSEUR: THE TRICK-OR-TREATER. At the tail end of every letter she doodled a delicate vine with wide-open heart-shaped leaves. At the tip of every leaf she drew a dripping dewdrop; around each dewdrop, three stars; and on the points of every star, a tiny peace sign. When the last peace sign was complete (there were one hundred and sixty in total), she planted the nib of her purple pen into the paper and stared into space, chewing the serrated edge of her thumbnail, and willed an idea — *any* idea — to come to her. She was supposed to have e-mailed Janie a detailed description of her bag concept by seven o'clock. She glanced at the blinking digital timer on her stereo: 12:53 a.m.

Maybe if she decorated each of her peace signs with a row of daisy petals, something would come to her.

Her bedroom window filled with a brilliant light, flashed, and then returned to pitch-black. Petra lowered her pen at the familiar purr of a polished black Audi pulling into the drive. There was a crunch of gravel, the slow crick of car brakes. . . .

They were home.

Date night (or "Hate Night" as Petra called it) was an idea introduced to her parents by their marriage counselor, Lisa, who suggested they "invigorate their marriage with a romantic ritual." Every other Thursday or Friday night, her father took her mother out to dinner in Malibu. The idea of them sitting across from each other at a cozy corner table — their faces imbued with candlelight and softened by smiles, a dwindling bottle of wine — was so surreal it was laughable. Petra could not imagine her parents sitting across from each other *at all,* that is, unless it involved a wall of bulletproof glass and a tattooed security guard with a nickname like Bones or Crazy-Eye.

The front door thudded shut. The shallow Waterford crystal dish by the door rang with the sound of dropped keys, and the marble hallway popped and echoed under her mother's stiletto heels. Petra could hear her father's voice, so low it was a vibration, and her mother's weaving through it, like a teakettle nearing a boil. After a while, her father stopped talking, and her mother's voice grew more and more fevered. Petra crept toward her bedroom door and pushed it open. She'd always had this perverse need to listen to their fights, and never more so than tonight. Had her father told her mother what he'd done? What he was *probably still doing?*

If only they were functional enough to get divorced, she thought. Lydia Whitman, Joaquin's mother, had been divorced *twice*, and she was probably the most emotionally balanced person Petra knew.

She practiced yoga every day, set an egg timer for her daily Camel light, and had a different gorgeous boyfriend every four to six months, all of them younger than her, and all of them tall and lean with strong veins in their forearms, tribal tattoos, black plastic bracelets, and silver rings. They padded around the kitchen in their bare feet. Drank her orange juice straight out of the carton. And then they were gone. Sometimes Lydia referred back to them, but never with malice or anger. Smiling from the corner of her sun-drenched living room couch with the Peruvian blanket draped across the back, she'd muse out loud: "Olivier was nice," or, "Cody was a sweetheart." She'd hook a lock of Petra's honeyed hair behind her ear, and push a playful finger into her chin: "You would have liked Raphael." She'd exhale a steady stream of smoke and smile a sleepy smile. "He was a dreamer."

Unlike her *own* mother, Lydia was at peace.

Petra emerged from her bedroom, tiptoed past her little adopted sisters Sofia and Isabel's bedroom, and continued down the oatmeal Berber-carpeted hallway, beckoned by the all-too-familiar sound of weeping. As she approached the top of the stairs, however, the sound became more clear, the change as subtle as a siren which, speeding past, changes from major to minor key. Petra strained her ears, struck by a startling revelation.

Her mother wasn't crying.

"Robert!" Heather Greene shrieked, sounding disconcertingly similar to one of the giggling idiot girls in her class. Petra crept down another few stairs, sliding and bumping along on her butt, until her parents came into partial view. Heather sat on their marble floor in a simple red shift dress, a black patent Manolo Blahnik stiletto on her right foot The other shoe hung from her father's fingers. "Give it back!" she gasped with laughter, swiping the air.

"Why don't you ask *nice?*" her father joked, dangling the gleaming black sling-back like stolen candy. He was wearing acid-wash Diesel jeans with distressed pockets and cuffs, and red-and-cream Prada sneakers. Across the chest of his Raw 7 T-shirt, in an ornate Biblical font, were the words: LIVE FREE.

"What are you guys *doing?*" Petra cried, immediately clapping a hand over her mouth, as shocked by the sound of her voice as her parents were. She stood up to flee, but it was too late. They were already staring up at her, stunned.

"Young lady," Robert intoned while Heather rose to her feet, tugging the skirt of her dress to cover her exposed lacy cream slip. She pressed her cabernet-stained lips together and stifled a laugh, burying her face in Robert's shoulder while Petra looked on with horror. That she thought this was *funny*. It was just so, like, *pathetic.*

"Go to bed, Petra," her father ordered while her mother snorted into his armpit. "Now."

"Don't" — Petra gritted her teeth, balling her ink-stained hand into a tight fist — "talk to me like a child."

"Petra!" her mother gasped in genuine shock. "How dare you?"

"How dare *I?*" Petra seethed, her tea-green eyes welling up with tears. "God, Mom. You don't know *anything.*"

"I know you're in deep trouble." Robert stepped forward, hardening his tone.

"*I'm* in trouble." Petra returned his threat with a menacingly contemptuous smile, and an expression of genuine concern flashed across his face. *Not for her,* her mind raced. *But for him.* His lips parted.

"Pet . . ."

But she'd already whirled on her heel and escaped down the hall. Rounding the corner that led to the maid's quarters, she thudded downstairs and within moments was in the backyard, streaking across their perfectly manicured lawn, the wet grass pushing up between her toes and sticking to her ankles in itchy thatches. She pushed through the thick Cyprus hedge and rounded the edges of their glowing green swimming pool, avoiding the painted grin on the duck decoy which bobbed on the surface, slowly dispensing chlorine. She had to get to her playhouse — not that it was hers, not anymore. Sofia and Isabel had captured it long ago, replacing Petra's green flag with their own pink one, and, for mysterious reasons all their own, rechristening it Mooyaka Baka.

Petra stooped at the tiny red door, with its heart-shaped window and real brass knocker, punched in Isabel and Sofia's top-secret code (P-R-I-N-C-E-S-S), and pushed into the castle's miniature interior. After a moment's fumbling, she flicked on the track lighting, mounted the spiraling stairs to the roof, and clambered up the silky rope ladder fixed to the castle's right turret, spilling into the crow's nest. Above a battery-operated lantern and a mini-arsenal of water balloons, an antique-looking toy telescope dangled on a hook. Petra took the instrument into her lap, twisting it counterclockwise until it fell into two parts. In one, she kept a blue Bic lighter and a small blue and green glass pipe. In the other, a baggie of weed.

She lit up and exhaled, watching the smoke slowly swirl, turn inside of itself, and disperse. She searched the night sky for the North Star and imagined she was at sea, where nobody judged you for drifting.

"Hey."

Petra ducked low into the crow's nest, sucking in her breath. Did somebody just say "hey," or had she imagined it? Above her, the pink castle flag whipped around in the wind, the nylon rubbing into itself, sounding small whirs of friction. She exhaled. *Just the wind,* she reasoned. *Playing tricks.*

"Dude!"

Okay. She swallowed hard. Had the wind just called her "dude"?

"Come on, man. I know you're up there. I can smell you from here."

With all the courage she could muster, Petra lifted her tousled head and peered over the edge of the crow's nest, scanning her night-cloaked backyard. "Over here," the voice instructed, punctuating his command with a splash of water. Petra redirected her gaze to a corner of her neighbors' Olympic-sized swimming pool, where a boy around her age grinned up at her, his finely chiseled face pale in the moonlight. He pulled right up to the pool's edge, the muscles in his arm tensing as he pushed a dripping mop of dark blue hair from his eyes. Petra couldn't believe it. She'd seen this guy before, months ago, from the corner of her bedroom balcony, and had looked for him every night for a week, but he'd never showed again. After a while, she filed him away under "vivid dream." It was either that or "hallucination."

She wasn't hallucinating now, was she?

"Oh shit!" He floated a little ways from the wall before yanking himself back again. "Are you, like, a *girl* up there?"

Petra forked her fingers through her tangled honey-blond mane and gave it a little tug, grabbing her brain by the reins. If he was a hallucination and she answered, wouldn't she technically be talking to herself? "Hey," she began slowly. "You weren't here before, were you? Like in July?"

"Probably," he replied, still gripping the wall. "My grandparents live here. What are you, some kind of spy pervert?"

"No!" she cried, appalled at the accusation. "I was just on my balcony, and I, like, *happened* to see you. It's not like I . . . I mean, I seriously didn't even think you were *real*."

"Man," he snorted after a pointed pause. "It's a good thing I know you're stoned. Otherwise I'd think you were retarded."

Petra laughed, allowing the insult to slide. "I even had a name for you," she confessed with a tiny shiver. The pot had made her skin hot and the night air liquid and cold, like forgotten bathwater. "I called you the Naked Moon God."

"The Naked Moon God?" He curdled with scorn. "Wait." He paused, plastering himself against the side of the pool. "Are you saying you saw me naked?"

"Well, yeah," Petra answered, bewildered. "I mean, you're naked now, right?"

He didn't respond, and was so firmly stuck to the side of the pool that he resembled one of those figurines, suction-cupped to a car window.

"Omigod," Petra realized. "Are you, like . . . *embarrassed?*"

"No!" he scoffed, venturing a few inches from the wall, as if to prove his point.

"Okay," she challenged. "If you're not embarrassed, then get out of the pool."

"No way."

"Come on," she urged him. "I'll roll you a joint that'll last you 'til January."

Naked Moon God cocked his head in interest, drifting farther from the wall. "February," he countered, treading water.

"January and a half," she countered back.

"Deal."

Before she could respond, he ducked beneath the surface, pushed off the wall, and propelled through the glowing green water, sleek and quiet as a seal. He rose with a gasp, drifted into the shadow of the diving board, and grabbed hold of the stair railing. He glanced up at Petra in the crow's nest, stalling for time, and her heart rose in her throat. She opened her mouth to call out — *forget it, never mind* — but his foot found a step she couldn't see, and he hoisted himself up and out of the pool. A pause passed between them, filled with sounds quieter than no sound: the crack of a twig inside a tree, a howling dog in the distance, and all that water kissing the walls of the two pools, the bobbing underbelly of the plastic duck, and dripping off the edges of this boy's perfect, perfect body.

"So, what's your name?" he asked, wrapping a white towel around his trim torso.

"Petra," she called, wrapping her chilled body with her arms.

"Petra." He frowned, squinting up at her. "Is that one of those fruity New Age made-up names? Like Shaleelo or whatever?"

"No." She frowned, fumblingly rescrewing the telescope. She could feel him watching as she descended the taut white rope ladder and leaped to the roof. "It's actually been around forever." She brushed her hands and turned to face him, but she was too low, and all she could see was the high woodplanked wall and its lush ramble of ivy. She missed the sight of him, she realized, but wouldn't dare return to the crow's nest and live up to her "spy pervert" reputation. Jumping from the low roof to the soft earth, she casually approached the fence. "Petra means stone," she explained. "In Latin."

"*Stone?*" He snickered behind the ivy. "Man, your parents had you figured out at birth."

"My parents have their own assholes figured out, and that's about it," Petra ruffled.

"Whoa," he laughed, impressed. "You got a streak of anger in you, Miss Stone?"

Petra blinked into the dark, stunned. Wasn't she the girl who floated around in mud-stained ankle-length cotton skirts, a dreamy, sad smile on her face, bifurcating blades of green grass with her thumbnail and answering basic questions with befuddled, but well-meaning, *"Whats?"* She loved petting zoos, naps outdoors, and harp music. Joaquin called her the Mistress of Mellow, and Theo, Queen Serene. No one in her sixteen years had ever called her angry, meaning no one (she now realized) had ever truly known her. Until this boy, who'd seen right through the fence, past the dark cascading ivy, and straight into her raging, smoldering soul.

"You *should* be angry," he proclaimed, his gravelly voice clearer somehow, as if he'd moved closer to the fence.

"I should?" Her heart throbbed.

"We all should," he affirmed.

"Listen" — she cleared her throat — "I can't roll a joint right now, so I'm just going to throw the bag over the fence, okay?" She pitched the baggie into the air, watching it rise into the night sky like a jellyfish, and then strained to hear it land. "Did you get it?"

"Yeah . . ." He groaned over a manic rustle of leaves. "Ow! Okay . . ."

She smiled as the rustle died down, and drew closer to the

fence. A weighty silence passed. "Hello?" she called, her heart beating in her ears.

"What?" he replied, his voice even more thrillingly close. He had to be right up against the fence, now. Just like she was.

"It's just . . ." She laughed, brushed aside a tangle of ivy, and flattened her palm against the exposed plank. Under the ivy, the wood was cool, moist with dew and rot, and as it warmed against her hand, she worked up the nerve to ask.

"What's your name?"

That night, as she lay in bed, it became an incantation. Should her parents return to haunt her head, all she had to do was say *Paul Elliot Miller,* and, in the wake of a deep, happy blush, they'd disappear, like vapors.

The Trick oR Treater

silver zipper →

mini gravel bedazzle

← larger gravel bedazzle

"TrickorTreat" pocket Flap →

TRICKORTREAT

Stringed gravel bead Fringe detail

gravel colors = marine emerald jet and Frosted platinum

← means stone ✓ rock ✓ gravel ✓

By PetRa Green

Materials: organic cotton
in different shades of bright blue
For "patchwork" effect
and
imported aquarium gravel

drawing Janie Farrish

The Girl: Melissa Moon
The Getup: Black velour yoga pants by Juicy Couture, jasmine blue tank by C&C, gold icon charm anklet by Dolce & Gabbana, white silk push-up bra by La Perla.

It was Sunday morning, and Melissa had yet to come up with a solid design for the Trick-or-Treater, which was seriously *not* okay, especially since Charlotte, Janie, and Petra had already turned in theirs, which meant Janie would start their drawings first, which meant — by the time she got to Melissa's — she might just skimp for time. That her design might receive unequal treatment! It was too unfair to think about. She tried to calm down with a brutal round of crunches, but even *that* didn't work. She'd had to keep fighting the disturbing urge to bite her own knees.

Vivien, of course, had cracked that Melissa needed medication. But her father rearranged a few letters and suggested something nicer: *meditation.*

"Always begin with *om*," he reminded her, stabbing into a plate of quivering egg whites, while Vivien plunked down a companion plate of two strips of Facon Bacon, a slice of gluten-free toast, and a glistening pink blob of antioxidant-fortified pomegranate jelly. "*Om* is the sound of infinity and immortality, which serves to *focus the mind.*" He picked up a strip of Facon and raised his eyebrows, pointing. "After that, you say *namo* — to *honor* and *appreciate.* For example, when I say, *'Om namo Shivaya,'* I am giving praise to the deity Shiva, gaining tranquil insight and destroying negative qualities."

With that, he bit into his Facon, chewing with the ambivalent, glazed expression cats get when they eat grass.

Melissa tried her father's mantra for a while, but as far as deities went, Shiva left her cold. She wasn't interested in tranquil insight. She wasn't interested in tranquil *anything*. She was interested in chaos, commotion, and craziness. Besides. Since her father went all "peace and love," hadn't his work paid a price? His latest single, "Buddha Be My Boo," completely and totally tanked.

Melissa wasn't about to make that mistake.

She stared hard at the smooth sheet of gold monogrammed paper on her desk, her crème brûlée Dior reading glasses glinting impressively on the bridge of her nose. Emilio Poochie lay sprawled across a sheepskin throw beneath her massive white-and-gold executive desk, and Marco Duvall, her boyfriend of four months, sat on her overstuffed pink floral Princess bed, staring slack-jawed at a digital dribbling posse of three-inch-tall Lakers. Melissa jiggled her foot until the moon-and-star charms on her anklet chimed. She fluttered her eyes shut and inhaled.

"*Om . . . namo . . . Kimora . . .*" She exhaled. "*Om . . . namo . . . Kimoraaa . . .*"

Marco muted the volume on the Lakers and flinched. "Excuse me?"

"Would you please chill *out?*" Melissa scowled, and rested her hands, palms up, on her folded knees. "It's my mantra. And don't eat those!" she snapped. "They're for POSEUR promotion."

"POSEUR promotion." Marco repeated with mock gravitas, and dropped the bulging multicolored pack of Starburst to the floor. He gazed over at his meditating girlfriend and frowned. "What are you, now . . . some kind of Ninja?"

Melissa's mahogany brown eyes flicked open like a jackknife. "Marco, I am trying to communicate with a *divine being.* And in case you're wondering? *That does not mean you.*"

Her boyfriend pushed a short burst of air through his lips and faced the TV. "Fine." He raised his hand. "Do your thing, Jackie Chan."

Melissa fluttered her eyes shut, inhaled, and prepared to allow whatever thoughts popped into her mind to pass by without resistance. "*Om . . . namo . . .* Kimoraaaa . . ."

"Wait a second," Marco barked a sudden, comprehending laugh. "You're not . . . 'Lissa, are you praying to *Kimora?* As in Kimora Lee *Simmons?*"

"I'm not *praying.*" She leaned back in her velvet upholstered office chair and avoided the question, but after a suspicious length of silence, opened her eyes. Marco was curled into a ball in the center of her bed, convulsing with mute laughter. *"Marco."* She folded her arms across her daunting double-D chest and frowned. At that, he positively wailed with laughter, tears of mirth streaming down his ecstatic, tanned face.

"Kimora Lee Simmons," he practically howled, causing Emilio to bark in staccato alarm. "*That's* your divine being?"

"It's not funny!" Melissa whipped her Dior glasses from her face and accidentally pitched them across the room. They swooped past Marco like a small skeletal bat, smashing with a cheerful and tragic tinkle against her sliding mirrored closet doors. Her jaw dropped.

"No!"

Pushing back her desk chair, she staggered across the floor and dropped to her velour-clad knees. "My glasses," she squeaked, cradling the broken frames in her arms. And then, to Marco's utter shock and sheer delight, she pivoted on her shins and threw her arms around his neck.

"I'm so sorry, Marco," she shuddered. "I'm just so stressed about the Trick-or-Treater."

"The what?" he asked, breathing deep the spicy nutmeg scent of her jet black ceramic straight-ironed hair.

"It's the name of our new couture bag." She gazed up at him with her best pouty face. "You . . . you think it's a cute name, right?"

"Oh yeah." He managed to nod and, at the same time, slip his thumb under the spaghetti-thin strap of her white satin La Mela thong. (Marco was nothing if not a master of multitasking.) "I was just thinking, like . . ." He stalled, having already blanked on the name of her bag (she did say "bag," right?) "That's cute."

"For real?"

"Baby" — he traced a lopsided circle in the small of her

back — "you've got to stop putting yourself under all this pressure."

"Putting *myself* under pressure," she repeated, stiffening in his embrace. Marco squeezed his eyes shut and bit the inside of his cheek. Had he really messed this up already? "I don't put myself under pressure, okay? *Pressure* puts *itself* on *me*. Pressure looked around and was like: who here has the *strength,* who here has the *commitment,* to take on *me?*"

"And then Pressure was like, *Ho!* That fine woman over there. In the blue T-shirt and the tight-ass booty jeans!"

"My shirt is *purple,*" Melissa sniffed, nevertheless melting back into his arms. Marco exhaled a sigh of relief, especially as her breast (he was pretty sure that's what that was) seemed to be pushing up under his left armpit. *A definite bonus,* he thought, fighting off a triumphant smile.

"Um . . ." He paused, choosing his words carefully. "You know one thing I heard that was good for, uh, when you're tense . . ."

She shifted her posture so that she was practically sitting in his lap. Her boob crushed against him in a way that would have been uncomfortable, except for the fact that, you know . . .

It was a boob.

"What's good for when you're tense?" she murmured into his neck.

At this juncture, Marco thought it best not to answer in words. Keeping his hands on her hips, he nuzzled into her fragrant neck, planted tiny kisses from her shoulder to the hollow behind her left ear, and, in a move he'd perfected on a dried apricot in the fifth grade, took her earlobe into his mouth and sucked on it — just a little. He made sure to be gentle, because a) the ladies like it when you're gentle, and b) he didn't want to gag on that baby-fist-sized diamond in her ear. Running his hand over the spiny bump of her back bra clasp, he pushed up under her cotton-stretch T-shirt and pinched the sturdy triple-hook clasp between his thumb and finger. He expected Melissa to protest, and when she didn't, he had to admit he didn't know how to proceed. Should he ask her if it was okay, or should he just go for it? On the plasma screen, a few key black and yellow uniform-sporting players gathered around their coach, hands on their knees, beads of sweat on their brows, the crowd behind them like a blur of pastel confetti. If only Marco could just . . . call a time-out, you know? Consult Phil Jackson for a few pointers?

As if he'd read Marco's thoughts, Phil Jackson peered through his wire-rim glasses, tugged his white Kentucky Fried Chicken goatee, and made direct eye contact with the camera. It was a sign! From the coach of the Lakers *himself.* Refusing to waste another second of precious time, Marco squeezed his eyes shut in concentration, pinched the three-hook contraption between his thumb and finger, and pushed the two sides together. The stretchy satin strap grew taut across her back, almost stubborn, and then — as if by magic — the clasp popped apart. He'd never, in his life, gotten this far before. "Oh my goodness!" Melissa cried in what he had to assume was unbridled ecstasy. "Marco, you're a genius!"

He grinned. He was aware some brothers had trouble undoing a bra, but Marco wouldn't say his finesse qualified him as a *genius*. Then again, he thought, why undermine his talents? *"Thank you,"* he replied, wondering if now would be a good time to get a condom. But before he could say *Durex Maximum Love,* Melissa sprung out of his lap and onto her feet.

"It's so simple," she declared, pacing the bedroom in a fit of excitement. "All I have to do is design a signature *clasp*. I mean, once you figure *that* out, the rest of the handbag is just sort of *secondary*."

At the word *handbag,* Marco experienced what he could only describe as an out-of-body experience. "Baby." His face crumpled in confusion. "What?"

"In order for POSEUR to become a major, like, *iconic* brand, the Trick-or-Treater needs *instant brand recognition.* And how does *that* happen? With a logo. And what do all the best logos look like?" She locked her hands together and raised her professionally tweezed eyebrows.

"A clasp?" Marco sighed, cheerful as a broken umbrella.

"Eggs-zactly!" Melissa kicked the air with excitement. "Like Gucci has those little interlocking G's and everybody's just like . . . *Gucci.* And Chanel has the interlocking C's. And Louis *Vuitton* has interlocking *L*'s and *V*'s, and . . ."

She widened her almond-shaped eyes and held up a Bliss high intensity hand-creamed hand — milking the drama of the moment. "What does POSEUR have?"

A beleaguered Marco stared into middle distance. "Interlocking P's?"

"*That come together like a bra strap.*" She squealed and clapped her hands, bouncing on her bare pedicured toes. "Oh, Marco. How hot is that?"

Marco watched her unclasped bra straps droop apart beneath her purple T-shirt and sighed. If only bras fastened in some other, completely un-purse-like way, like with duct tape, then she never would have had her "big idea." She'd still be stumped, tense, vulnerable . . . and utterly under his sway.

Melissa plopped into her custom-made office chair (a champagne-velvet upholstered throne — on wheels with adjustable seating and lumber support) and got to work, which, as far as Marco could tell, meant scribbling on a piece of paper, shaking her head, and chanting the word "buh-zilliant." He sighed, faced the silver-lined plasma screen, and grabbed the remote.

"You know who should get into fashion design?" he muttered, punching a rubbery blue button to unmute the TV. "Me."

But the game was already over.

The Guy: Jake Farrish
The Getup: Faded red-and-black-plaid flannel shirt,
used gray cords from Wasteland, and black Converse
All-stars.

Monday morning and here they were again: inching uphill on
Laurel Canyon in their black 240 Volvo sedan, stuck in morning
traffic. Behind them, the San Fernando Valley stretched out, gray
as the ocean and with only the occasional palm tree to break the
flatness, rising up like SOS flares. Jake, for one, appreciated the
metaphor.

He was, after all, a sinking ship.

A heavy sky hung over the horizon, clouding the canyon view,
and he was grateful. For once, the weather matched his mood. Rain
swept the slick road in gusts and muddied the hills; tall mustard
grasses leaned together, bobbing and tipping their heads, and rivers
of brown water gurgled by, skipping over rocks and upsetting orange construction cones. Jake leaned forward and squinted, wiping
the windshield with the back of his plaid flannel sleeve. The Volvo's
trusty defroster roared with the force of forty Boeing jets, and yet
had managed to clear no more than a butt-print patch of glass.

God, he hated this car.

"Why'd you turn it off?" his sister asked as Jake withdrew his
hand from the round plastic knob on the dash and returned it to
the wheel. "We just had it fixed."

"Oh really?" Jake tugged his invisible beard in contemplation. "We just had it fixed, you say?" Thrusting his indignant finger to the misted windshield, he wrote in squeaky, wet script: *my sister says you're fixed*. As his words fogged over, Janie frowned, straining against her seat belt. She wrote: *you are ridic*.

"No, *you're* ridic," came Jake's pithy reply.

"How am *I* ridic?"

Jake fixed his eyes on the black Audi directly ahead. The cold heat of brake lights glowed red in the rain, and he muttered, "I can't believe she said she was in love."

Janie hid her face in her hands and moaned. She couldn't believe she'd told her brother. Then again, had it really been her fault? From the moment she'd returned from the Viceroy, Jake had done nothing but relentlessly demand she recap everything Charlotte said. He insisted there was something she wasn't telling him, even though she swore there wasn't, and fed him the same line every time: "We talked about our periods."

But Jake was like a Stasi officer in 1960s East Berlin, asking her the same day-old questions — over and over, again and again — until at last she'd cracked. She'd been faced with a choice: either confess to Jake and hurt his feelings, or peel her own face off. As the latter hadn't really been an option (she was almost convinced her face was starting to get pretty), she'd surrendered, confessing one teeny-tiny illicit detail:

"She said you never really challenged her and she's in love with someone else; the end."

Okay. Maybe "one" and "teeny-tiny" weren't the best word choices.

"And she didn't say who?" Jake asked her now, slouching in his tan weathered vinyl seat. His faded red-and-black-plaid cowboy shirt wrinkled around his narrow hips, and the scuffed toe of his black Converse eased on the brake. "Come on, Janie. Does he go to our school?"

"I already *told* you. . . ." She looked out the window. "I don't know."

Jake eyed her with suspicion. "Is it Luke?" he asked. "Is it Theo? Is it, oh God . . ." His boyish face crumpled in disgust. "It's not that little Emo tool, Tim *Beckerman*, is it?"

Janie tightened her mouth like a disapproving nun.

"I can just see it," Jake continued, undeterred. "You guys are sitting there. On swively little bar stools. Drinking your girlie Cosmos, or whatever." He scowled, slouching deep into his seat. *"Giggling."*

Janie looked at her twin brother in disbelief. He'd seriously said "giggling" as though it described the act of pooping on a breakfast plate.

"You're insane," she realized out loud.

"Yeah." Jake nodded, as if taking her diagnosis into serious consideration. "But you know who I bet's *not* insane? Tim Beckerman."

Janie groaned. *"Jake."*

"And I bet he's *challenging,* too. In fact, that's all he does . . . just goes around . . . challenging people." He swiped the turn signal, which flipped to attention like a middle finger. "Well, good for you, Tim. Good. For. You."

"Okay, would you please *stop*?" Janie groaned. "I promise it isn't Tim Beckerman. He doesn't even go to our school, okay?"

"Awesome," Jake replied, even though he sounded anything but. The last time she saw him look so haggard was two years ago, when he came home to discover Dog-Breath, their goldfish of nine years, floating belly up in his fish tank.

"Hey . . ." She jabbed the side of his faded gray corduroy–clad leg with the corner of her textbook. "If it makes you feel any better . . ."

"If it makes me feel any *better*?" Jake cut her off. "Feeling better implies I feel bad, okay? And I don't feel bad. *I'm fine*."

"Okay." Janie lifted her hands in surrender. She couldn't believe this. It was like he and Charlotte had lifted the same lines from their *How to Live in Denial* handbooks.

As she lowered her hands, a mass of gray and white clouds parted, and the sun poured out like liquid gold. The dismal California landscape revived like a black-and-white movie gone Technicolor: magenta bougainvillea blossoms tumbled from the vine, glowing ripe oranges dangled from trees, and hedges of white Oleander burst like popcorn. As the Spanish-tiled roof of Winston Prep's assembly hall appeared on the lush horizon, Jake slowly shook his dark tousled head.

"Stupid weather."

The Girl: Charlotte Beverwil
The Getup: Are you jealous yet?

Charlotte opened the heavy door of her cream-colored mint-condition 1969 Jaguar and swung her delicate ankles into the sparkling, post-rain sunshine. She emerged from the car and stretched her long neck, shaking her chaotic mane to the small of her ballerina back. Having shut the door, she circled the car, her eyes fixed to the depths of her black vinyl Chanel shopper, and pretended to rummage, smiling a secret, self-satisfied smile. Every single guy in the Winston Prep parking lot had his eyes on her right now — she could just *feel* it. Their gazes warmed her face like rays of a distant nuclear blast.

She was wearing a body-skimming, low-cut slip dress in midnight-blue silk, black appliqué tights, and pearl gray mid-calf Barbara Bui button-up-the-side boots. A very thin silvery scarf looped about her neck, plummeted the length of her five-foot-two frame and unraveled into loose, swinging fringe. Soft coal pencil lined her pool-green eyes, smudging around the lids to create a smoldering bedroom look, and her cheeks were stained tuberculosis pink. Most remarkable of all, her glossy french roast hair reflected a new subtle red hue — the result of an organic henna rinse Don John had applied the night before. In Victorian paintings, prostitutes were often depicted as women with red hair, and Charlotte thought: why not follow suit? Not to say she wanted to look like a whore (puh-lease), but merely meant to suggest, in her own secret way, that yes . . .

She was back on the market.

Scanning the Showroom, she spotted Jules, chatting away with frumpy old Ms. Dewitt, Winston's Geology teacher, and — apparently — wannabe cougar. Charlotte narrowed her eyes. Didn't Dewitt realize she and Jules *had* to be flirting when Jake arrived any minute? If she'd learned anything from Janie that stressful night at the Viceroy, it was this: Jake was *still* not jealous, which meant Charlotte had to move her "little project" from phase flirt to phase *date.*

"Jules!" She swooped in the moment Dewitt tottered off smiling her overstuffed chipmunk smile, her black wool stretch pants creasing into smile-lines across her sagging pear-butt. Charlotte smiled, fluttering her inky black eyelashes. "Hi."

"Charlotte," he said, rewarding her boldness with a pleased bob of his thick black man-brows. His amber eyes floated about her face, both bored and alert — like a lion's.

"How was your weekend?" she asked, widening her eyes like a baby gazelle.

"Very educational," he informed her in his unplaceable accent. "Ms. Dewitt organized a tour of Los Angeles for me and other exchange students from different schools. We went to the La Brea Tar Pits and also to the Hard Rock Café."

"Oh?" she replied, swallowing her horror. "I just love restaurants," she mused. "I wish I went to them more." She paused, waiting for him to acknowledge her cue, but he just stood there, posture perfect as a coat rack. "Sometimes," she decided to add for good measure, "I think I'd go to a restaurant with *anybody*. I mean, if they asked."

"Really?" Jules tugged his licorice black ponytail and frowned. "I'm not sure if I have the same passion for restaurants, but . . ."

"We should go to one and find out!" she trilled, jumping the gun. She couldn't help it — the Volvo was *right there*.

"Charlotte . . ." Jules looked genuinely confused, and for a second she worried he was going to decline. But then he took her hand in his, guided her knuckles to his curving mouth, and brushed them with his lips. "You take the words from my mouth."

"Oh." Charlotte instantly smiled. She glanced around the Showroom, taking quick account of her witnesses: Tim Beckerman, Theo Godfrey, Luke Christie, Joaquin Whitman. Of course, at the moment of her attention, they pretended to be looking at something else; only Kate and Laila, both leaning on the fender of Kate's pink and white Mini Cooper, gawked directly. Charlotte offered her two best friends a tiny how-does-this-kind-of-stuff-always-happen-to-me shrug, but they just stared, too stunned to respond. Charlotte, meanwhile, continued to scan the Showroom. There was only one person she wanted to catch watching her, one person she wanted to be jealous above all others, one person who would elevate Jules's hand kiss from "kind of weird, actually" to "paradise on Earth."

But he was nowhere to be found.

He didn't have a destination, just a motive: get as far away from Winston Prep as possible. Where he was going was beside the point, a dismissible side effect of the real issue: what he had to leave behind. Or, more accurately, what he was escaping: the sight of his girlfriend — okay, *ex-girlfriend* — subjecting her hand to the probing, possibly oozing lips of Sir Ferrari-pants. Jake's first impulse had been to laugh (he was kissing her *hand*? Who did he think he was, a *musketeer*?), but then he caught a glimpse of Charlotte's face, and the laugh curled into a tight black ball and died like a burnt hair. Even from a distance of forty feet (Jake had stationed himself behind an oleander hedge, careful not to be seen), he could see the details of her smile: the sweet dimple in her left cheek, the teasing tilt of her tiny chin. She used to smile at him like that, usually right after they kissed, or right after he made her laugh, or right after he delivered his report on mitochondrion in AP Biology. Okay. Right after he did pretty much *anything*.

She hadn't looked at him like that for a while.

Before he could think twice, he beelined back to the black Volvo 240 sedan, flung the door open, and hurled himself inside. He started the engine and pulled out of his spot. All he wanted to do was tear out of there. But he couldn't. There were too many obstacles: Joaquin Whitman and his hackey-sack crew. Melissa Moon and her flip-flopping entourage. Seventh graders bursting from the depths of the Locker Jungle, thumbs wedged under the thick straps of their bulky backpacks, and bobbing about his car like a herd of porpoises. Jake weaved through them, slouched low into his seat, quiet as a shark festering in a stagnant pool of resentment. He could have handled the sight of his ex-girlfriend's hand in the grip of a guy *who wore loafers without socks.* He could have handled it! Except for the fact that, minutes before, Janie told him the guy in question didn't even go to this school.

He eased into the dip of the driveway, nosed into traffic, flipped his blinker, and took a deep breath. Behind him the school bell rattled awake, ringing louder than he'd ever heard it ring before.

He yanked the car into the road, and took off.

The Spanish tile roof of Winston Assembly Hall bobbed along his rearview mirror, ducked behind a row of Cyprus trees, and disappeared from view. He flipped on the radio — the White Stripes — and punched the dial, changing the station. The White Stripes made him think about black stripes, which made him think about black-and-white stripes, which made him think about prison. And okay, he knew outside of Elvis movies and Looney Tunes prisoners didn't wear black-and-white stripes. He also knew ditching school wasn't a criminal offense. But who cared what he quote unquote *knew?*

This was about how he *felt.*

He slid his eyes from the road to the passenger seat, where his cell vibrated on the vinyl like a Mexican jumping bean. He swallowed. Was it his parents? The dean? He turned the phone over, braved the illuminated screen, and read the name of his caller. With a rueful laugh, he dropped the phone back on the seat.

Of course.

The Girl: Nikki Pellegrini
The Getup: Pale blue cardigan set by Ralph Lauren,
knee-length white cotton skirt by Lacoste, white
ballerina flats by Tory Burch.

For her first day back to Winston Prep, Nikki Pellegrini con-
structed an outfit of angelic whites and palest sky blues. She parted
her long, flaxen hair on the side, plaiting it into two simple braids,
and but for a dab of cover up on a post-traumatic stress pimple
between her eyebrows, wore no makeup. The plan was to look
chaste, innocent, and pure . . . that is, the opposite of a "two-faced
slut," the exact phrase she'd just discovered scrawled in bright red
lip liner across her light green locker door. It was 7:53 a.m., and
a predictable rush of pre-school activity filled the labyrinthine
locker rows with noise: the *click* and *whir* of combination locks, the
rattle-clang-slam of locker doors, the *zip-unzip-zip* of backpacks, the
low, burbling rabble of conversation . . . and laughter. Nikki winced
at a particularly explosive shriek (was it Anna Santos?) followed by
an appreciative cackle (Zoey Bloch?) followed by a hyperventilation-
style titter (Olivia Lu?). *What were they laughing at?*

   Were they laughing at her?

   "Excuse me."

   Nikki glanced over her shoulder, where tiny Sunrise Roche,
eighth-grade gymnastics freak and proud owner of the bottom

locker to Nikki's top, cocked an impatient, overplucked brown eyebrow. Her tight-bunned head cocked firmly to one side, and her terrifyingly cut forearms braided across her convex chest. "Can you move?"

"Hey, Sunrise!" Nikki ignored the request, plastering herself against her locker like a human censor strip. The toe of Sunrise's gold Adidas Y-3 ballet flat tapped in perfect time to the beat of Nikki's own panicked heart. "Wow." She grinned. "I *really* like your shoes. Where'd you get them?"

"Um . . . a whore?" Sunrise replied with an exaggerated roll of her green-gray eyes. Nikki's heart shriveled inside her chest like a snail in a bucket of salt.

"At a . . . at a what?"

"At a store, at a *store!*" She stamped her gilded foot in irritation. Nikki bit her lower lip in disbelief. True, Sunrise had a reputation for being hostile (rumor had it she was on steroids), but this was the first she'd been rude to Nikki. She watched in fear as the gymnastics queen took a step back and went completely rigid, her hands stiff at her sides, as if at any moment she might launch into the air, execute a triple-twist back flip, and land smack in the middle of Nikki's terrified face. Before she could think better of it, Nikki spun on her heel, balled the sleeves of her cardigan into her hands, and rubbed vigorously at the door of her locker, smearing the lip-linered epithet into the luxurious soft blue fabric, and ruining her best cashmere sweater forever.

"Thank you," Sunrise groused, squatting to her knees as Nikki stepped aside. As Sunrise yanked the combination lock toward her broad chest, her face grim with concentration, Nikki returned her frightened gaze to the illegible red streak on her locker door. Wasn't it possible, even *probable,* that her locker had been confused with someone else's? Perhaps her locker (top row, second from the right, aisle *seven*) had been mistaken for, let's say, Amanda Bishop's locker (top row, second from the right, aisle *eight*). Nikki slid her eyes to the locker in question, where Amanda Bishop herself unloaded her textbooks, tipping them into an over-pinned black canvas backpack with all the enthusiasm of a gravedigger. Her limp almond-brown bangs veiled her sleep-deprived mascara-smudged eyes, grazing the bridge of her freckled farmer's daughter nose, and a wine-red bra strap slipped down her right shoulder. All it took was one glance at Amanda's exposed butt crack, stuck like a soda straw above the waist of her too-tight low-rise Joe's jeans, and Nikki was convinced. Whoever wrote "two-faced slut" wrote it for Amanda, *not* her.

Cheered by her theory, Nikki quickened her pace, the heels of her white ballet flats slapping the pavement, and made a beeline for the Kronenberg Theater, where she and her two best friends, Carly and Juliet, were to spend first period making posters for the annual Hallow-Winston Carnival. The pumpkin fest was just around the corner, and it was up to them, the Student Decorating Committee, to drum up proper enthusiasm. She swept through the theater doors, and at the warm sound of her friends' voices burbling

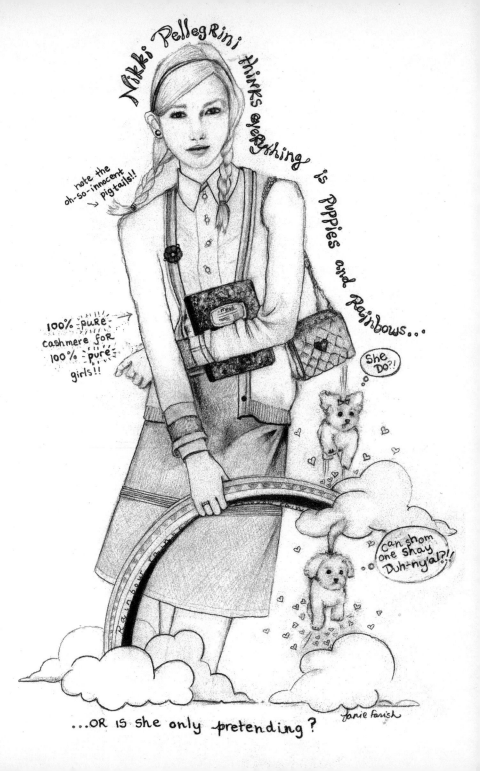

at the end of the hall practically cried with relief. But then she pushed open the door and stepped inside.

Relief died like a bug on Raid.

"Are you Nikki?" Melissa Moon slid her Juicy Couture denim-skirted butt from the edge of the fold-out table on which she was perched, and folded her arms across her epic chest.

"Yeah . . . ," Nikki answered after a moment's hesitation.

"I'm Melissa," she unnecessarily introduced herself. "You and I have some important things to discuss."

Nikki glanced to a corner of the faded blue carpet, where Carly and Juliet sat together, surrounded by markers, glue, glitter, stencils, and long narrow tubes of butcher's paper. Juliet stared deep into the depths of her freshly lobotomized pumpkin, extracted an impressive glob of oozing orange guts, and dropped it onto the spread-out newspaper with a loud *splap*. Carly smoothed a black-cat decal on a piece of poster board, pushing three stiff fingers around in concentric circles. Nikki waited for either of them to meet her eyes, but neither of them did.

"Sorry, I'm late!" gasped a voice directly behind her. Nikki clutched her notebook to her chest and turned around, locking eyes with, of all people, Venice Whitney Wang. "I brought you a double-skim, one-pump vanilla latte," she panted, redirecting her gaze toward Melissa, to whom she offered a steaming Venti cup of Starbucks. As the cup exchanged hands, Nikki noticed their fingernails were painted the exact same shade of Chanel Paparazzi pink.

"Do you people know Venice?" Melissa asked, sliding her gaze between the three younger girls. Nikki observed Juliet and Carly share a glance. Of *course* they knew Venice; she'd practically been salivating to insert herself into their clique since the first day of seventh grade. To be honest, Nikki had considered her a good candidate, but Carly and Juliet eventually wore her down. "No *way* is she in," Carly had repeatedly sniffed. "She wears cartoon Band-Aids, and her name rhymes with 'penis.'"

"*Almost* rhymes with penis," the more careful Juliet had pointed out. "But *still*."

"Venice is my new fashion intern," Melissa continued, tipping some Starbucks into her glistening MAC'ed-out mouth. "And I expect y'all to treat her with the same respect you'd treat Miss Paletsky, who assigned her to this position. Venice has been working very hard to answer some difficult questions about what happened at my party the night of September thirtieth."

Venice swished her straight-ironed jet-black hair behind her body-shimmered shoulder and pouted her lips.

"Nikki," Melissa sighed. "Do you know why you're here?"

Nikki automatically glanced at her friends, who continued to ignore her. Weren't they all here to decorate? "I . . . I'm not sure," she offered at last.

"You're being indicted," Melissa calmly explained. Nikki took a moment, repeating the word in her head: indicted. *In-die-dead.* She willed a definition to come to her, but nothing rang a bell. Melissa sighed, squeezing a dollop of L'Occitane hand crème into her smooth palms, and rubbed her hands together. The air blossomed the unlikely mingled scent of lavender and pumpkin. "Venice" — Melissa rescrewed the cap and cleared her throat — "can you please explain Nikki's situation in terms she can understand?"

"Definitely!" Venice beamed, and proudly extracted a tube of white parchment from her colorful Murakami Louis Vuitton canvas tote. "I drew up an affidavit."

Affa-david. In-die-dead. Seriously, Nikki fretted. *Is this even English?*

Venice shimmied a Goodie No Snags rubber band down the length of the tube in one swift motion, and with a snap of her bangled wrist, unfurled the paper with a flourish.

"It's in calligraphy," she pointed out for Melissa's approval.

"Would you mind reading it out loud?" Melissa folded her arms across her bountiful chest. Venice nodded, clearing her throat.

" 'I, Nikki Pellegrini, hereby confess to the deliberate sabotage of the contest organized on the thirtieth of September by the . . .' "

"Wait — *what?*" Nikki burst out without thinking.

"Please, don't interrupt," Melissa sternly advised. "Venice, go on."

" 'I, Nikki Pellegrini,' " Venice repeated the first line with restored authority, " 'hereby confess to the deliberate sabotage of the contest organized on the thirtieth of September by the Fashion Label currently known as *POSEUR.*' "

"But I didn't!" Nikki gasped, clasping her hands and retreating a step toward the back wall.

"Really?" Melissa asked, unfolding her toffee-toned arms. "Because Venice has been working on this all week, and she swears you did."

Nikki noted a lilt of worry in Melissa's voice, and for the first time realized how genuinely she wanted to know the truth.

"I swear to God!" Nikki swallowed, emphasizing her innocence by touching the modest gold cross at her neck. Melissa cocked her head toward Venice, raising a beautifully arched you-better-explain-yourself eyebrow.

"Juliet," Venice quickly addressed Nikki's dark-haired friend, "didn't you say Nikki disappeared at 11:30?"

"Yes." Juliet nodded, glancing at Nikki. "Well, you did."

"And the crime occurred between eleven and midnight." Melissa frowned, refocusing on Nikki. "And so far, everybody *else* can be accounted for. Can you explain that?"

"I . . ." Nikki bit her bottom lip, the same bottom lip that had found it's way so easily into Jake's mouth, the same bottom lip that he'd tasted with his tongue, sending little pulsing jolts of electricity throughout her entire body. "I was . . ."

"She was kissing Jake Farrish," Carly impatiently snipped from her position on the floor. *"Gawd."*

Melissa gaped, looking her up and down. "That was *you?*"

"Yeah, but . . ." The panicky Venice tugged Melissa's bronzed arm for attention. "Juliet said she was gone for practically an *hour*. No *way* were they kissing the entire time."

"I was *not* gone for an hour!" Nikki insisted, gaping down at her double-crossing friend. "Juliet, *tell* them."

"All I know is you were the one who invited me to that party and then you totally left me stranded," she sniffed.

"But I . . ." Nikki flushed as her friend lowered her pumpkin-slathered ice cream scoop to the floor and furrowed her dusky forehead. Omigod, she *had* abandoned Juliet, she realized with a pang of guilt. But it hadn't been *intentional*.

"Juliet," Melissa addressed her in soothing tones. "Try to put your emotions aside and think. Was Nikki really gone for an *entire* hour?"

"I wasn't wearing a watch so I don't know." She frowned into the lobotomized pumpkin skull and slowly nodded. "All I can say is that's what it *felt* like."

"But," Nikki beseeched her redheaded friend for support, "Carly . . ."

"Don't look at me." She raised a marker-stained palm and hotly huffed. "*I* wasn't even *invited* to that party, *remember?*"

"But . . ." Nikki's face crumpled. "You *knew* I could only invite one person."

"And you invited Juliet, so *I'm* staying out of this." Carly uncapped a blueberry-scented marker with a *pop!* "Sorry."

"Listen, Nikki," Melissa interrupted. "We all *want* to believe you, but you have to admit . . . your case does not look good." She smoothed Venice's swirling calligraphied affidavit on the wooden fold-out table, and clicked open a ballpoint pen. "Why don't you just sign this, so we can all move on with our lives?"

"Because I didn't do it," she replied weakly.

"Okay." Melissa unclicked her pen and dropped it into her purse. "I'm going to give you *one* week. If I were you, I'd do everything in my power to locate one of the vandalized tags. If the handwriting doesn't match yours, then you're off the hook."

"But what happens if I don't find one?"

"That's not really my problem," Melissa breathed airily, checking her pink crocodile watch, and shoving her half-drunk latte into Venice's waiting hands. "All right, ladies. I'm out."

"Good luck finding those tags." Venice smirked as Melissa's sharp footsteps faded down the hall. "I spent every day last week looking up and down Rodeo . . . and nada, *muchacha*."

"I need VitaminWater," Carly sighed to her feet, brushing off her denim-clad knees. "Juliet," she addressed her friend, "Focus, Endurance, or Multi-V?"

"I'll go with." Juliet sprung to her feet and joined her at the door.

"Can I go, too?" Venice asked. Carly and Juliet shared a quick glance.

"A'course," they replied in unison.

As her friends disappeared down the hall, Nikki swallowed a hard lump in her throat, and — against all logic — checked her pink Nokia phone. Had he called her back? Of course he hadn't. She stared at the blue carpet, noticing for the first time a water stain in the shape of a whale, and her friends disappeared down the hall, Venice in tow, her cornflower-blue eyes stung with tears. The whale-shaped water stain wavered at her feet, expanding and contracting. If only it would expand into the size of a real whale, she thought. A great blue whale, like the one in *Pinocchio,* to swallow her whole. She would live there, surviving on seaweed, krill, and plankton. She would listen to the lonely slosh of ocean waves, text-message by the light of a kerosene lamp . . .

It wouldn't be so bad.

For their first date, Charlotte recommended dinner at Campanile, the ultra-sleek see-and-be-seen restaurant on La Brea Boulevard (a far cry from the see-and-be-*shot* Hard Rock Café, thank you very much). The breezy interior of the ivy-covered building boasted such historical details as terra-cotta tile floors and elegant abbey-like walls of exposed grayish brown brick. Sage green rafters supported a peaked glass roof through which one could glimpse a square bell tower with secret-looking windows, a wraparound balcony, and a glinting silver sundial. Charlotte had been seven years old the first time she'd come to Campanile; her father had taken her to celebrate her first ballet lesson. They'd ordered Russian tea with dark cherry preserves, raspberry financiers, flaky ginger scones, and while Charlotte ate, her actor father gesticulated dramatically to all corners of the room, narrating the history of the place. The building, he'd told her, was built *all the way back* in nineteen twenty-nine by none other than Charlie Chaplin, who planned to use it as an office. He never got to work there, however; just as the structure neared completion, he lost it in a scandalous divorce from his wife, Lita Grey, whom Chaplin had married at sixteen. Which was to say, *she'd* been sixteen. Chaplin, Bud Beverwil informed his daughter with a chuckle, had been thirty-five.

And now it was Charlotte who was sixteen, catwalking the Campanile restaurant floor like she owned it. She shrugged out of her high-collared butterscotch-brown Milly faux-fur coat, allowing four dozen sets of eyes, both male and female, to linger wistfully on the confident jerk of her hips, the elegant angle of her neck, and the tumble of glossy black curls between her ivory shoulder blades. As usual, Charlotte ignored her audience, pausing only once to measure the gaze of someone she recognized, or thought she recognized — a middle-aged man with amused hazel eyes, a closely cropped salt-and-pepper haircut, and a deeply lined smile. He was so familiar, Charlotte turned as she passed him, rubbernecking like a motorist at the scene of a gruesome accident, and, noting her attention, the middle-aged man cocked a groomed eyebrow and smirked. She turned away, realizing at once who he was.

Never mind; there was Jules, waiting at the polished bar just half a room away. He slid off his barstool, eyeing her with rapt appreciation, and Charlotte batted her soot-black eyelashes in thanks (the only time she'd seen Jake get to his feet out of respect was during the National Anthem at Dodgers Stadium). *Nice to be dating someone with manners,* she thought as he hung her coat next to his.

"You look beautiful," he whispered into her ear, sending a thrill to the base of her spine. "And you smell like a fig."

"Thank you," she replied, affecting a modest blush. Following the advice of her bosom friend and fashion confidant, Don John, she'd chosen to wear something in keeping with the restaurant's Roaring Twenties history: a vintage Lanvin drop-waist emerald-green satin frock with draping sleeves that fluttered as she moved. Jules, she noted, wore fitted dark gray chinos and a black cotton V-neck — all very fine — but it wasn't until he sat on the barstool and wedged the heel of his polished black Ferragamo on the horizontal bar below his seat, cinching his pant cuff ever-so-slightly, that she gasped with final approval.

"Your socks!" she exclaimed, and fixed her chlorine-green eyes to the article in question. Jules lifted his right foot to examine his ankle, frowning in confusion, and Charlotte's little heart skipped a beat. Here was a definite, *definite* sign, she thought, mingling Jules's amber gaze with her own. "They match my dress," she informed him. "Like, perfectly."

"Oh," he laughed with relief. "I thought there was something wrong."

Charlotte smiled. How could anything be wrong when everything was right? What were the chances of arriving in two outfits that not only didn't clash, but coordinated *perfectly*? She had no head for percentages, but the chances had to be slim. *Like being struck by lightning,* which was, incidentally, exactly how it felt, staring into Jules's electric amber eyes. Charlotte decided his socks and her dress knew something they didn't, but soon would:

They belonged together.

And so, as he divulged the details of his life before Los Angeles, she listened with rapt attention. He attended *L'Ecole Internationale de Genève,* a French-speaking boarding school in Switzerland, where he cultivated interests in everything from skiing to birding to fine wine to Italian opera. But so wide-ranging and eclectic were his tastes, he feared he would never focus on *just one thing.* Yet *focus,* he told her, was a necessary and important step toward adulthood. Not just any adulthood, of course, but the kind of adulthood to which he aspired: *a necessary and important adulthood.*

So, rather than waste time fretting, he took a comprehensive aptitude test which determined a list of career choices based on his "natural strengths" and "innate talents." And low and behold . . .

"I am a natural filmmaker." He wrapped up his monologue with a little blasé shrug. "So I move to Los Angeles. Why not?"

"Yay!" Charlotte burst into a mini round of applause, to which Jules lifted a modest hand. Indeed, he'd conveniently forgotten "filmmaker" had been nineteenth on his results list.

"Dentist" had been his first.

"But tell me, *Charlotte,*" he continued, pronouncing the "ch" in her name like "children" (Charlotte imagined they'd have four, all girls; the fifth, a boy, would die tragically in childbirth). "I want to know all *abowchoo.*"

Charlotte unhooked her platinum Christian Dior stiletto heel from the horizontal leg of her barstool, and rested it on his. "Well . . . ," she began with a coy, flirty smile. "I enjoy long, romantic walks on the beach . . . waking up to the sound of the rain . . . and laughing with old friends."

Jules responded with a solemn nod of his handsome head. "I too enjoy laughing with friends," he informed her, sounding grave. Charlotte dangled a few absentminded fingers into a dish of salted nuts, and gazed fleetingly at a nearby burbling fountain. She'd intended her clichéd response to be taken as a joke (hadn't that been obvious?), but somehow Jules had missed it. What to say next? She found herself at a loss.

She crammed a fistful of nuts into her mouth.

"We must laugh at man," Jules boomed with unexpected force, causing Charlotte to gag quietly on a cashew, *"to avoid crying for him."* He bobbed his thick black man-brows, assessing the level of her awe while she nodded, dabbing her watering eyes with the edge of her napkin.

"Do you know who said that?" he ventured at last.

"Um . . ." She bit the corner of her petal-pink bottom lip. "You did?"

He chuckled, touching her softly on the elbow. "It is a quote," he explained. "Napoleon. You know who he is, yes?"

Charlotte narrowed her pool-green eyes. Did she, Charlotte Sidonie Beverwil, honorary French Citizen of the Hollywood Hills, know who Napoleon was?

"Um . . . he's dating Mischa Barton, right?"

"No," Jules answered with a sympathetic smile. "He is . . ."

"I know," she blurted, holding fast to the seat of her stool, "who he is. I was *joking*."

"Oh." Jules blinked, looking stunned. And then, without warning, he burst into a fit of giggles. Seriously. *Giggles.* Charlotte flushed to the roots of her hair and glanced around, queasy with embarrassment. "You are *funny*!" Jules informed her in an exhilarated voice, while a blonde at the end of the bar smirkingly pretended to examine her fingernails.

"I'm really not." Charlotte cringed, bugged her eyes at the bartender, and mouthed the word "martini." The bartender, a white-haired man with a nose like a turnip, raised his gray caterpillar eyebrows, judging her age with classic bartenderly suspicion.

"Yes." Jules pounded his Rolexed fist into his open palm. "Of all human qualities, humor is the most important. More important than *strength,* than money, than beauty, than *strength* . . ."

"More important than repeating yourself?" Charlotte couldn't help herself.

"Perhaps," Jules went on, blissfully unaware of her gentle jab. "Even more important than food. Because food only nourishes this." He pressed his wide hand to his firm abdomen, and for one delicious moment Charlotte's appreciation for rock-hard mandriff overwhelmed her urge to die. But then he said:

"The tummy."

Charlotte blanched with numb horror. The *tummy*? Was he a

guy, or an unusually overdeveloped *Teletubbie*? She sent the bartender another imploring look. *Please,* her eyes pleaded, and she actually clasped her hands. *Please, take pity.* The bartender sighed, and with a casual *whaddowhycare* shrug of his black suspender-clad shoulders, twisted open a bottle of gin.

"So!" Charlotte blurted, desperate to change the subject. "What's your favorite movie?"

"Oh." Jules frowned, baffled as to why they changed topics of conversation. (The laughter thing had been going so well!) "Well, that one is easy for me. *Garden State.* Have you seen this film?"

Charlotte bit the inside of her cheek, hard, hoping to distract herself from an unwelcome memory. She and Jake had rented *Garden State* on their first official second date; Charlotte had thought it was okay, actually, but Jake had *hated* it. He'd staggered around the rest of the day with this glazed, wide-eyed expression on his face. "Look at me," he'd say. "I'm Zach Braff. I just go around, like, *feeling* stuff." And when she'd hit him with her pillow, he'd whine. "Sto-o-op! Don't you realize I'm Zach Braff and I'm *sensitive?!*" And when she'd pressed her lips against his to shut him up, he'd clutch his stomach and say: "Ugh . . . I'm gonna braff. Oh God, I just braffed myself."

She'd never laughed so hard in her life.

"You see that guy over there?" she blurted, desperate to change the subject once again. Jules stared at her for a prolonged beat, and Charlotte realized he was beginning to think she was schizo. "By the fountain," she instructed, inexplicably lowering her voice.

"Yes." Jules frowned, observing the small, candlelit table in question.

"You know that girl Petra?" Charlotte evenly continued. "That's her father."

"Oh." Jules nodded with another blasé shrug. "He is a handsome man, no?"

"Yeah, well . . . see that woman he's with? Definitely *not* her mother. And they're still married, so . . . you put it together."

Jules furrowed his black eyebrows, joining Charlotte in observing the scene. The man who was Petra's father stabbed a toothpick into a small ceramic dish, offering his mysterious brunette companion a dripping green olive. Smiling, she tilted across the table, sunk her teeth in, and slowly slid the olive from the tiny wood skewer. Her oversized, thin oatmeal cashmere sweater slipped down her shoulder as she leaned back into her seat, rolled her prize inside her still-smiling mouth, spat the pit into her cupped palm, pinched her tapered fingers, tilted across the table a second time, and dropped it — like a coin — into the right breast pocket of his expensive-looking denim cowboy shirt.

"Isn't that just so . . . *ew?*" Charlotte delicately inquired.

Jules swiveled in his seat, exhaled an expressive burst of air between his pouting French lips, and squeezed his eyes shut. "Nothing disgusts me more than this," he intoned. "To do such a thing to your wife . . . it is despicable."

"Really?" Charlotte winked her left eye with suspicion.

"Of course!" Jules pinched his fingers to his temples, springing them apart. "People who go around like loyalty is *nothing*? It makes me sick. When I am with a woman, I am *with* her."

"So, you mean" — Charlotte swallowed — "you've never cheated?"

"Never." he frowned. "Marguerite, my ex . . . we were together for five years, and she betrayed me with a man like *this*." He indicated Petra's father, and spewed. "She is too young! You despicable *pig*."

At the word "pig" Charlotte could no longer restrain herself. Gripping the edge of the bar, she tilted forward on her high stool, touched his flushed, chiseled cheek with her hand, and kissed him.

"I am *so* sorry," she gasped moments later, settling into her seat and smoothing her glass-smooth brown hair. She fluttered her eyelashes and smiled. "Are you traumatized?"

"Of course, *no*!" Jules clutched her knee, locking her into a look of grave concern. "Why do you apologize?"

Charlotte took a breath. Okay, so the guy had no sense of humor. You know who had a sense of humor? Jake. And look how well *he* turned out. What if, instead of *judging* Jules, she decided to join him? It could be a relief: to be serious, to be treated seriously, and not (as Jake had treated her) like a joke.

"You're right," she observed with a serious nod. "It's so silly to apologize." As if to reward her decision, the bartender slid two martinis in her direction and she smiled, lifting her glass by its delicate stem. Clear liquid sloshed about the rim of the glass, spilling a drop to her lap, which bled into her satin dress and transformed the brilliant emerald green into something darker, like the color of mold. With Jake, she would have incorporated the spill into a toast. "To dry-cleaning," she'd joke. "To wetting my pants." But she wasn't here with Jake. She was here with Jules. Good, loyal, *serious* Jules.

"To new beginnings," she offered, clinking his glass. He smiled.

A PIECE OF CANDY COUTURE

Materials:
emerald silk exterior
leather interior
brass and glass beads for clasp

← art deco clasp
inspired by Paris
Metro Stations

diluted dye
"water stain"
detail

No visible label (keep it subtle)
style = clutch

chez Charlotte Beverwil

inspiration: martini-stained silk dresses

drawing: Janie Farrish

If only everyone spent Tuesday night dining at Campanile, but they didn't. Janie Farrish, in particular, dined at an establishment so exclusive, only four people (and, occasionally, a disobedient cat) ever ate there.

Her kitchen.

"Mom." Janie swept the pink and gray eraser boogers from her open sketchbook, and glared — for maybe the umpteenth time — at the kitchen wall. "When are we going to get that fixed?"

"Get what fixed, honey?" Mrs. Farrish murmured, removing the lid from a large pot of boiling pasta, and tilting her tired face toward the steam.

"That." Janie pointed to the kitchen wall by the fridge, or, more accurately, the utter *lack* of wall by the fridge, a vestige of Tyler Brock's new puppy, a French bulldog named Beluga, whom they'd babysat last year. At night, they'd made a bed of towels and confined her to the kitchen, blocking the door with a baby gate. She'd whimpered the whole night, and come morning Janie discovered her passed out in the corner — a saucer-sized hole in the wall, incriminating flecks of plaster still clinging to her rubbery, black lips.

"Janie." Her mother lifted the heavy pot from the stove and furrowed her damp brow. "Your father plastered it over months ago."

"Yeah, but haven't you noticed? It's a completely different color than the rest of the wall."

"You want to repaint the whole kitchen?" her mother scoffed, dumping the pot's steaming contents into a large dented strainer. "Be my guest."

A sour bubble surfaced inside Janie's stomach and threatened to burst. Weird, but certain words, which before Charlotte's friendship had meant nothing, now meant *everything* — to the point where they made her physically ill. Take her mother's word, "guest," for instance. What if Charlotte came over? Janie looked around, seeing her whole house with a brand-new set of eyes — *her* eyes — and all the details she'd never noticed before — the tear in the screen door; the old, matted carpet; the boxy smallness of the kitchen; the sagging, pet-haired arms of the living room couch — pulsed outward in vivid Technicolor. It wasn't merely that the furniture was *falling apart,* but that it had never been that great to *begin* with. What would Charlotte, whose bedroom was lit by not one but *three* antique chandeliers, think of Janie's square ceiling light fixture, complete with tiny, fried moth corpses by the bulb? What would Charlotte, who spent her nights sweetly tucked into a four-poster mahogany bed, think of Janie's standard IKEA fiberboard single?

What would Charlotte think of *fiberboard*?

And then, on top of all of that, there was *the weirdness factor.* Like the potted cactus her mom decorated with red chili-pepper lights. Or the collection of dried wishbones on the kitchen windowsill. Or the eighteen PROPERTY OF JAKE stickers stuck at random on the front door, a vestige of his Dymo label maker days in the fourth grade.

How had she not noticed this before? How had she not *cared*?

Jake knowingly chortled as she explained her issue, his eyes bolted to their boxy black TV. He was deeply entrenched in a crucial game of *Grand Theft Auto: San Andreas,* his sole respite from thoughts of Charlotte, and therefore his current addiction.

"You're wearing Winston goggles," he explained, blasting a parked white car with his machine gun.

"Winston goggles?" Janie winced as her brother rattled another vicious round of bullets into a hapless palm tree. "You mean, like, beer goggles?"

"Yeah." He paused to wrestle with his controls, punching buttons like a lab rat on crack. On the screen, a shrieking blonde ran down the street. "Except instead of everything looking better, everything looks worse."

"But Jake" — Janie ripped a cuticle from her thumb — "things look, like, *way* worse."

"Yeah, but whatever." He lowered his controls to his lap while his character, C.J., bench-pressed at the gym. "I mean, imagine you grew up in a shantytown." He raised his eyebrows for effect. "In, like, *Honduras.* You'd probably think our house was some kind of paradise."

"Very nice!" Mrs. Farrish clattered in the kitchen, and Jake and Janie shared a glance, bracing themselves. "Honduras" — she stomped into the living room, wiping her hands on her green checked dishcloth — "is one of the most *destitute* and *impoverished* regions in the world. Is picturing yourself there *really* necessary for you two to appreciate life in this house?"

"I guess Honduras is a little extreme," Jake deadpanned. "What about . . . Rwanda. One of the nice parts?"

"What?" His mother gaped, eyeing the TV with sudden suspicion. "Is that that *terrible* video game again?"

Jake glanced at the TV, where C.J. sat flexing his 50 Cent–caliber biceps in a warehouse of deathly rocket launchers. "Uh . . . no?" He grinned, attempting to block the TV with his scrawny body. "I mean, it *is* a video game. But not the one you're thinking. It's Mrs. Pac-Man."

His mother narrowed her eyes.

"The next generation," he added.

"You," she said, pointing her finger. "Turn that off and take out the trash. You," she addressed Janie. "Set the table."

Janie was far too busy thinking about Winston Goggles, and all that it implied, to eat, and went to bed without dinner. What if, she wondered, flipping through her sketches, Winston Goggles also applied to her designs? She'd worked far into the night interpreting and reinterpreting the Trick-or-Treater proposals, brewing enough Yogi Stomach Ease tea to steep a blue whale, and yet, come Wednesday morning, doubt continued to weigh on her mind. She blinked into the not-quite-morning dark, hugged her blankets to her chin, and shivered.

With its lush lawns, evergreen hedges, and brimming pools, you could forget Los Angeles is a desert — but then, nothing quite reminds you like the morning. At night, the temperature plummets, and by dawn, the lawns and hedges are gray with frost, and the pools are sharp as mirrors. For Janie, getting out of bed was more than "a challenge"; getting out of bed was, like, a total aberration of nature. Her limbs grew stiff, her movements slow, her breathing labored — almost like she was part reptile — and every bodily cell begged her to find a nice sun-warmed rock, somewhere to flatten her chilly lizard belly and gape.

Working up her will, Janie whipped aside her bedding, and thought better of it, snatching her red-and-black-checked comforter and wrapping herself inside. Grabbing her sketchbook, she shuffled out of her bedroom, the tail end of her makeshift robe trailing along the linoleum, and headed toward the kitchen. Her brother sat at the table, staring grimly into a bowl of Peanut Butter Bumpers, and so thoroughly swaddled inside his comforter he resembled a gigantic larva.

"Ha." The gigantic larva pivoted in its chair. "You look like a gigantic larva."

"And you look like a bee-yoo-ti-full princess," Janie rejoined, slapping her sketchbook to the linoleum table.

"Seriously," Jake scoffed, hugging his gray T-shirt cotton comforter close. "Can we *not* put on the heat for *five* minutes?"

"Go for it." Janie raised her eyebrows. "If you want to die by the hands of Mom."

"Why do we have heat if we can never use it?" he moaned, withering into his cocoon. Janie sighed, blinking into the glowing depths of the fridge. Her dad had remembered to bring home her favorite Stonyfield low-fat lemon yogurt, and yet, the sight of it made her sick. She shut the door, surrendering to another wave of queasiness.

She plopped down next to her brother, slid her sketchbook across the table, and flipped it open. "Can you tell me what you think of these?" she asked, locating the drawings in question. "They're designs for the POSEUR bag," she explained, biting her nail.

"Oh yeah." Jake nodded, and promptly returned to his Bumpers. "They're good."

"Jake." Janie's tongue clucked in dismay. "You didn't even *look*."

"Dude." He winced. "They're purses, alright?"

"I'm just," she sighed, removing her nail from her mouth. "Do you think Winston Goggles apply?"

"How do you mean?" Jake frowned, examining the cereal box for new fun facts.

"I mean . . ." Janie leaned on her elbow, tucking her sleep-tousled bob behind her left ear. "Do you think the girls at school . . . I mean, they're so used to wearing, like, *designer* stuff. Maybe they'll think these purses look . . ."

"Poor?" Jake suggested.

"No, not *poor*." Janie drew her eyebrows together. It was ridiculous to think of themselves as poor — they bought organic yogurt, for god's sake. "But just like, not . . ."

"Rich," he offered, causing her to cringe. "Rich" was one of those déclassé words, right? That *poor* people used?

"Okay, well, for the sake of argument," she surrendered in a rush. "Do you think they'll think that?"

Jake returned his attention to her sketches, frowned for a long second, and shook his head. "Dude." He scooted his chair from the table. "I'm sorry, but they all look the same to me."

By the time she got to school, all she wanted to do was find a quiet place in the shade to lie down and vomit. But such luxuries weren't available to her. "Janie!" Charlotte cried the moment she emerged from the underground elevator, and broke free from her Jaguar orbit. She scampered excitedly to Janie's side, pinning her chlorine gaze to the sketchpad tucked underneath her long and lanky arm. "Are those *them?*" She squealed, clapping her little hands. Janie hugged the sketchpad to her chest, attempting a smile. "Can I see? Can I see, puh-lease?"

"Um . . ." Janie lowered the sketchbook to waist level and slipped her thumb under the first page. Her stomach dropped. "Actually," she croaked, retreating a step, "they're kind of not ready."

"Come on," Charlotte begged, and teasingly reached for the sketchbook. "Can't I just see what you have so far?"

"No," Janie squawked, whipping the book from Charlotte's light grasp. Charlotte retreated a tiny step, fluttering her soot-black

eyelashes — stunned. At some distance, Kate and Laila, who'd remained wilted across Charlotte's shining Jaguar hood, shared a bemused glance. "I'm sorry." Janie flushed, sweat prickling her armpit. "It's just . . ."

"Charlotte!" Jules called from the opposite end of the Show-room, diverting her attention. Janie seized her window and escaped, her sketchpad flapping against her flat chest, Pumas pounding the pavement. A basketball rolled by and she stumbled into it, kicking it clear across the Showroom and under Evan Beverwil's forest green Range Rover. "Yo!" Marco Duvall bellowed in dismay. But she had no time to apologize, let alone retrieve the ball and risk running into Evan, whom she'd been avoiding since their totally awkward "moment" together at the Viceroy.

She felt sick.

"What are your symptoms?" the school nurse inquired in a cereal-crisp voice, subjecting Janie to a calculating once-over. Nurse Jackie wore her silver hair in a short, angular bob that never seemed to grow out or be cut, and appeared to subsist on a strict diet of Pepsi One and York Peppermint patties, nibbling around the edges like a rat at a wheel of cheese. Her fake-baked rail of a body, with its galaxy of sunspots across the arms and chest, earned her the nickname "Nurse Crackie," which everybody used, including some teachers. She was in her sixties, but still dressed sixteen — a cause of major distress for Winston's more fashion-forward fe-males. Nothing quite compared to the trauma of arriving to school in the same outfit as their sour-faced school nurse, an experience collectively referred to as "crack," as in, "*ew-uh* . . . my pink Bur-berry driver's cap is totally on crack!"

But Nurse Crackie restricted her purchases to luxury retailers like Barneys, Saks, and Ted Pelligan, so the chances of Janie ap-pearing in her clothes were slimmer than Crackie herself. Today, for example, the school medic wore light blue high-waisted jeans (Stella McCartney) with a wide fruit-roll-up-red belt (Marc Ja-cobs), a patterned navy blue blouse with puffed sleeves (Nanette Lepore), cherry patent-and-cork pumps (Tapeet), and plastic ban-gles (Jessica Kagan) that clacked when she extended her bony arm to slide the thermometer from Janie's waiting pursed lips.

"You don't have a fever," she remarked, shaking the thermom-eter with a decisive flap of loose underarm flesh. She observed Janie with an appraising look. "Would you like to lie down?"

"Okay," Janie nodded weakly, crawling across the crackling butcher-papered cot. She sent Nurse Crackie her bravest smile. "Is it okay if I call my mom?"

"Of course," she replied, and swiveled in her seat, returning to her gray computer. Janie unearthed her cell phone from her crocheted bag and pressed 1.

"Hello," answered a breathless voice on the first ring. Janie smiled into the phone.

"Hi, Mom."

"Sorry?"

"I'm at the nurse's office," Janie explained, lowering her voice.

"Oh!" Amelia cackled with comprehension. *"Faker."*

"I'm actually not." Janie frowned, peeling the lid of a mini Kozy Shack rice pudding. "I actually feel really nauseous."

"Oh no." Amelia mulled this new information over. "Have you immaculately conceived Paul's love child? Are you Juno?"

"Amelia!" Janie yelped, almost dropping her Nokia. She glanced in the direction of Nurse Crackie's workstation, expecting a hard and reproving stare, but the nurse was plugged into her Nano and engrossed in her MySpace profile, oblivious to every word. "Amelia" — she lowered her voice a harsh whisper — *"tell me he did not hear you say that."*

"Omigod, Janie," Amelia laughed. "He's a *million* miles away, I swear. And you'll never guess what he's doing."

"What?" Janie licked her floppy foil pudding lid with great melancholy.

"Making a daisy chain."

"He is?" Janie smiled. She *knew* Paul had a sensitive side.

"Puh-*lease* don't sound like that," Amelia chastised. "This is seriously disturbing shit. Like, the other day? He was listening to *Devendra Banhart.*"

"Um . . . Amelia?" Janie lowered the foil lid to her lap and clutched her stomach.

"I just hope his weird hippie phase doesn't affect Creatures of

Habit," she blathered on. "It's, like, *you* are the lead guitarist of a *punk* band. There are no *daisies* in punk."

"Amelia," Janie whimpered, "you think my drawings are good, right?"

"Omigod," Amelia slowly replied. "I was just talking about Paul Elliot Miller, and you *changed the subject*." She paused, letting it sink in. "You're, like, *dying,* aren't you."

"It's just it occurred to me, you know? Maybe I'm not that good. . . ."

"Janie," Amelia scoffed, "part of being talented is feeling like a fake. If you walked around, like, *I'm so great* all the time, you'd be that girl. *You* know. From the Art Fair?"

Janie smiled, knowing exactly to whom her scornful friend referred. Despite a severe case of tone-deafness (or perhaps because of it) Deena Yazdi genuinely considered herself the next Christina Aguilera. The Showroom, the girls' bathroom, the end of the Breezeway, the back of the school bus — no place was safe. Without warning, she'd cup a manicured hand to one ear, flutter her brown eyes shut, and unleash her atonal howlings upon the world. As for the Art Fair to which Amelia was referring, she'd performed Celine Dion's "My Heart Will Go On" to an audience of five hundred. At the most dramatic moment in the song (the part where Celine thumps her chest), Theo Godfrey unleashed a warbling dying-dog yowl, and the entire auditorium dissolved into laughter. But Deena remained onstage, completely unfazed.

"Ugh," Amelia groaned at the memory. "I actually think confidence goes hand in hand with utter lack of talent."

"Yeah, except . . . you're the most confident person I know."

"*And* I'm talented," Amelia agreed, stunned. "Okay, so my theory doesn't work. But who cares? You're still the best artist I know."

"Yep." Janie gulped and lurched, clapping her hand to her mouth. Glancing about the room in a panic, she dropped her phone, leaned over the edge of the cot, and — in the spirit of Deena herself — began to spew.

The Guy: Evan Beverwil
The Getup: Forest-green board shorts from Val-Surf,
black cotton J.Crew t-shirt, black havianna flip-flops,
and pewter "Celtic Knot" dog-tag necklace.

The only place where he truly felt, like, *good* was the beach. Yeah, yeah . . . his little sister was always correcting him on that. "You're supposed to say you feel *well*, Evan, not *good*. Don't you even know basic grammar?" Not that he dignified her stupid-ass comments with an actual response, but: he meant what he said. Something about the SoCal beaches — the air, the sand, the gloomy gray Pacific — he actually felt like a better person. Purified on a spiritual level. He didn't feel well. He felt *good*.

Maybe that's why he felt so out of his element at school. Winston was like this landlocked island — and things could get pretty existential. One time, when he ducked out of class to get this book he left in the Brat (the Brat was what he called the Porsche; the Rover was just the Rover), this seagull came cruising by and landed straight up in the middle of the Showroom — pretty crazy when you thought about it. Bird had to have traveled some serious mileage, and yet he didn't look tired, or lost, or anything. He strutted about, gray wings tucked behind his back, chest puffed up like he owned the place. And when he spotted Evan, he flexed his hard yellow beak and let out a little bird-yap, like he was indignant, like, *where have you* been? Evan had to laugh. "I been in freakin' *bio,*

bitch," he replied. (Why not? No one was around to judge him. Everyone was in class.) That seagull just tilted his ruffled white head in total confusion: *yap, yap!* "I *know,* dude," Evan shook his head. "Tell me about it."

Later, when he got out of class for real, the seagull was gone. Evan waited around for it to come back; he even ditched bio once or twice, heading out to the Showroom to scan himself some sky. But that was it. One day, the beach came to visit. The next day, it was gone.

That is, until he met her.

Janie Farrish, man. Ever since that night at the tar pits, that girl had been *killing* him. Her *eyes*. People were always talking about his eyes, his sister's, too, about how bright blue and green they were, like swimming pools, or whatever. Evan didn't get it. Janie had eyes like the sea. Yeah, he knew it was cheesy, but it was *true*. And not just like any sea, but the SoCal Pacific — the only sea that mattered. The SoCal Pacific wasn't comforting, like those bright blue Bermuda beaches on postcards; it was dark, murky, and un-readable, shifting from blue to gray to silver and back again. Her eyes were like that, man. Moody. He'd asked his friends — Joaquin, Theo, Tim, *all* those guys — what they thought of her, but they all just shrugged, like, *what was there to even think about?* Evan nod-ded, like, *yeah, I feel you.* Even though he didn't. Not even close.

Why do people go for swimming pools when the ocean's, like, right *there*?

But she wasn't into him, that much was clear. She'd practically told him off that one night in the Brat, and then, man, the Viceroy. He was boring — she'd all but told him so, straight up. Not that he'd argue her point. He could be pretty quiet, and well . . . yeah. He was quiet. If he hadn't been so good-looking (he was just say-ing), he'd probably have girls say he was boring all the time. But he *was* good-looking and lots of girls were fooled. It's just the way it is. Good looks are interesting, even if the person behind them isn't; he could be honest with himself about that.

But Janie wasn't like other girls. Her ocean eyes saw right through him. And there was no escaping them, either. Just last weekend he was surfing, and he caught this deeply righteous wave. Like, the water came churning up under his board and just, like, *launched* him. And there he was, sailing through this perfect salt-gray tunnel of glass, all exhilarated, when suddenly, he thought, *I'm inside her eye.* And then his board kicked up under him, and the wave came crashing down — just this *rush* of water, man — pounding on his body, his ears, and generally kicking his ass. Everything was this blue and gray, shadow and light, like, *swirling.* But it was all good. *I'm inside her eye,* he'd told himself. And just surrendered.

Sometimes, instead of heading out to Baja Fresh with his buddies, he'd spend lunch alone in an empty classroom. A couple of times, he'd arranged the desks into weird alien formations, like crop circles and pyramids and shit, which accomplished the double mission of pissing off teachers and making kids laugh — two birds with one stone. But most times, he'd just kick up his legs, peel a banana, pop open a bag of goldfish crackers, and listen to his iPod. Lately, he'd been on this Bob Seger kick — okay, he was *always* on a Bob Seger kick — but there was this one song in particular that he just kept on playing. If you keep listening to one song, he noticed, it's like waves weathering rocks to sand. Individual words disintegrate into long, blended sound. For a while he'd zone out, forget to listen — but a few words always pulled him back. Words that no matter how many times he listened refused to disintegrate and disappear.

Like: *I lost my way.* Or: *Searchin' for shelter. The secrets that we shared. There in the darkness . . .*

Janie was lovely . . .

It goes without saying she skipped lunch. Nurse Crackie advised her to go home, but Janie assured her she was completely fine, really, and headed straight to 201B, the classroom where the weekly POSEUR meeting was held. She'd decided to set up early and get her mind in the right place. She *would* get this over with. Even if it killed her.

She pushed through one of the two heavy doors, and entered the Main Hall. The long corridor stretched out, all arched ceiling and tall windows, patterning the polished tile floor with white trapezoids of sunlight. She relished the flickering flashes as she walked, the echo and ricochet of her blue ballet flats, all of which conspired to add *just* the right amount of drama. So, yeah, maybe this day wasn't dramatic in any *global* sense, but it *was* dramatic for her. And it was sympathetic, in a way, for the Main Hall to get into the spirit of things.

She cracked open the dark green door, peeped her head in, and slid her gray eyes about the room. The teacher's desk, established territory of Melissa Moon, remained unmanned, as did Charlotte's narrow length of windowsill and Petra's blue corner of carpet. Confident she was alone, Janie swung the door open, kicking the doorstopper with the toe of her foot and securing it to the wall. She turned around. Now it was just her, her sketches, the recycling bin . . .

And Evan Beverwil.

There by the corner window: his lean, golden body folded into one of the small student desks, his flip-flopped feet kicked up on the seat of another, his sun-kissed hair flipped sweetly about his ears as he pursed his lips and clenched his fist, bobbing his head in time to music she couldn't hear. His eyes were squeezed shut. All he had to do was open them, and he'd be looking right at her.

She wasn't about to let that happen.

Still clutching her sketchbook and overstuffed folders to her chest, she tiptoed backward toward the open door, pivoted her foot, and turned to escape down the hall. But then, without warning, and scaring her half to death, Evan howled, "Against the *wind!* I'm still running against the *wind.*" She shrieked, and he cracked his eyes open, opened them wider, and quickly removed his headphones.

"Hey." Janie froze in the open doorway, exploded folders and scattered papers at her feet. "Sorry," she recovered, sinking at once to her knees. As mortifying as it was to pick up dropped papers in front of Charlotte's brother, it was an easier task than looking at him (that is, looking at him looking at *her,* in that weird, judgmental way of his). She blushed at the sound of his approaching flip-flops, and then — so much worse! — there they were. The tanned skin, the hair on his ankles, the sort of long toes. God, his feet were so, like . . . *naked.*

"Lemme help you," he said, bending to his knees. She could hear his headphones, draped across his neck — the tinny sound of whatever song he'd been listening to. He smelled exactly like salt and sun-warmed wood.

"Whoa," he said. "Did you draw this?"

"Oh." She looked up so quick she got a head rush. "Yeah . . . ," she admitted, blinking back the blotches and reaching for the paper.

"It's really good," Evan said, holding on to it, transfixed. "Who is this?"

"It's, um . . ." Seriously, could she just *die*? Like, right *now*? "It's my mother," she explained. Evan bobbed his eyebrows in approval.

"She's hot."

"H-ha," Janie stammered. Was he joking? "Yeah . . . *your* mom's really hot."

"Aw, man." Evan's face crumpled in disgust. "I can't think about my mom like that."

"Oh." Janie's voice heightened to a disbelieving squeak. "But you *can* think about *my* mom like that."

"Well . . ." His chlorine-green eyes locked into middle space, and he grinned. *"Yeah."*

"Ew," she laughed, batting him on the arm with a floppy black folder; their eyes met for about a millisecond before she glanced away. Once her parents had been in the market for a new house, and looked at one with a swimming pool. It had been way out of their price range, but they seriously seemed to think about it, and when they finally "came to their senses" (as they put it), Jake and Janie were crushed. Evan's eyes were like that swimming pool: all she ever wanted, and all she'd never have.

"Okay," she breathed, rising to her ballet-flatted feet, and hugging her messily arranged papers to her chest. "Thanks." She blushed again. "I guess I'll, um, go."

"No, wait. I'll go," Evan insisted, getting to his feet. "I mean . . . you're here to, like, work or something, right?"

"Kind of." Janie nodded. "I've got to set up for this, like, presentation. And I'm kind of nervous about it, so . . ." She covered her face with her hands and briskly shook her head. "I have no idea why I'm telling you this."

"Hey, it's cool." Evan began to reach for her elbow, and stopped himself, lifting his hand to the back of his head. "I mean" — he forked his fingers through his hair — "you got to talk someone, right?"

"Yeah." Janie couldn't resist a rueful laugh. "Like a therapist, maybe."

"Or you could be like Margaret," he suggested, clasping his hands at his heart. "Are you *there,* God?"

Janie angled her face in bemused suspicion, sputtering a tiny laugh. "Okay, *how* do you even *know* about that book?"

"You know," Evan admitted with a sheepish shrug. "I just, like, *read* it."

Their eyes met again, and this time for keeps (aka a good three seconds.) "What?" Evan angled his face and furrowed his brow, taking his turn at suspicion.

"You're just . . ." Janie paused, searching for the word, and when she found it, shook her head, embarrassed. "Never mind."

"No, what?" he insisted. "What am I?"

"I don't know." She shook her head again, allowing her slinky light brown bob to fall around her eyes, and laughed, hoping to excuse the total lameness of her next word. *"Interesting."*

Evan frowned, nodding to himself, and scratched the back of his neck. He looked up, locked her into a smile, and walked slowly backward, exiting the room. Out in the hall, he lifted his chin in salute. "You too."

"I can't believe this," Melissa gasped, clutching Janie's sketch and holding it to the beaming fluorescent light. Her perfectly gelled eyebrows knit together, and she shook her head in slow disbelief. Janie sighed, still too focused on Evan to care. So, Melissa hated her design. Big deal. Did Janie really want to be responsible for bringing *yet another designer handbag* into the world? No, she did not. There were enough handbags as it was, waiting around in malls, in need of some kind person to notice them and take them home. But no . . . POSEUR had to design their own.

It was pretty selfish, when you thought about it.

"It's perfect," Melissa breathed, lowering the drawing to her desk. "It's, like, *exactly* how I wanted it to look."

Janie blinked out of her stupor, stunned. "It is?"

"Like, *exactly* exactly!" She returned her gaze to the drawing, shaking her head with slow amazement. "For real, Janie? It's like you went inside my *head*."

Janie smiled, imagining the tiniest of doors — situated right behind Melissa's diamond-studded ear — swinging open. And there she'd be, Mini-Melissa, all decked out in thimble-sized furs and Barbie bling. "*Hay*-ayyyy!" She'd beckon a shaky handheld camera inside, beaming her mini-watt smile. "Welcome to my *head. Ah-hahahah!*"

"It's true," a cool voice intruded into Janie's fantasy. Charlotte looked up from her own drawing, eyes shining. "It's exactly what I pictured."

"How did you do it?" Petra beamed. "I love it *so*urdough pretzel sticks."

Janie laughed. "Sorry?"

"BBQ corn nuts." Melissa glanced at Petra, nodding her head in agreement. "Mint Milano Mentos, Baked Cheeto bagel chip? *Frooty Booty.*"

Janie swallowed. Now that the pressure was off, it seemed her appetite had returned all at once — massive, and all eclipsing — like the airborne anvil in cartoons. She could no longer talk, or even think. The anvil came crashing down and smashed her brain to pancake.

Mmm . . . *pancake.*

"Um, you guys?" She abruptly pushed her desk chair back and sprung to her feet. "Sorry, but do you mind if I run to the vending machine?"

"That's *my* job," Venice piped up from the back of the room, eager to be of service. She flipped open her sparkly white notebook (an exact match to Melissa's) and looked up, blue bubble pen poised. "Snicker chip bagel stick?"

A sound, like a baby pterodactyl, reared from the deepest part of Janie's stomach, and she bolted for the exit.

"Hey-uh!" Venice cried, gaping at Melissa for some kind of explanation. Melissa widened her dark brown eyes, crumpling her forehead like an accordion. "I would've done it," Venice sniveled.

"Don't worry about it, Venice," Petra sighed from her place by the blue recycling bin. "Janie doesn't need to make you do things she's perfectly capable of doing herself." She cocked a serious eyebrow in Melissa's direction. "This isn't the Court of Versailles."

"Don't remind me," Charlotte pouted, turning the gold bracelet on her wrist.

"Venice." Melissa snapped her fingers, and a glittering rhinestone sprung from her nail and disappeared. Her intern stood at attention, resisting the urge to scan the floor. "Would you please post our designs on the bulletin board?"

Darting like a hummingbird from girl to girl, Venice dutifully retrieved the four sketches and secured them to the bulletin board with clear plastic tacks. Once the drawings were attached, she retreated to her corner of the room and resumed the mystifying task of separating Emilio Poochie's dog kibble into three piles by color: red, yellow, and brown.

Melissa narrowed her eyes, squinting at the drawings. "Charlotte . . . ," she began slowly. "This is a joke, right?"

"What?" Charlotte swung her legs from the windowsill and

landed lightly — the daintiest of dismounts. In four quick steps, she was at Melissa's side, examining the sketch in question. "Of *course* it's not a joke." She frowned.

"You want to make this bag out of stained silk." Melissa bugged her eyes in disbelief. "*Stained.* For real."

"I don't see the problem." Charlotte folded her arms and knit her porcelain brow.

Melissa flew her hands to the crown of her head and began to pace, stomping to an abrupt stop. The spiky heel of her silver Isabella Fiore boot ground into the gray-blue rug. "Who in their *right* mind is going to want to buy a handbag — a *new* handbag — that *already has stains on it*?!"

Charlotte inhaled, bracing herself for combat, but just as she opened her acid mouth, Petra joined them at the board and interjected.

"I can't *believe* this," she reprimanded, fixing Melissa with a reproving stare. "You're seriously upset about a little stain?"

"*Thank* you," Charlotte exhaled, but Petra rewarded her gratitude with a scathing glance.

"Do you have any idea" — she trembled — "where silk even *comes* from?"

Charlotte fluttered her eyes shut and sighed — already bored.

"For every gram of silk . . ." Petra pinched her fingers and squinted her eyes like a jeweler. "For every single *gram,* fifteen silkworms are killed!" She paused for effect. *"Boiled alive in their cocoons."*

"Petra." Charlotte couldn't hide a bemused smile. "Forgive me, but . . . they're *worms*."

"Seriously, Petra." Melissa folded her arms and shook her head. "What are you gonna do if you get a tapeworm? Give it a name and throw it a Frisbee?"

"That's different." Petra glowered. "Silkworms aren't hurting anyone."

"Hey, look." Melissa raised her hands in surrender. "I'm on your side, alright? You don't want silk. I sure as hell don't want stains. Charlotte?" She removed Charlotte's sketch from the bulletin board and, in her best Heidi Klum accent, pronounced: *"Yer owt."*

"I'm out," Charlotte ruffled like a tiny owl. "What about you?"

"Well, *my* bag is canvas. So unless there's some *canvas* worm I haven't heard about . . ."

"Mm . . . no." Charlotte smiled with wincing contempt. "But there's something called a tasteless, *tacky* worm? And by the looks of this bag" — she gazed at Melissa's design, pressing her fingers to her throat — "no life was spared."

"Did you . . ." Melissa held up a hand and squeezed her eyes shut. "Did you just call my Trick-or-Treater *tacky*?" Charlotte clasped her hands into a steeple and pressed them to her chin.

"Yes."

"I can't *believe* this!"

"Oh come *on,* Melissa." Charlotte planted her hands on her hips. "It's one thing to put 'POSEUR' on every available inch of space, *and* in more colors than a Benetton ad — but on top of that," she added, perusing the drawing a second time, "*gold* zippers, *gold* chains, *studding,* charms, *and* that hideous *gold clasp?*" She paused. "It's like 50 Cent's *chest* with a *shoulder* strap!"

This time, Petra stifled the laugh, and Melissa whirled around, setting her jaw. "You *agree* with her?" Petra hesitated as, behind her, Charlotte discreetly removed the tacks from Melissa's drawing. The paper curled, flopped forward . . .

"It *is* a little much," she admitted.

The paper slipped along the wall and smacked to the floor. *"Whoops!"* Charlotte smirked, still pinching the final tack between her fingers.

Melissa swept her design from the floor and pressed it to her hip. "Just so you know" — her dark eyes flashed — "you're siding with someone who decorated *her* bag with *gravel!*"

"Oh, she did not," Charlotte laughed, sidestepping to examine Petra's design. Within half a second, the laughter died on her lips. "Oh."

"What?" Petra defensively folded her arms.

"What do you mean 'what'?" Melissa scoffed. "You realize there's a difference between *runway* and *driveway,* right?"

"She's kind of got a point, JLo." Charlotte locked eyes with Petra and cringed. "The rocks that you got? They're kind of just *rocks.*"

"I *know* they're *kind of just rocks,*" Petra imitated her. "That's the whole *point.*"

"Okay, *that* point? Is crazy," Melissa informed her.

"Oh, is it?" Petra flushed, leaping to her feet. Inside the recycling bin, a glass bottle shifted with a fragile-sounding *chink*. "How is decorating my bag with stones any less crazy than decorating yours with gold? Who's to say gold is any more valuable or . . . or *worthy* than any other random rock you happen to pick up?" Her tea-green eyes filled to the brim and wavered, glassy and bright. "What *idiot* decided that gold, or diamonds, or *pearls,* or any of that crap is worth *anything at all*?!"

At that, she stormed from the room, nearly colliding with a stunned Janie, who stood clutching an assortment of candy bars, a bottle of iced Peach Oolong tea, and a half-eaten bag of Potato Flyers. She staggered backward as Petra squeezed past her, tearing down the corridor, the cheerful jingle of her gypsy belt in contrast to the dramatic sound of sobbing.

"What *happened?*" Janie gasped, spewing potato flecks.

"Nothing!" Charlotte and Melissa chanted in unison.

"But . . ." Janie's eyes darted toward the door.

"Look," Melissa snapped. "None of the designs work, okay? End of story."

"*None* of them?" Janie's jaw dropped in disbelief. "What do you mean?"

"Apparently," Melissa huffed, as if never in her life had she had to say something so absurd: "My Trick-or-Treater is *tacky.*"

"And mine" — Charlotte bobbed into a sarcastic curtsy — "is *worm genocide.*"

"Right." Janie swallowed, sucking the salt off her finger. She noticed neither of them so much as *considered* her design, which remained on her desk exactly where she'd left it — ignored. She figured now was not the time to bring it up. The tension in the room was so thick, you could cut it with a knife. Or maybe dip it with a chip? (Her mouth watered at the thought.)

"The Hallow-Winston Carnival is now in *two* days." Melissa expanded her hands on either side of her frustrated face. "And I have worked very hard to have promotion ready. I do not want to promote something that's just not going to happen, you hear me?"

"Okay, listen," Janie attempted to calm her down. "I'm sure if we just take a moment to think this over, we can come up with a . . ."

The bell rang its hysterical interruption, and all along the hall, doors swung open, striking the walls in a succession of hollow thuds: *boom-boom-boom-boom-ba-ba-boom.* After a second of silence, a clamor of voices rose up and swelled, surging the corridor like water.

And so before Janie could say "compromise," Melissa and Charlotte were swept up by the tide.

Hallow-Winston Thursday had arrived at last, and — thanks to the united efforts of the Student Council — the Showroom had completed its transformation from a glossy parking lot to a hay-choked, peanut shell–infested, soon-to-be bass-thumping carnival ground. Among other things, this meant those popular students whose daily right it was to park in the Showroom were forced to park underground, with — as they so charitably phrased it — "the rest of the cave dwellers." Their exodus forced a certain segment of said cave dwellers from their allotted spots, which in turn forced a *second* segment of cave dwellers from *their* allotted spots, until, at last, there came that pathetic last segment of cave dwellers with no place to park at all. Among this sad sector, yellow parking passes were distributed, entitling them to reserved spaces at the Yum-Yum Donuts down the street. As they lugged their bulging backpacks the three-and-a-half blocks from Yum-Yum to campus, their superiors zipped by in Audis, Porsches, Range Rovers, and BMWs, and assailed their poor sensitive ears with explosive honks, cackling laughter, and howlingly expressive *WhoooOOOOO*'s.

If you'd asked him last year, Jake would have said his future on Donut Trail was guaranteed, and perhaps it would have been, if not for Charlotte's sudden and frankly discomfiting interest in his sister. To his and Janie's mutual relief, they got a spot underground, on the *top* level even, their banged-up sedan sweetly slotted between Bronwyn Spencer's dark red Porsche Cayenne and Marco Duvall's ridiculously tricked-out black Escalade. Their SUVs were ginormous, bulging well over their respective double yellow lines, and forced him and Janie to *squeeze* from their cracked car doors, suck in their stomachs, and shimmy their respective ways to freedom.

It had been a small price to pay.

"Jake," Janie called after her brother, who, as usual, refused to wait for her. "Elevator's this way?" She gestured to the stainless steel double-doors, only a few feet away from the car.

"I'll take the stairs," he explained as the elevator clicked into place, sounding its customary *bing!* Janie watched her brother steam ahead and sighed. He'd been taking the stairs all week, and she had yet to understand why.

It was weird. Jake used to confide in her about everything.

"Where is he?" the bespectacled Tyler Brock asked as she squeezed into the crammed six-by-six-foot cube of space. She shrugged, and he tilted outside, stopping the doors jarring *kuh-klunk*. *"Dude,"* he called to Jake's retreating flannel-clad back. "Elevator!"

Jake's already hunched shoulders tensed, but he ignored his friend and continued to walk.

"Come on, dude!" Tyler persisted while his fellow passengers groaned with impatience. "Don't deprive me of my one pleasure in life. *Please?*"

"Man," Jake sighed a few seconds later as the elevator doors glided shut. He glanced at Tyler and shook his head. "Aren't you sick of this yet?"

The grinning Tyler caressed his scraggly excuse for a goatee, and shook his head while a thoroughly mystified Janie looked on. *"What* are you guys talking about?"

"Dude feeds off my misery," Jake ruefully explained under his breath. The doors sighed to a stop and shuddered open, depositing its passengers into the thick of Locker Jungle. Because upper classmen stored their stuff in their cars, Locker Jungle was a seventh, eighth, and ninth-grade stomping ground. They buzzed around and cackled, oblivious to outsiders — that is, until they spotted her brother. In that moment, Janie noticed, their eyes, like, *glinted* — like yellow-eyed bats in a dimly lit attic.

"Get ready," Tyler warned as a redheaded eighth grader stepped boldly forward.

"Hijake!" she cheeped, alerting the rest of her glittery-eyed comrades. Jake lifted his hand in greeting, and they dissolved into fits of shrieks and chirping:

"Hijake!hijake!hijake!hijake!hijake!hijake!hijake!hijake! hijake!hijake!"

"Make it stop!" Tyler swiped the air around his head and shrunk to his knees, screaming, while Janie spun around, hiding her laughter in her hands. "For the love of all that is holy, make it *stop!*"

Jake smiled, always happy to amuse — even at the expense of his own dignity. Ever since he'd made out with that girl Nikki, he'd become something of a cult figure among seventh- and eighth-grade girls, most of whom were desperate kissing virgins, and *all* of whom seemed to be thinking, *if he did it with her, would he do it with me?* Jake took the stairs to avoid them, but mostly to avoid Nikki, who — even though he hadn't responded once — had continued to text-stalk him for, like, *two weeks.* The first thing he did when she came back to school was take her aside and explain, in as kind a manner as possible, she needed to *back the hell off.* The thing was, she *did,* and, after an initial wave of relief, he felt guilty. *Really* guilty. More and more, he let Tyler bully him into these trips to Locker Jungle in hopes that he'd run into her, and, if not apologize, at least, you know. Say hey.

Just so she wouldn't think he hated her.

"You're going to the carnival, right?" Janie asked him, once Tyler and the cheeping bats dispersed for the rafters.

"Where else would I be?" Jake frowned, rising on the scuffed toes of his Converse. He glanced around, scanning the aisles.

"I don't know," Janie mused. "Ditching?"

Jake scowled, falling back on his heels. "Would you just, like, let that die?"

Janie cocked an eyebrow. "Just promise you'll come to the POSEUR booth." She shifted her brown canvas Manhattan Portage tote to her hip, digging through it. "My shift is two 'til three."

"Sure," Jake absently replied, back to scanning the lockers. Of course, now that he was looking for her, Nikki was never around.

Where could she be hiding?

The Girl: Molly Berger
The Getup: Oversized black-and-white MC Escher T-shirt from the MOMA gift shop, purple cotton leggings from the Gap, and orange Crocs (with nifty frog-charm gibbets).

Some people could disappear and nobody ever noticed. Eighth grader Molly Berger was one of these people. She was the kind of person who blessed herself when she sneezed. She walked on the balls of her feet, her posture disconcertingly erect, craning her long neck like a leaf-seeking dinosaur. Her vocabulary gravitated toward old lady words, like "prudent," "sensitive," and "fragile," which may have explained her devotion to delicate and useless things, like sea dollars, decorative bath soaps, antique thimbles, and maple-syrup candies shaped like Amish women. Choosing one of her crushable collections to bring to school, she'd arrange the items about her during lunch, sitting on the desolate cement stoop outside the computer lab. In keeping with Longstanding Dork Tradition, she always ate alone.

And then, out of nowhere, Nikki Pellegrini asked to sit with her.

"Why?" Molly looked up at her, squinting, and Nikki shrugged, struggling to smile. *Because I have no other options!* (It was all she could do not to scream it out loud). All this week, Carly and Juliet had *refused* to eat with her. "Sometimes we just need to be alone," they'd explained, annoyed. *Which makes perfect sense,* Nikki thought, considering *they* were eating lunch together, while *she* was eating alone. She'd hovered around other groups of girls in hopes some kind member might take pity, but they too ignored her (in her presence, they'd grow quiet, communicating solely by eye contact). Not that Nikki blamed them. Everyone knew she was Melissa Moon's primary suspect (Venice had wasted no time spreading the word). Who'd want to be seen with someone that not one but *two* popular sophomores happened to hate? It was social suicide.

As was eating lunch with Molly Berger when everybody else was at the carnival. But, at this point, what'd she have to lose?

"It's just . . ." Molly grimaced, stabbing her strawberry-milk box with a stiff white straw. To her left, a horizontally cut turkey sandwich sat neatly on a flattened paper bag. To her right, a collection of small- to medium-sized geodes sparkled purple in the sun. "I don't think it's right," she explained, after a gasping sip of milk, "to ask to eat lunch with me as a last resort."

"What makes you think you're a last resort?" Nikki asked, attempting innocence.

"Well, because you've been ostracized." Molly shrugged, taking a gigantic bite out of her turkey sandwich. Off of Nikki's blank look, she continued, "That means you've been rejected in the most extreme way possible."

"I know what it means," Nikki lied. A nearby drinking fountain buzzed awake and shuddered, and she shifted her weight from one leg to the other, exhaling a short, impatient breath. "So, can I eat with you or not?"

Molly winced. "I guess."

Nikki swallowed a sigh of relief, mounting the cement steps to the computer lab stoop. "Just a moment," Molly ordered, popping the latch of a blue-and-gray tackle box. One by one, she wrapped her geodes in sage-green velveteen cloths, packing them inside. Nikki gestured to help, but Molly rejected her offer, hulking over the stones like an overprotective bird. "I'd prefer it if you'd just let me handle them," she explained in a strained tone. "These stones are very fragile."

"Oh." Nikki's hand retreated. "Sorry."

"It's okay." Molly resumed loading the stones. When the last one was safely tucked away, she locked the tackle box and set it to the ground, sliding it to the plaster wall with the side of her orange Croc. Satisfied, she looked up at Nikki and smiled. She kind of had a pretty smile if you could ignore the glob of mustard in the corner of her mouth.

"So," she said, once Nikki assumed her place next to her on the stoop. She lowered her voice to a confidential level. "Did you do it?"

"No," Nikki sighed, peering into a humid baggie of baby carrots. "I don't know why everyone thinks I did."

"I think it has something to do with being a slut," Molly offered. Nikki gasped, her cornflower blue eyes wide with shock.

"What?"

"Not that being a slut means you'd vandalize contests." Molly ripped into an apricot fruit leather and shrugged. "I mean, that's like saying, 'that girl's obese so she's more likely to rob banks.'" She snorted with laughter. "Absurd."

"But who says that?" Nikki trembled. "Who says I'm a slut?"

"I don't know." Molly tore into her fruit leather and chewed. "People."

"But I'm not!" Nikki wailed.

"What does that have to do with anything?" Molly leaned back in her seat and flinched. "*I'm* not a dork. Does that prevent anyone from saying I'm a dork?"

Before she could think better of it, a small yet combustible word escaped Nikki's lips. "But."

"*But what?*" Molly huffed in two hot puffs of strawberry-milk breath. Nikki shook her head, reverting her gaze to her baby carrots. "No," she persisted, crossing her blotchy pink arms across her oversized M.C. Escher t-shirt, "what were you going to say?"

"*Omigawd-uh!*"

There — in the center of a nearby alleyway, her eyes fixed to the two unlikely lunch companions in appalled horror — stood Carly Thorne. Juliet stood off to one side, her hand clapped to her mouth, and Venice Whitney-Wang leaned against the cinderblock wall, a fuchsia-legging leg kicked behind her, and Dita sunglasses glinting in the sun. Carly closed her mouth, remoistened her lips, and opened it again.

"You're eating lunch with *her?*"

The world around Nikki seemed to ripple. All she wanted to do was leap to her feet, run toward Carly, and hug her forever. But, in respect for Molly's feelings, she restrained the impulse.

"Aren't you going to the carnival?" Juliet frowned in confusion.

Nikki beamed. "I just thought —"

"Not *you*," Carly interrupted. *"Molly."*

Nobody moved except for Venice, who lowered her leg to the ground. A sparrow fluttered down to the cinderblock wall, hopped once, and cocked its sleek feathered head in interest.

"I don't see the point of carnivals," Molly started to explain. "They —"

"Why are you doing this?" Nikki blurted, interrupting Molly's sure-to-be tedious observation. Her eyes danced between Carly and Juliet, wounded and bewildered. "You guys are supposed to be my *friends*."

"It's not like we haven't tried." Carly folded her arms across her padded chest and stared at the ground. "But it's kind of like, you've made it impossible."

"Seriously, Nikki." Juliet flashed. "This isn't all about you."

"That is *so* not fair," Nikki pleaded against all better judgment. Nothing annoyed her friends more than accusations of unfairness. Sure enough, Juliet rolled her eyes, readdressing Molly.

"You want to go on the Moon Bounce?" she asked. "I think there's this new rule, like, you have to go in pairs of four."

"Really?" Molly furrowed her brow in thought, stuffing the remains of her half-eaten lunch into a brown paper sack. One crushed milk box, two mustard-stained husks of sourdough bread, a semi-gnawed fruit leather, and two wax-sealed Baby Bell cheeses later, she replied. "Okay."

"But we were going to have lunch!" Nikki reminded her, desperate beyond all reason.

"We can have lunch tomorrow," Molly informed her, stuffing her bulging paper lunch sack into her backpack. "If you so desire."

Nikki grabbed her by the bony elbow. "I hope you realize," she croaked with emotion, "they're only asking you to go on the Moon Bounce to make me feel bad. It's not 'cause they actually *like* you."

Molly drew herself up and gazed down the length of her narrow nose. Her skin had the blanched quality of uncooked macaroni. Her nostrils were so pink they glowed.

"You know what?" Her pale eyes winked with disdain. "You're a really *mean* person."

Before Nikki could defend herself, Molly pivoted the toe of her orange Croc and propelled her wedgie-butt toward the New Nicarettes. The three girls walked slowly, bumping into each other, laughing, taking their time, and Molly loped in their wake, squinting at the sky, and oblivious to her blue-and-gray tackle box, which — in what had to be a historical first — she'd left behind.

With a shuddering breath, Nikki lifted the box into her lap. She popped the latch, lifted the light plastic lid, and pinched aside a corner of sage-green velveteen fabric, revealing a small corner of the gray stone. She hesitated, bracing for Molly's frantic return, before lifting the geode from its folds of velveteen. She liked the way it sat inside her palm, the eggish shape and dense weight of it, the way the purple crystals glittered in the sun. She turned the stone over and examined the rock shell, an ordinary gray, scarred in places by more ordinary grays. Before long tears spilled down her cheeks, raining like lemmings from the edge of her chin, splattering to the quiet asphalt, and dissolving everything in sight, even the geode, which she continued to turn in her hand until both sides looked the same.

With the exception of a spastic white ghost creature whipping around the inflatable roof, the Haunted Barn Moon Bounce was the same as all Moon Bounces. Puffy plastic walls creased, bowed, quaked, and trembled, a massive air pump droned, and, inside, a mass of seventh and eighth graders tossed about in chaos, masks of unbridled glee on their squealing pink faces. If they'd paused to look, they might have noticed Jake Farrish, his doleful face smashed against the net, observing them with the glazed eye of a trapped tuna. *Junior high . . .* he thought with a wistful sigh.

Such a happier, simpler time.

"Hands off the net!" a crackling voice bellowed from behind the ticket booth, and Jake looked up. The Carnie couldn't have been older than nineteen, but with his tattooed, sunburned arms, and massive, burly chest, he looked about thirty. Jake watched as one

of these arms dislodged from its coordinate armpit, moved like a crane toward a large scuffed buzzer, and punched the button, sounding an alarm.

Needless to say, Jake's hands were off the net. "Sorry," he apologized.

"Step *away* from the Bounce," the Carnie replied, and Jake took a few obliging steps backward. *"Did you hear what I said?"*

"Dude," he winced, indicating his size twelve Converse. "I *stepped.*"

"Alright," the Carnie gritted his teeth, and steamrolled toward him, fists swinging. "What's your name?"

"Why?" Jake asked, flinching in the hot gale of Carnie breath.

"Once again," he continued, cricking his neck. He didn't appear to speak so much as tear words from the open air, gnashing them like meat between his teeth. "What. Is. Your. *Name.*"

"No way, man." Jake held his ground. "I didn't *do* anything."

"Will someone here tell me this guy's name?" He roared, whirling to face a gathering crowd of goggle-eyed kids. Jake's eyes darted around in panic. It was only a matter of time before a teacher, sensing the commotion, intruded into the scene, and then . . . and then *what?* He hadn't done anything!

"His name is Zach Braff."

The crowd parted and she stepped forward, dressed for the season in a strapless orange silk organza mini dress and black patent-leather heels. Her tumultuous curls, restored to their original black coffee hue, were pulled back into a stem-green double-rope headband to which she'd sewn two delicately crocheted, matching green leaves. Her frosted lips, an iridescent cupcake color, matched her fingernails, which lined like pearls along her dainty hips. Not that Jake noticed this crap. All he saw were her eyes, which — in the half-second they rested on his — sparkled and snapped, alive again with their old familiar light.

"He's my brother." Charlotte returned her cool blue-green gaze to the Carnie.

"Really." He grinned, eyeing Charlotte up and down. "*Someone* hogged the looks in the family."

"And brains, unfortunately," she sighed, once he'd finished laughing at his own joke. She returned a sisterly gaze to Jake, sighing with sympathy. "He's a little . . . *challenged*."

"No kiddin'." Carnie mulled over this new grain of information, scratching his sturdy trapezoid of a neck. Charlotte straightened Jake's collar, brushing some invisible lint from his shoulder.

"Zachy." She shook her head and touched his cheek. "We didn't eat too many pumpkin cookies, did we?"

The Carnie pushed some air between his lips. He wasn't stupid — he knew he was being played — but he wasn't in the mood to argue with a girl, especially one this pretty. Later that night, he'd heat up a pot of Campbell's chicken noodle and stir and stir, dreaming up their life together. It would be an isolated life, deep in the heart of an uncharted forest. He would loft the

Moon Bounce in the highest part of the forest canopy and invite her there to live, surrounded by brilliant blue sky, moss-covered tree branches, chattering parrots, kindly sloths, and the sound of dripping rain.

He turned toward Jake and, without warning, button-punched his scrawny boy-chest. "No more pumpkin cookies for *you.*"

"*Ow . . .*"

"Come back later." Carnie ignored him, returning to Charlotte with a mild wink. "I'll give you a free bounce."

"Ooo!" she trilled in an effort to disguise her inner *ew.* Then, affecting an air of saintly patience, she led her "brother" away by his elbow. Jake happily allowed her to guide him (if she'd needed to declare him mentally deficient to save his ass, he might as well return the favor by playing his part). He gazed about the carnival, offering the world an uncomprehending smile. His brown eyes shone with wonder. A small petal-white butterfly fluttered by.

"*Bird!*" He pointed. "Bird! *Bird!*"

Charlotte yelped with laughter, ducking her face into her hand — and then quickly threw his arm from her grasp, chastising herself. "Don't make me laugh." She shook her head, flashing her eyes. "This isn't funny!"

Whirling on her tiny heel, she stormed toward Kate and Laila — who, after mutual steely looks in Jake's direction, closed behind her like double doors. Jake stood for a few seconds, numb with confusion, and in a flash of frustration, followed his ex-girlfriend to the POSEUR booth. Melissa sat behind the table, lording over a thumping black boom box. On either side of her, Petra and Janie stood on plastic foldout chairs, mounting their blue-and-gold-silk POSEUR banner.

Charlotte found her seat next to Melissa, while Jake steamed ahead, pushing his way through the gathering mob of fashionistas. "What was that?" He panted, laying a hand on the wood table. "Why did you just *do* that?"

"I don't know." Charlotte frowned, ripping into a bulk pack of Starburst while the rest of the girls looked on, curiosity piqued. "I hate to see an old friend in trouble."

"No way." Jake shook his head, his voice husky with stress. "You didn't just do that to save my ass." Charlotte tipped the bag on its side, raining the rainbow candy into a waiting Waterford crystal bowl. "Admit you miss me."

"Ew." Charlotte pinched the empty bag at either corner, snapping it clean. "I think you should leave."

"No," he replied, with a simple bob of his eyebrows. "My sister told me to come."

"You did?" Charlotte flashed, causing Janie to drop a corner of the banner and wobble in her chair.

"I told him between one and two," she explained in a rush. "During your break."

"During her *break?*" Jake observed. "Gee, Janie. Way to bend over backward."

"I just . . . I didn't want it to be awkward!" she stammered.

"We're *not* awkward," Jake and Charlotte cried in unison, aggressively avoiding eye contact.

"Um, excuse me?" Melissa planted a manicured hand on her hip, temporarily halting her distribution of pink-and-black POSEUR buttons.

"We're promoting POSEUR awareness," Petra explained.

"And you two are *not* representing," Melissa bristled. With a hard look, she raised a bullhorn to her lips. *"Free Starburst!"*

"What I don't understand . . ." Charlotte locked eyes with Jake and resumed her rant at a low hiss, stuffing candy into anonymous outstretched hands. ". . . Is the way you just, like, *go around.* Like nothing ever happened."

"*I* go around like nothing happened," Jake scoffed in abject disbelief, looping the periphery of the booth. Eager to escape his advance, Charlotte sprung from her seat, scurrying to the foot of the table. Jake instantly rooted himself in his tracks; it was one thing to argue with your ex in public, quite another to chase her around a booth. From either end of the long table, they faced each other, eyes narrowed like rival tennis champs.

"*You're* the one who's in love with someone else," he informed her, lobbing the first ball.

"Oh please," Charlotte sent it flying back. "I never said we were *in love*."

"Really," Jake retorted with an expert backhand shot. "That's not how Janie tells it."

"He forced it out of me!" Janie explained, descending from the wobbling chair to safer ground.

"Well," Charlotte sniffed. "Fine. Maybe we *are* in love. So?"

"So?" Jake gripped his face and sort of smeared it around. A rueful laugh escaped his lips. "We broke up, like five minutes ago!"

"As if you care." Charlotte tightened her jaw. "Janie told me all about how *happy* you are."

"You *did*?" Jake turned to his sister, agog.

"Omigod." Janie covered her face in her hands. "Please, don't put me in the middle of this."

"You're not in the middle!" they cried again in unison.

"*You wanna know who's in the middle of this?*" Melissa blasted into her bullhorn, causing every person in a fifteen-foot radius to cringe, clapping their hands to their ears. "Me. *And I do not want to be here.*"

"Fine." Jake scowled, shoving his hands into his beat-up corduroy pockets. And then, to no one in particular, he muttered, "See you around."

"Don't forget your free Starburst!" Melissa bellowed, and Charlotte shot her a defensive glance. Removing her heels, she took off at a sprint, chasing Jake down. She waved her hand above her harried head.

"Jake! Wait!"

Melissa unwrapped a yellow Starburst and popped it into her glossy pink mouth. "That was crazy," she pronounced with a bob of her perfectly groomed eyebrows.

"I don't know what to do." Janie shook her head and solemnly chewed. "I don't think I can take it."

"Oh, come on. Stiffen up." Petra smiled, unwrapping a green Starburst. "I've seen way worse."

"Marco and I *never* fight," Melissa informed them proudly, after a disapproving glance in the direction of the slowly turning, spastically flashing Ferris wheel, where Jake and Charlotte continued to rave, gesticulating wildly. "Those two need to learn to resolve their conflicts in a mature manner."

"You mean like us?" Petra scoffed at the irony. "We can't even decide on a *bag* without death threats."

"Please." Melissa slapped the air with her hand. "This is not the time."

"Um . . . it kind of is," Petra pointed out. "October thirty-first is Monday. And today? Is Thursday. If we plan to have a bag ready, we better make a decision, like, yesterday?"

"Actually," Janie timidly intruded. "I have a possible solution?" Melissa and Petra waited, solemnly sucking their Starbursts. "I just thought," Janie continued, blushing at their attention, "instead of choosing *one* design, we could, like, take the best elements of *all* our designs and combine them into one. You know . . . come to some sort of . . ."

But before she could say "compromise," they were distracted by a long and terrified scream.

Thursday, October 27 — 7:33 p.m.

Are you there, Tom? It's me, Nikki.

I have been a member of MySpace for more than 13 months (I wasn't allowed to join until seventh grade or else I would have been a member for much, much longer ;-)). I remember when I first joined MySpace and my page said "you have 1 friends" and that friend was you! I was excited but at the same time a little freaked out because a) I didn't know who you were and b) you're way, way older than me (Happy 32nd, btw!!!) Anyway, the combination of these two things meant I was worried you were a cybermolester and/or i-Perv.

To be on the safe side, I called my best friend (*ex*-best friend now) because she'd already been on MySpace for two months and I figured she'd know what to do. But she just started laughing like, "Oh my God, you're not talking about *Tom,* are you?" And I was like, "What?" And she was like, "Nikki! He *started* MySpace. He's an *automatic* friend, not a *friend* friend!"

Well, then I felt pretty dumb.

But a lot has changed since then and I have totally changed my attitude. I realize I should have never felt dumb or embarrassed — that feeling excited was the right way to feel. Because when you think about it, it's a lot like how my grandmother says it is with God. I mean, she says God accepts everybody no matter what — so does that mean we should all be like, "Oh yeah. *God.* He accepts everybody so He doesn't count?"

Answer to my own question: No!!! LOL!

Basically I would like to apologize for not thinking of you as a "real friend." And please don't think I'm only writing you now because you're my only MySpace friend left (besides celebrities and my cousins in Florida) because that is so *not* the reason. The real reason is *we have so much in common*. For starters, we both don't smoke, are from L.A., and have "General Interests" such as karaoke and finding new food!!! Also, we are both air signs (you're a Libra, I'm an Aquarius) and like Whitney Houston, Kelly Clarkson, and movies such as *Beauty & The Beast* and *Gladiator*.

Okay, this comment has gotten waaaay too long. Sorry! Basically I just wanted to say I'm looking 4-ward to getting to know you better. And please write back soon!!!!:-)

Luv <333

Nikki

P.S. Happyyy Halloweennn!!!!

Thursday, October 27 — 7:37 p.m.

Are you there, Tom? It's me, Nikki.

Sorry!! I know I only wrote you four minutes ago, LOL!! But I just wanted to say that *just* because I wrote you a super-long comment does *not* mean you need to write me a super-long comment back!;-) Even if you wrote me a small to medium-length comment back, that would totally, totally make my day!!

    Luv <333

    Nikki

    P.S. I heart your sideburns!!!!

Thursday, October 27 — 8:58 p.m.

Are you there, Tom? It's me, Nikki.

    So, so sorry I'm writing you again! *Please* don't think I'm psycho — I totally get that you have 213,957,272 friends and your mood is "busy," so it's not like I expect you to write me back right away!! It's just I happened to be looking at your profile again and I *just noticed* that under "About Me" you wrote: I'm Tom and I'm here to help you — send me a message if you're confused by anything. And even though I know you probably mean "confusion about MySpace," and not "confusion about life in general," I still thought maybe you could help with just one thing?????

    Last Thursday, I was supposed to eat lunch with this kind of nerdy girl but she left and forgot to take her geodes with her (geodes are like rocks but with crystals inside). I knew she'd be super upset so I decided to return them to her, but when I walked up holding her blue tackle box (that's where she keeps her geodes), she was like, "You stole my geodes!" I was like, "No, I didn't. You left them behind!" but she refused to listen and started to cry. Like *really* cry. Like her nose turned pink and her eyes puffed up like those fat goldfish with puffy eyes and at one point a huge snot bubble came out of her nostril. Pretty soon a big crowd formed around her with everyone looking at each other like, "Why is she crying?" with these "How sad" expressions on their faces even though *I know for a fact* they'd all made fun of this girl a million gazillion times!!! Then I heard this *new* girl say, "Nikki stole her geodes," and right after she said it the nerdy girl cried *really loud* so of course everybody thought what she said was true. Then somebody called me a bad word (the same bad word had been written on my locker, FYI), and I turned around to see who it was and something cold and slimy hit me on the face. At first I thought it was a loogie (sp????) except the only boy I know who can make a loogie that big is Casey Madigan and he lives in Denver now. Before I could wipe my face, more of them hit me all over my back and my neck and my knees, and there were all these splattering noises, and I screamed really, really loud. I ran and ran until I was in the girls' bathroom and these two ninth-grade girls stared at me and the one with brown hair said, "Ew," and the one with blue hair started laughing and it wasn't until then that I looked into the mirror. I was covered in pumpkin guts. Big disgusting globs of orange pumpkin guts and pumpkin seeds all in my hair and my face and all over my favorite white Lacoste shirt.

I ended up going home early.

The thing is, there's this hard, hard ache feeling inside my throat and behind my heart that won't go away. In science class, we learned about petrified wood — which is what happens when trees get buried in the ground where there isn't any oxygen and they turn into stone. For the last three days, I've felt like I haven't been able to breathe, which probably means I haven't gotten enough oxygen, and meanwhile the ache feeling is getting harder and harder and I can't help but wonder . . . are there such things as petrified human beings?

Okay, now that I wrote it down I can tell I'm being com-puh-lete-ly overdramatic!!!! But still, it would be so helpful if you were like, "Nikki, you're being dramatic!" Also, that things won't feel this way forever. And that things will get better (soon!).

For some reason it doesn't help *at all* when I tell myself these things.

Luv <333

Nikki

"Bravo! Bravo!" Vivien cried from the edge of the embossed gold velvet settee, springing to her feet. She was auditioning pianists for her all-important engagement party, and Seedy had insisted Melissa be there, because, quote-unquote, it's real important to Vivien. Uh-huh. More like "real important to Vivien" to *ruin* her Saturday morning *and* afternoon.

Melissa wrested her attention from her Apple iPhone — she'd been updating her Web site MoonWalksonMan.com — to focus on her soon-to-be-stepmother's clapping hands. *She's still doing it.* Melissa narrowed her eyes, carefully unwrapping a leftover pink Starburst. At first, she'd thought it was only her imagination, but after a week of cold, hard observation, she now knew for sure it wasn't. She glanced at her father. *Am I the only person seeing this?*

Now that six-foot-high, fake-purple-eyed Vivien Ho had a twenty-six carat ring to show off, she'd reassigned all hand-related activity from her right hand to her less-inclined left. She waved with her left. Answered her cell with her left. Opened doors, smoothed her hair, and applied lip gloss with her left. But because *she was actually right-handed* (it was all Melissa could do not to scream this fact out loud), even the most basic gestures looked plain *off*.

She can't even clap *right,* Melissa realized, fluttering her eyes shut. Woman looked like an underfed porpoise with a double-fractured flipper.

"Ah . . ." She stopped clapping and returned to her seat, tucking a white Juicy Couture pompom boot under her A&G pink denim miniskirt-clad butt. "Wasn't that just *so* pretty?" she proposed, landing her left hand on Seedy's knee.

Ms. Beauchamp, the latest in Vivien's long string of applicants, turned on the round white leather piano seat, her hard coral fingernails pressed firmly to her plump, burgundy slacks—covered thighs, and attempted a smile. Blobby pearl earrings gleamed in her saggy, soft ears, and a ruffled gray silk blouse spilled over her enormous breasts. She looked like the kind of woman who kept a bird, covered her couches in plastic, and refused to "forgive Charles for what he did to Diana" — and she was.

Vivien discovered Ms. Beauchamp in the Nordstrom's shoe department, where she played piano every Saturday from two until five p.m., limiting herself to a repertoire of upbeat jazz renditions of such classics as "Strangers in the Night" and "People." On occasion, someone asked her where the bathroom was, or a small child materialized at the corner of her keyboard to watch her hands with wonder; but for the most part, she passed her Saturday afternoons at Nordstrom ignored. Imagine her surprise when Vivien Ho swooped in, dropped her shopping bags, and proceeded to gush like a teenaged fan. "You *have* to audition for my engagement party," she'd insisted, and Ms. Beauchamp had been too stunned to decline.

"What's that one called again?" Vivien asked, still squeezing Seedy's knee.

"Pachelbel's Canon," Ms. Beauchamp reminded her with a strained smile, careful to avoid the menacing gaze of the positively criminal-looking man next to her, not to mention his wild-eyed creature of a daughter. Vivien seemed like a nice enough girl (of course, she *might* do with covering herself up a bit more); what was she doing mixed up with such *dreadful* people?

"Was that the one you were playing at Nordstrom?" Vivien inquired.

"Why, yes," Ms. Beauchamp nodded her assent. In truth, she'd been playing "The Lady in Red," but that song was far too personal to play *here*. "Pachelbel's Canon is very popular for weddings."

"Oh," Vivien fretted, glancing between her and Seedy. "This is an engagement party."

"It serves its purpose just as well," Ms. Beauchamp assured her, raising a hand. "*Very* appropriate."

"I just *love* classical music," Vivien fluttered, returning her fawning attention to Ms. Beauchamp. "It's just so . . ." She hesitated, in search of the perfect word, and broke into a smile. "*Classy.*"

"Sure is." Seedy nodded, and cleared his throat. "Melissa," he exhaled, checking in with his daughter while Vivien sighed in frustration, rolling her eyes. "What'd you think?"

"It was nice." She looked up and quickly tucked her iPhone under Emilio's snoozing belly. "But, you know. Not really my thing. No offense," she told Ms. Beauchamp with a contrite glance.

"None taken," the pianist assured her with another strained smile. "We all have different tastes."

"What are you even asking her for?" Vivien addressed Seedy in a burst of exasperation. "You *know* she hates everything I like no matter what it is."

"Daddy!" Melissa gripped the arm of her armchair, defiant. "That is *not* true."

"Oh really?" Vivien challenged her. "Name one thing you like that I like."

"Rag & Bone." Melissa bobbed her eyebrows. "I still like Rag & Bone even though you like Rag & Bone."

"Please," Vivien scoffed. "*Everyone* likes Rag & Bone."

"Ms. B." Melissa cocked an unconvinced eyebrow at the pianist. "Do you like Rag & Bone?"

"I'm afraid . . . I'm afraid I don't . . ." Ms. Beauchamp drew a sharp breath to quell her nerves. Rag & Bone: wasn't that the name of a notorious, bloodthirsty street gang? *Yes.* She was almost *sure* of it! Oh dear, oh dear . . . was she really supposed to say that she "liked" a *gang*? How terrible! Unless . . . wait. Perhaps this was all some sort of elaborate setup. Perhaps they were trying to trick her into confessing loyalty to a *rival* gang. Oh, but why would they care about *her* allegiances?

What in God's name did they *want* with her?

"Ms. Beauchamp." Seedy noted the pianist's increased discomfort with concern. "You okay?"

"Yes, of course," she rasped weakly, the color draining from her face. By the time she rose to her feet, clutching her purse to her soft bulge of stomach, she'd achieved the sickly pallor of a withering grape. "Please excuse me," she apologized. "I have an appointment."

"Please," Vivien offered. "I'll walk you out."

"Oh no," Ms. Beauchamp assured her, turning quickly for the door. "I can find my way."

Despite her mild protests, Vivien caught up with Ms. Beauchamp at the foot of the white marble stairs and escorted her to the exit. As their contrasting figures disappeared into the hall, Seedy sighed, returning his attention to his daughter.

"Rag & Bone," he repeated with a bemused arc of his eyebrow. "What the heck is that — some kind of chew toy?"

"Daddy, *what?*" Melissa laughed, rousing Emilio from his slumber. "No! It's a *designer.*"

"Baby, don't you remember?" Vivien sailed into the Meet-and-Greet room, a fresh Diet Coke in hand. "You bought me a pair of their jeans last week."

"Yeah," Melissa muttered under her breath. "Right after I bought the exact same pair."

"Seedy?" Vivien pouted, ignoring Melissa's comment, and sucked in her long and toned torso, centering the gold buckle of her new Gucci belt. "You'll never guess what Ms. Beauchamp told me just now," she sighed, turning to check her adjusted reflection in their gilded floor-to-ceiling mirror.

Seedy settled into the settee, pushing some air from between his lips. "She isn't available to play the engagement party?"

"How did you *know* that?" Vivien gasped in an accusing tone, as though knowledge had made him responsible

"Just a guess," he replied as Vivien folded her arms across her chest.

"Why would she come all this way to audition, and then say she wasn't available?"

"Let me put it this way." Seedy cleared his throat. "Woman likes her *white* keys on one side of the board, *black* keys on the other."

Vivien knit her eyebrows together. *"Excuse me?"*

"Vee." Seedy closed his eyes. Did he really have to spell this out? "Woman was a racist."

"She *was?*" Melissa widened her eyes and craned around in her seat, half-expecting Ms. Beauchamp to materialize in a burst of flames.

"Seedy, oh my God." Vivien dissolved into a fit of cackles. "You are so paranoid!"

"I am *not* paranoid!" Seedy defended himself. "Did you not see the look on her face when I came in and introduced myself? She looked at my hand like I was holding a loaded glock!"

"She *probably* looked at your hand like it has a big ol' tattoo of Melissa on it." Vivien rolled her eyes. "Which it *does.*"

"I can't believe you're arguing me on this." He sat back in his seat in disbelief. Melissa bit the insides of her cheeks, restraining a smile. Finally, it had happened. They were *arguing.* Which was almost the same as *in a fight.* Which was practically the same as *calling off the engagement.*

Okay, maybe that last bit was a stretch.

"You know what?" Vivien planted her hands on her hips and frowned. "This whole argument is just an excuse."

"Excuse for *what?*" Seedy's face crumpled in confusion.

"You don't want a pianist at our engagement party." She whimpered, and Seedy sighed, bowing his head into his hands. "Even though I've *always* wanted a pianist at my engagement party. Ever since I was a little girl!"

"Alright." Seedy gripped his knees and tried to get his bearings.

"I admit, I am confused as to why it's so important for you to have classical music at our engagement party. It's like rap, hip-hop — that's all good for the *everyday*. But when it comes to a *special* occasion? Ho no. We got to sit back and subject ourselves to some 'Taco Bell Canon,' written by some three-hundred-year-old white dude."

"We are getting *married*." Vivien's voice dropped to a restrained tremble. "*Rap* music isn't appropria —"

"Okay, would you listen to yourself?!" he erupted, bounding to his feet, and all but ejecting Emilio Poochie from his daughter's lap. The little dog landed in a heap, scrambled to his feet, and skittered wildly down the marble hall. "Rap music isn't 'appropriate,'" he continued. "Rap music isn't 'classy.' Vivien, do you even know how pathetic and self-hating this sounds?"

Vivien gasped, and even Melissa had to admit, she was equally shocked. If anyone in this world loved herself, it was Vivien.

"I cannot *believe* you just said that," she intoned.

"Vee," he pleaded with her. "It'd be one thing if ever, in my *life*, I heard you listen to classical music. You know — if I thought it meant something, like, *deep* for you. But you and I both know that's not what this is about."

"Oh really." She breathed in deep, protruding two fake breasts as rock-hard as her will. "What *is* this about?"

Seedy sighed, massaging his aching eyelids. He and Vee had been rock solid for eleven months, but ever since they got engaged, something had changed. More and more the question nagged his mind: *were they right for each other*? Of course, he chastised himself. Of course they were, but . . . why this sudden hating on rap? Where did that even *come* from? When they first got together she'd been all *about* it. Had it all been some kind of act? And if *that* was an act, then how far did it go?

"It's just I have this feeling," he beseeched her, lowering his hand to his side. "Like sometime in the last couple of weeks we just stopped being *real*. Do you ever get that? Like our real selves are someplace else, and you and I are just . . ."

Melissa bit the tip of her Paparazzi-pink thumbnail. "Po-seurs?"

The doorbell chimed like a game show sound effect: *that answer is correct!* Melissa glanced between her father and Vivien, waiting for either of them to react, but neither of them moved. She cleared her throat.

"I'll get it!"

Squaring her bare, body-glittered shoulders, she padded brightly down the white marble hallway. Her father's awards, plaques, photographs, and platinum records decorated the walls, gleaming impressively behind thick panes of glass. Melissa admired the many tiny reflections of herself — darting schools of tadpole-sized Melissa Moons — on the array of polished surfaces, before trotting up another short flight of stairs and sailing into the foyer. A woman in a too-tight eggplant tweed blazer stood facing their lush antique tapestry of *Cheonjiyeon,* a famous waterfall in South Korea, a royal blue velvet scrunchie secured to the mousy ponytail at the nape of her neck. At the sight of that scrunchie,

Melissa winced, and quickly stared at the cute black bows on her new Juicy Couture sandals. Bad fashion is a lot like a stiff shot of tequila: you have to ease the effects with some kind of chaser.

"Melissa?"

Melissa looked up from her sandal in surprise. "Miss Paletsky!"

"Ch'ello!" Miss Paletsky greeted her in a shaky, if cheerful, voice, hugging a sheaf of paper to her chest. "Ch'ow are you?"

"I'm okay," Melissa replied after a moment's hesitation. She wasn't in trouble, was she? "How are you . . . ," she asked slowly, growing queasy.

"I'm good. I mean *well*." She smiled, revealing her overlapping eyetooth. "Although a little nervous," she confessed in a confidential tone, cringing behind her LensCrafters. "Is your father home?"

"Miss Paletsky." Melissa flushed, sputtering a nervous laugh. "Is this about asking Venice to color-code my dog's dog kibble? Because I can totally explain that."

"Lena!" Seedy boomed, mounting the final stair to the foyer. He grinned, landing a hand on his daughter's shoulder and extending the other. "So glad you could make it."

"Yes." Lena shook his hand and blushed. "I'm sorry for being so late!"

"No, you're right on time," Seedy assured her, giving Melissa's shoulder a final squeeze before gesturing down the hall. "The piano's just down this way, so . . ."

"*She's auditioning?*" Melissa realized out loud, soliciting a mutual burst of quiet adult laughter.

"What'd you think?" Seedy teased, ushering the ever-blushing Miss Paletsky across the foyer. "You were in trouble?"

"*No,*" Melissa scoffed. "I just . . ." She pattered downstairs and addressed her pretty young teacher directly. "I didn't know you played piano, Miss Paletsky."

"Oh." Miss Paletsky glanced over her left shoulder as the three of them continued down the hall and into the Meet-and-Greet room. "I don't really —"

"Hello," Vivien sang in an everything-is-fine tone, interrupting Miss Paletsky midsentence. She planted her Diet Coke on the glass coffee table and extended her left hand, forcing Miss Paletsky to clumsily shift her sheaf of music from the crook of her left arm to her right. "I'm Seedy's fiancée," she said, shaking her hand. Noticing the cool flicker of judgment behind Vivien's violet contact lenses, Melissa bristled, instantly protective. So what if Miss Paletsky wore opaque L'Eggs Suntan pantyhose with dove gray peep-toe pumps and reeked of Suave hairspray?

At least she was nice.

"So." Miss Paletsky set her papers on the piano, and smiled. "Let me begin by saying I am so *pleased* to meet someone who appreciates classical *mewsic.*" Vivien smiled, avoiding Seedy's gaze, but Miss Paletsky continued, far too nervous to register the tension. "Can I ask, please: is there a period you like more than another? Baroque period? Romantic period? Modern?"

"Um." Vivien flipped her spiraling jet-black extensions with her left hand, shifting her weight from one long leg to the other. "Yes."

"Oh." Miss Paletsky nodded, meeting Seedy's eyes. She flushed, quickly looked away. "I was thinking a piece from the Impression-istic style. *Mewsic* from this period sounds very much like . . . how do I put this. What it sounds like to be underwater."

"I don't know if Seedy told you," Vivien laughed. "But this is an engagement party. *Not* a pool party."

"Forgive me . . . I miscommunicate." Miss Paletsky smiled, reaching to squeeze Melissa's arm. "Sometimes, when I play for my *stewdents,* I try to give them images to keep in their head. In case it gets too boring."

"That's nice," Vivien replied with a tight smile. "But you real-ize today isn't about your students."

"Vee . . . ," Seedy intruded.

"It's about me," she pushed on, ignoring him. "So . . ." She glanced at her white gold Rolex, raising her penciled-in eyebrows. "Should we get this show on the boulevard?"

"Of course." Miss Paletsky nodded politely, sweet as always. But Melissa noticed it — a brief but glittering heat behind her eyes — proof that she wasn't the only one in the room who found Vivien to be a truly horrible human being. *At last!* Melissa smiled as her trustworthy teacher plunked down on the white leather stool, arranging her sheet music into a crisp overlapping row. *She wasn't alone!*

Miss Paletsky lifted her small hands, her fingertips caressing the polished ivory board, took a breath, and began to play. She exhaled, and her hands exhaled with her, sinking into the keys, dancing in place like elegant, long-legged spiders. From the depths of the grand piano, notes spiraled into the air, arranging themselves into startling patterns, floating high above their heads — a complicated canopy of sound that shifted, and shifted again. Miss Paletsky stopped playing and the canopy shattered, the notes drifting down, and landing at their feet. It was quiet.

"Oh." Vivien pressed her hand to her heart, looking at Seedy for the first time since their tiff. "That was . . ."

"Beautiful," he agreed, dropping his arm across her shoulders.

"Yeah," Melissa begrudgingly admitted. As much as she enjoyed the piece, it was hard take pleasure in what had just resulted in Vivien and her father making up. She gazed at the ceiling, wincing at the swampy sound of their kisses.

Having peeled his lower lip from Vivien's temple, Seedy returned his attention to Miss Paletsky, shaking his head. "You know what's crazy?" He laughed. "I never listen to classical music, and I *swear* I heard that before."

Melissa hugged Emilio to her chest. "I thought that, *too*."

"Here we go." Vivien rolled her eyes, resting her head on Seedy's waiting shoulder. "Now she's an expert."

"I never said I was an expert," Melissa seethed. "It's just . . ."

"I'm just glad you liked it, baby," Vivien purred to Seedy,

changing the subject. She poked his cheek with her ring finger. "Didn't I *tell* you?"

"Yeah, you did . . ." Seedy grinned, planting another kiss on her temple. "You were right."

"I'm always right." She fake-pouted.

"Lena." He slapped his hands to his knees and got to his feet. "Please tell us you'll play at our engagement party."

"Of course." She smiled, gathering her sheet music into a pile. "It would be my pleasure."

Later, as Seedy and Melissa walked her to the door, he remembered to ask: "That piece you played . . ." He scratched the back of his neck. "Who wrote it, again?"

"Well . . ." She gazed at the polished marble floor. "Remember the day you came into my office, you told me you wanted one type of music, but your fiancée wanted something else? Well, I thought, why choose? Why not *combine* the two types of music into something completely new?"

"Okay, *combine* rap and classical piano?" Seedy began to laugh at the notion, but the laughter died on his lips. "Wait . . ."

"Omigod," Melissa gasped. She turned to Miss Paletsky in awe. "It was 'Bi Bim Bitches,' right?"

"It can't be." Seedy gripped his forehead, humming the refrain under his breath. "Wait a minute." He exploded into a wonderful triumphant laugh. "It *is,* isn't it?"

Miss Paletsky nodded, sheepish but proud.

"How did you even *hear* that song?" He grinned, his eyes shining. "Isn't it, like, locked up on the B side of some EP they only sell in Japan?"

"Well," she confessed, embarrassed, "yes."

"I cannot believe this," Melissa laughed. "Miss Paletsky: secret hip-hop junkie."

"I wouldn't say *that*." She blushed, fanning her hands on either side of her face. "In fact, this kind of music . . . Okay, I *hated* it. But your father changed my mind. Just a *little*."

Seedy laughed, and bumped her fist. "I hope this serves as a lesson to you." He turned to Melissa with a stern look.

"Um . . . Miss Paletsky's awesome?"

"*And,*" her father prompted. "Amazing things come out of compromise."

"Oh right." Melissa nodded as he ushered Miss Paletsky toward the door. She smiled, repeating his words in his head. With a sudden wave of urgency, she ran upstairs, down the hall, and into her bedroom. She belly-flopped across her mattress, snatched her rhinestone Sidekick from her pink satin pillow, and punched 6.

"Hey," she answered when Janie picked up. "I have an idea."

"Thank you all for putting aside your personal agendas to attend this emergency meeting," Melissa intoned as Petra, Charlotte, and Janie gathered round the beige plastic table. They'd decided to meet at the Whole Foods on the corner of Santa Monica and Fair-fax, conveniently located equidistant from all four girls' houses, as well as providing free Internet access.

"Well, this better be important," Charlotte sighed, smoothing a paper napkin on the beige plastic bench. She sat down, tucked her long, pink tights–clad legs under her seat, and rolled her perfectly coiffed head on her long neck. "I'm missing a ballet class for this."

"And *I'm* missing my nap," Petra yawned, tugging the straggled ends of her honey-gold, chlorine-scented braids. According to a tacit understanding, she and Paul had gotten together every night, meeting up in his grandparents' kidney-shaped pool, treading the temperate, dark-as-night water, and keeping their gasping voices low. Until they got sick of talking. Then they floated on their backs, blinking at the moon, water lapping into their ears — and bumping into each other, always by accident. She hadn't gone to bed before two in the morning for over a week (not to say she had regrets).

"I'm not missing anything," Janie announced with a cheerful shrug.

"Thank you, Janie," Melissa said, reaching into her silver nylon Batkier tote, "for having the right attitude." Extracting her reliable Tiffany gavel, she loudly rapped the hard plastic table, causing a nearby female shopper in purple baggy-butt sweatpants to gasp in alarm. "So." Melissa flipped open her glitter white notebook, scratching a note to herself in the margin. "I've been doing a lot of thinking since our last meeting, and I think maybe we were all a little too rash. Thankfully, part of my duty as executive officer of public relations is to take the *rash* . . . and turn it into the *rational*."

"*Stellar* wordplay, Meliss," Charlotte mused, dropping a green straw into her glass Orangina bottle. "It's like having lunch with Shakespeare."

"Obviously," Melissa ignored her, "we all have very different ideas of what the Trick-or-Treater should look like. But *what if*," she postulated, cocking a savagely gelled eyebrow, "instead of choosing *one* design, we took the best parts of each and *combined* them, designing something completely new? Like a hybrid super bag."

"You *have* to be kidding me." Janie dropped her whole-wheat cinnamon roll and gaped. "You're suggesting a compromise?"

"What's wrong with that?" Petra frowned in confusion.

"Nothing, except . . ." *Except I'd been trying to suggest a compromise all week, and no one would listen!* "Except nothing," she sighed, grinned at the irony, and stuffed her cinnamon roll into her face.

"Okay." Melissa gently yanked a Xerox copy of Janie's sketch from her folder, sliding it across the table for her perusal. "Janie: if you could only save *one* element from your Trick-or-Treater design . . . which one would it be?"

Janie stared down at her drawing and frowned, finding herself torn between two design elements: the color of the purse, a glaring bright yellow, which she'd chosen in homage to Paul "Electric Banana" Miller, and the cotton cord lace-up detail, inspired by Evan Beverwil's board shorts . . . that one night at the Viceroy. She'd go with the color, she resolved. She'd loved that yellow for as long as she could remember.

"The cotton cord lace-up," she blurted, flushing at her answer. The words had leaped to her lips, surprising her.

Melissa poised her pen. "You sure?"

Janie swallowed, shaking her head. "Yes," she assented, surprising herself again.

"Cotton cord lace-up it is," Melissa announced, and with a kick of her poor, baffled heart, Janie watched her write it down. "Petra?" Melissa solemnly slid a second sketch across the table. "You're next."

"Definitely the color," she replied, returning the sketch without looking. She recalled the name of Paul's dyed hair color with a dreamy, secret smile. "Atomic Turquoise."

"Oh yeah . . ." Janie furrowed her brow. "Isn't that a Manic Panic color?"

"Done!" Melissa trilled, scrambling to write it down before Petra changed her mind and decided to keep those damn rocks. "Okay, Charlotte . . ." She presented her sketch with a flourish. "That leaves you."

"And you," Charlotte pointed out, fluttering her sooty eyelashes into a downward gaze. She wrinkled her porcelain brow. "I'm attached to the stained silk," she confessed, the smallest note of apology for Petra's benefit. "Sorry."

"Stained silk is *two* elements," Melissa sighed, her earlier triumph with Petra all but ruined by Charlotte's stubborn attachment to insanity. "It's the stain or the silk, French Fry. And you *know* my vote."

"Okay, see my dress?" Petra got to her gold flip-flops and circled the perimeter of table, planting herself at Charlotte's side. "It totally looks like silk, right?"

"Well, yes," she admitted, reluctantly admiring Petra's floor-length, empire-waisted ruby-red gown.

"Seriously." Petra stepped forward. "Touch it."

"My fingers better not smell like patchouli after this," Charlotte warned with a playful squinch of her ski-slope nose. The moment she rubbed the fabric between her ginger fingertips, her expression melted from skepticism to surprise. "That really isn't silk?"

"No," Petra answered with a proud smile. "It's a bamboo, cotton, soy blend."

"*C'est magnifique.*" Charlotte bobbed her eyebrows at Melissa, impressed. Melissa buried her face in her hands, grief-stricken. "I'll keep the stains," Charlotte informed her. "But only if we make the purse from that fabric," she insisted, indicating Petra's skirt.

"You might remember my bag's made of *stain-proof* canvas?"

Melissa uncovered her face, and huffed. "What if I want to keep *that* for my design element?"

"Ah, *what if,*" Charlotte sang. "But you won't."

"Fine." Melissa gritted her teeth, committing their final decisions to paper. "But if you keep the stains, then I'm keeping my interlocking double-P clasp."

Charlotte shrugged, rolling a flimsy green rubber band along her clear plastic sushi container. "*C'est la vie,* I guess."

"And when you're designing this bag," Melissa addressed Janie in an all-business tone, "keep one thing in mind, and one thing only. *Instant brand recognition.* This means I want that POSEUR label *on* the bag. Not embroidered in teeny tiny your-name-on-a-grain-of-rice sized letters *inside* the bag." She narrowed her almond-shaped eyes at Charlotte. "This is our premier couture handbag, and it has to be noticed."

"Hurrah." Charlotte chewed, drumming the air with her chopsticks. "Death to subtlety!"

"Subtlety," Melissa repeated, shaking her head in a show of contempt. "That word riles me, ladies. And it should rile you, too — with that pansy-ass silent letter. POSEUR isn't about *silence.* Our letters will be loud, proud, and *in your face!*"

"Okay, I already have something in mind," Janie confessed, gray eyes agleam. She rubbed her hands together. "Ah!" She squealed. "It's gonna be *so good.*"

"Can you have it done by tomorrow morning?" Melissa inquired.

"First thing," she beamed, still excited. "I'm halfway done already."

"I hope so, because if we're going to call it the Trick-or-Treater, we *have* to launch it *on* Halloween." Melissa leaned forward, locking Charlotte into intense eye contact. "Seamstress Charlotte. Be completely honest. Can you really do this in one day?"

"Omigod," Charlotte frowned, raising her small hand. "For toats."

"Because I came up with this totally phenom teaser." Melissa continued to look stern. "But once it's out, it's *out,* and we're do-or-die committed."

"We're *committed,*" Petra assured her.

"*Straight*-jacket committed," Janie emphasized.

"*Couture* straight-jacket committed," Charlotte amended. "Of course."

"Okay!" Melissa laughed at last, gaveling the table with all her might. A tiny man in a woolly scarf and nipple-revealing tank top looked up from the salad bar, his chiseled face sour with scorn, and good ol' Baggy Butt — squeezing and sniffing oranges this entire time — looked up from her latest victim, shaking her head in slow disgust.

"Uh-oh," Petra tittered under her breath. "I think we've upset the natives."

"Really," Melissa intoned, with a defiant bob of her eyebrows. She pinched Charlotte's green rubber band from the table, looped it around her thumb, and shot. Baggy Butt continued to sniff her fruit, oblivious to the assault — as well as the green rubber band clinging to her baggy butt–pants butt.

"As I was saying," the straight-faced Melissa continued, as Charlotte, Janie, and Petra collapsed to the table, stifling their giggles in their arms. "This emergency POSEUR meeting is officially dismissed."

The Girl (sometime last century): Nikki the First, aka "Nonna"
The Getup: Full, knee-length skirt and wide-collared swing jacket in matching beige silk jacquard by Escada biscotti brown midheel pumps by Ferragamo. Navy quilted handbag by Chanel, semi-sheer control-top nude stockings by Wolford, and top-secret brassiere by La Perla (La Mela's oldest and greatest lingerie rival).

In addition to her pink Nokia cell phone, Nikki also owned a mint-condition princess phone from nineteen fifty-five, a relic of her grandmother's first marriage. The candy blue phone hunkered on her white side table, the size and shape of a curled-up cat. Because it never rang, Nikki assumed its purpose was decorative — much like the broken grandfather clock in her father's study. Imagine her confusion at 8:42 that Sunday morning, when the phone rattled her awake with a terrifying *brrrrriiiiiinnnnggggg!* She sat up with a start, blinking behind a tangled veil of flaxen hair. The phone rang again, and whipping aside her butterfly-patterned Tommy Hilfiger duvet, she swung her longish bare feet to the plush white carpet, and half-walked, half-stumbled her bleary-eyed approach. As she neared the phone, the ring seemed to increase in volume and urgency. Slowly, slowly, she lowered her hand, her fingers gripping the vibrating receiver until — kuh-*click* — she picked it up, and the thing went dead in her hand. She raised the heavy plastic receiver to her ear and took a deep, fortifying breath. Maybe it was irrational, but . . .

"Tom?"

"Nicoletta!" a disappointingly familiar voice rasped on the other line, and Nikki exhaled, her cornflower-blue eyes smarting with disappointment. "What are you doing up there? You are on the Fruit Machine?"

Nikki sighed. Her grandmother referred to anything developed after medieval times as "machines," including but not limited to televisions, microwaves, Dust Devils, toaster ovens, cars, and those kids' shoes that blinked red lights when they walked. Nikki once tried to demystify her Apple laptop to her grandmother, but the only detail retained was the machine's all-important relationship to fruit. Within just a short amount of time, "Apple Laptop" became "Apple Machine" became "Fruit Machine" and, finally, just plain "Fruit."

"The Fruit is *no* good," her grandmother cried into the phone. "It is bad! You have not come out of your room in . . . how long, Nikki? Days. *Weeks.* You need sunlight, *cara.* Fresh air. You need *people!*"

"Nonna." Nikki forced a smile, attempting an optimistic tone. "Please, don't worry about me. I'm fine."

"Ha! Fine, she says. *You are not fine,* cara, you are *sique*! The Fruit eats up your thoughts and then holds you like a hostage!"

"Just leave me alone!" Nikki wailed helplessly into the phone.

And then she did the unthinkable — she hung up on her grandmother. Eight seconds later, the phone rattled to life, and Nikki flung herself to the bedroom floor, grinding her hot cheek into the plush white carpet, and breathed in the pleasant, vaguely mineral scent of residual vacuum breath, covering her gold-studded ears with her hands. When, at long last, the phone stopped ringing, she turned her face upward. Her white laptop snoozed on her painted oak desk. On the lower panel, a little Tic Tac of light brightened and darkened, breathing in, breathing out. Sliding into her simple ladder-back desk chair, she punched the space bar, and the laptop buzzed awake. She felt herself relax, beginning to type.

`Are you there, Tom . . . ?`

She took a moment and smiled, weakened by the opiating effect of those four little words. Except they weren't words anymore — they were an addiction. She resumed typing, fingers atremble, and succumbed fully to the heavy-yet-light sensation of giving in.

`It's me . . .`

"Nicoletta!"

Her white bedroom door sprung open and *thwacked* against the adjacent wall, upsetting her very favorite framed Anne Geddes photograph. The baby-in-a-lettuce-cup slammed to the floor with guillotine-blade finality, the glass pane cracking in three places.

"Get away from The Fruit Machine," her grandmother rumbled, pointing a waxen finger. Nikki closed the laptop with an obedient click. Nikki the First hadn't ventured from her bedroom, let alone *upstairs,* in as long as she could remember. She was almost *always* in bed, to the point that Nikki hardly perceived them as distinct, separate entities. Like a mermaid, or a minotaur, her grandmother was a glamorous creature of myth: half human, half mattress.

"Get dressed," she ordered, raising a shakily drawn crayoned eyebrow. Gone was the virgin white, lace-trimmed nightgown, and in its place a matching skirt and jacket in beige silk jacquard. Biscotti brown pumps molded to her small, knobby feet, and nude stockings wrinkled about her matchstick-thin ankles. Bright orange coral lipstick and slapdash streaks of blue eyeliner made her wrinkled face pop, and a shining helmet of hair clamped to her head like a vise.

"Nonna." Nikki struggled to button her pink-and-green Ralph Lauren cardigan. "Are you . . . is that . . . are you wearing a wig?"

"What," she chuckled, patting the blond orb with her hand. "You think I grow this overnight?" She coughed, thumping her upper chest with her fist. "Of course, we call it a wig only between us. Once we are outside, it is my *real* hair. *Capiche?*"

"Outside?" Nikki's hands dropped to her sides, appalled. "What do you mean?"

"I am taking you out," her grandmother declared, popping open her navy quilted Chanel purse. She extracted a ball of used tissue, held it to her nose, and sniffed. "You need to see the world! Appreciate nature, air, art . . . humanity!"

"But . . ." Nikki's eyes darted to her laptop.

What if Tom sent her a message, and she wasn't here to receive it? What if she didn't write him back right away? Maybe he'd think she wasn't serious about their friendship. Maybe he'd . . .

"Do not even *look* at The Fruit," her grandmother interrupted her thoughts, clutching her arm. She tugged her toward the open door. "You are coming with me!"

The Girl: Janie Farrish
The Getup: Unisex black-and-white wide-stripe cardigan and black leggings by United States of Apparel, and Red flip-flops by Havaianas.

"Janie," Mrs. Farrish murmured, training her eyes to the pile of junk mail in her lap. "That's the third time you've brushed pencil sharpenings on the floor."

"Sorry," Janie muttered in her seat at the opposite end of the dining room table, still squinting at her design.

"Unbelievable," her mother clucked, shaking her messily ponytailed head in dismay. "These *people* with their 'one-time-only' credit card offers. I swear . . ." She pushed another envelope into the shredder, listening with satisfaction to the resulting chainsaw buzz. "They're like *drug* dealers."

Janie stared at her drawing and blew, pursing her Carmex-slathered lips. At the noise, her mother looked up, blinking behind her turquoise cat-eye reading glasses.

"You *do* realize you're cleaning that up."

"Obvie," Janie sang, just as her cell phone flashed awake, buzzing across the table like a dying bee.

"Obvie?" her mother repeated, as her daughter lunged. She grimaced. "Is the word 'obviously' really too much of an effort?"

"Hey, Charlotte," Janie answered, scooting back in her chair and padding into the kitchen. The digital microwave clock read

8:48 a.m. "I was going to call you, but I thought you'd still be asleep."

"No, how's the design?" Charlotte's delicate voice chimed on the other end, whipping in and out of a breeze. The tangerine tree outside Janie's kitchen window rustled its leaves. "Are you done?"

"Just finished." Janie nodded, pacing back to the table. She pinched the corner of her sketch, lifting it to the light. "I just need to pack up, and I'm on my way."

"No, no . . . I'm in the Valley!" Charlotte informed her, still chiming in the wind.

"What?" Janie blanched. Maybe she'd misheard. Maybe she'd said, *No time to dally!* Janie wouldn't put it past her.

"My friend Don John's acting class is about five minutes from where you live," Charlotte explained, crushing Janie's hopes in an instant. "I thought he could drop me off at your house and pick me up after?"

"You want to come *here?*" Janie's entire circulatory system pulsed in horror. Mrs. Farrish glanced up from her bills. "Um, I . . . I don't know. . . ."

"It's fine," her mother silently mouthed, wagging her palm. Janie hugged her ribs and frowned, turning toward the wall.

"He says his class is only . . . what was it again? Oh, an hour and fifteen minutes. I thought if I came by we could go over your sketch together . . . make sure we're on the same page?"

"Oh, right. Yeah," Janie replied, her voice hoarse. "Okay, sure. *Bye.*" She clapped her phone shut, covering her eyes with one hand.

"Was that *Charlotte*?" her mother's wry and all-knowing voice rose behind her.

Janie dropped her hand to her side and turned. "Yeah."

"So, she's coming over?" Mrs. Farrish stacked her remaining bills into a pile.

"I . . . I don't know exactly." Janie shrugged, still hugging her ribcage with her arms. Off her mother's baffled look, she continued. "I mean, she *might,* but it . . . it all kind of depends on this friend? I don't really know. She was kind of unclear on the phone."

"Well, make sure you clean up that mess," her mother instructed, scooting back in her chair. "Whether or not she *does* come."

"Uh-huh." Janie swallowed, glancing into the kitchen to recheck the time. The microwave was splattered with spaghetti sauce, and the plastered hole seemed to eclipse the entire wall. She reached for her phone.

"Oh, and do you have any laundry?" her mother called from the opposite side of the house, pervading the ring in Janie's waiting ear. "I'm doing whites!"

"Hey," Jake's recorded voice clicked into gear. "This is Jake Farrish. Please leave a message. And don't be embarrish."

Beeeeeeep!

"Jake, hey . . . ," Janie murmured, cupping the mouthpiece with her hand. "I know today's your day to have the car, but I really, really need it. Please come back as soon as you can, *please?*"

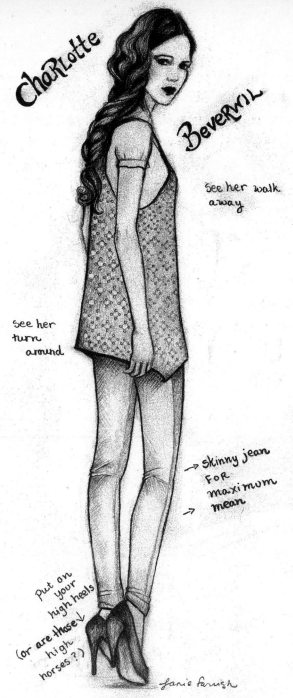

Charlotte

Beveryl

see her walk
away

see her
turn
around

→ skinny jean
for
maximum
mean
→

Put on
your
high heels
(or are those
high
horses?)

Janie Farrish

see her turn into a pillar of sulk

The Girl: Charlotte Beverwil
The Getup: Dark blue skinny jeans by Chloé, blue dot-print shirt by Rebecca Taylor, brown suede T-strap sandals by Oscar de la Renta, and heart-patterned neck scarf in nutmeg, gold, and sapphire silk by Christian Dior (courtesy of Jules).

The Farrishes' house was small and square, with two front-facing windows and a triangle birthday-cap roof painted a cheerful robin's-egg blue. The rest of the house was pale yellow. To the left, a pocked gravel driveway, occupied by Mrs. Farrish's much newer white Volvo station wagon, a not-quite-spherical basketball, and a looping sprawl of garden hose, sloped to the gray residential street. The lawn, though browning in patches, was neat, and freshly mown, and a leafy walnut tree offered shade. By the end of October, a fair amount of fallen nuts attracted a posse of neighborhood squirrels — they dawdled, poking about the stiff winter grass, pausing every three seconds to sniff whatever it is squirrels sniff.

Charlotte pulled her 1969 Jaguar to the leaf-littered curb and slowly braked, allowing the gleaming cream car to lumber. As the great French songstress Edith Piaf warbled and emoted inside her speakers, she checked a crinkled sheet of antique-toned paper in her lap, peered across the quaint suburban street, lowered her Havana brown Dior sunglasses, and squinted.

"Car ma *vie* . . . ! Car mes *joies* . . . ! Aujourd'*hui* . . . CA COMMENCE AV —"

"Well . . ." She finger-punched the stereo, cutting Edith off mid-climax. "This is it!"

Nineteen-year-old Don John looked up from his Juicy Couture Sidekick, tilted forward in his passenger seat, tipped his Dolce & Gabbana aviators to the end of his well-exfoliated snout, and winced. "Yes, but . . ." He winced again, returning his sunglasses to their rightful place. "*What* is it?"

"It's a *house,* Don John," Charlotte sighed, shutting off the engine. "Obvie."

"Wait, like a house where you *live?*" he gasped, bulging his light gray Bette Davis eyes to maximum capacity. "It's so *small!*"

Charlotte drew herself up in her seat, flexing the great ballerina muscle of social consciousness. "You know what? *Small is relative.*"

He yanked his gelled eyebrows into a puzzled knot. "Y'all are relatives?"

"No," Charlotte groaned. "What I mean is *just* because it's not a ten-bedroom estate does *not* mean it's quote-unquote *small.* Compared to another structure," she ventured, "it might look quite large."

"Compared to *what* structure?" Don John snorted, unconvinced. "Ashley Tisdale's nose?"

"You are *not* funny," Charlotte snapped. But a ghost of a smile twitched behind her peony-pink pout as she glanced into her lap, unzipping a quilted white leather Chanel makeup bag. "So," she said a moment later, fixing her trusty MAC compact with a haughty glare and applying another layer of lip gloss. "You'll remember to pick me up at eleven o'clock, right?"

"Oh yes, yes!" Don John agreed, clasping his hands on the polished walnut dash. At *last,* stingy old Beverwitch had agreed to let him borrow her car (he'd only asked three *million* times, and she'd always replied, "Can't you just borrow Mort's wheelchair?"). Her timing could not have been more perfect. He was desperately in love with Jamie Law, his Advanced Acting for Television teacher, who (despite Don John's boyish good looks and *indisputable* razzmatazz) remained bewilderingly aloof. He absolutely *had* to get Jamie to notice him, and the cream-colored Jag was his last and only hope.

Nothing says "Love me back, bitch" like a hundred-thousand-dollar car.

Charlotte detached the silver key from her purple squiggle bracelet, dangled it to Don John, and pushed open the heavy car door. She'd barely let go of the handle when he turned the ignition and revved the engine, scattering the squirrels in an instant (except for the fattest of the bunch, who merely froze).

"Ta!" her dear friend cried, flinging his polo-clad arm in farewell. And then, before Charlotte could tell him he had lip gloss on his teeth, there came a whirl of autumn leaves, car exhaust . . .

And he was gone.

Charlotte squared her puffy-sleeved shoulders and crossed the street. The quiet house appeared to watch her, its rectangle windows opaque yet curious, like the eyes of a long lost friend. Drawing closer, she succumbed to nostalgia, as if on some unconscious level, she *did* recognize this place. But how was that possible? How could a house she'd never seen before feel familiar? She reached the sidewalk, and a gentle breeze rustled the leaves of the walnut tree, sending a fleshy green pod to the earth with a hollow *thwop*. . . .

And it hit her.

She'd drawn this house in kindergarten — always a square, two windows, and a triangle roof. (Okay, most kindergartners drew that house, but *still*.) Arriving home from school, she'd dutifully surrender the drawings to their *dame de la maison,* Blanca, who secured them to the stainless steel doors of the Sub-Zero refrigerator. As soon as Charlotte went to bed, however, Blanca would remove them, returning the fiberglass starfish magnets to the shallow cutlery drawer and the crayon drawings to a clear plastic bin labeled STORAGE.

Georgina Malta Beverwil disapproved of clutter.

When Charlotte awoke to find her houses gone, she drew another. And when *that* house disappeared, she drew another. How many hundreds of triangles had leaped from the tip of her crayon, how many thousands of squares, before that fateful day in first grade when Madame Lefevre, her ballet instructor, changed her life? "I wee-quire all my students to do zaire own *mending,*" she'd informed Charlotte in her croaking French frog-voice, handing her a painted tin box. Inside, she'd found eight gleaming spools of thread, a pair of mother-of-pearl fabric shears, two fresh needle packs, a felt tomato pincushion, and — most precious of all — a pewter measuring tape no larger than an oyster's shell. Without a moment's hesitation, she traded her crayons for needles, her paper for bolts of fabric, and resolved "from now on" to create only what she could *wear*. That way, wherever she went, her creations went right with her.

And she'd never wake to find them gone.

"Charlotte!" Janie swung the screen door open and serenely glided to the front porch — which is to say, tripped over the welcome mat and crashed into a set of hanging wind chimes. As the agitated metal pipes clamored for attention, she cringed: *how* did her mother find that sound soothing? All she could think of was runaway ice cream trucks and psychotic clowns.

"Ha!" she gasped, attempting a "cool girl who could laugh at herself" sort of thing (she sounded more like the actor who gets stabbed offstage in a Shakespeare play.) "You're *early*," she observed through gritted, smiling teeth.

"Well, early is the new late!" Charlotte chirped, kissing each of her flushed cheeks. She eyed the black folder in Janie's hand, and beamed. "Is that . . . ?"

"It *is*." Janie linked Charlotte's petite arm with her own, guiding her like a blind man down the porch stairs.

"Oh, before I forget" — Charlotte patted her hand — "Melissa wants us all to wear formal gowns for tomorrow morning. She wants us to present the Trick-or-Treater in costume, but like *themed* — so we're all dressed like Oscar winners."

"You mean, like, *dead* Oscar winners?" Janie asked, lowering her voice.

"She didn't specify." Charlotte, too, lowered her voice and frowned. "Why are we whispering?"

"No reason." Janie brightened as they achieved a fair distance down the drive. "I just thought we could take a walk. See the sights."

"Oh," Charlotte exhaled in disappointment, craning around. "I was kind of looking forward to seeing where you lived. Your house is so charming."

As Janie measured Charlotte's chlorine gaze for glimmers of irony, a familiar putter sounded at the end of the street. She looked up, all but wilting with relief.

"Jake!" She released Charlotte's arm, scampering to the curb. Her brother eased on the brake and buzzed down the passenger seat window, blasting the air with music — something over-the-top angry and drum-infested. "Did you get my message?" Janie yelled.

"Ye-es," he replied, gazing past her shoulder to meet Charlotte's ready-for-a-challenge gaze. "Thanks for being so specific." He grimaced at his sister, increasing the volume. "I'll be going now."

"No, wait!" she cried as he eased on the gas. She staggered alongside the slowly moving car, clutching the bottom of the window. "Can't I borrow the car?"

"No Volvos for Judas." Jake fake-smiled. "Besides," he braked. "I told Tyler we'd meet up at Pins on Pico."

"Omigod." Janie fluttered her eyes shut, balling her hands into fists of prayer. "Charlotte's house is *right on the way*. Can you please just drop her off?"

"Janie!" An appalled Charlotte squared her shoulders and rapidly approached the car, immaculate brown suede shoes a-clacking. "Did you just ask him to give me a *ride*? Don John's picking me up in an hour."

"I know, but . . ." Janie glanced between them both, scrambling for an explanation. "Mom's really sick," she confessed, focusing on Jake.

"She is?" both of them replied, briefly united by concern.

"It's just a bad headache," Janie amended, going for realism. "But, maybe it's not the best time for guests. And I should probably stick around, you know, in case she needs something?"

Through the open car window, Jake and Charlotte locked eyes. Janie could tell Charlotte was waiting for her brother to make the first move, but he just sat there, brain-dead as always, while the stereo barfed a continual stream of testosterone.

"You know what," Charlotte snipped, returning to Janie, "I think I should just . . . wait on the lawn, or something."

"For an hour?" Janie fretted.

"I'll be fine." Charlotte narrowed her eyes at Jake. "I think I have a receipt or something I could read."

"Okay, why are you guys *being* like this?" Janie clenched her fists, stamping her foot in frustration. "Charlotte." She whirled to face her unlikeliest friend. "Did you *not* just tell me yesterday that Jake's the only person who makes you laugh?"

Charlotte's dainty jaw dropped in indignation, but rather than allow her the time to retaliate, Janie thrust an accusing finger at her brother. "And he cried into his *cereal* about you, so don't *even* think he doesn't realize how stupid he was."

Charlotte closed her mouth and glanced at Jake, who gripped the steering wheel and stared at the horn, humiliated beyond belief.

"It's the *truth,* Jake," Janie barked. "You *miss* her. And Charlotte, you miss him. So why don't you two just get over yourselves and be friends so I can stop being in the middle of this starting *now*. Charlotte?"

Charlotte blinked, fiddling the ends of her heart-printed neck scarf. "Yes?"

"Get in the car!"

Less than twenty seconds later, Janie sailed into the house, kicking the door shut behind her. She leaned against it, heart pounding in her chest, exhilarated by a sense of her own awesomeness. She couldn't *believe* she'd just done that. She couldn't believe it had actually worked! Without another peep of protest, Charlotte slid her annoyingly perfect butt into the cracked vinyl front seat, Jake politely lowered the music, and together they took off for the hills. Janie smiled, congratulating herself for a job well done.

But just as she traipsed toward her bedroom, eager to call Amelia and share her latest exploit, her mother pushed out of the laundry room, a bunched white towel in her hand, and blocked her cheerful path.

"Janie." She frowned, pinching the white towel at either corner and shaking it out. "What is this?"

"Oh." Janie hesitated, taking a small step backward. She bit her lower lip and cringed. "It's a dress?"

"Did you use one of my *best* bath towels for this?" her mother asked, balling the dress into her hip. She shook her head in slow amazement as Janie stared at the floor, quiet.

"I can't believe this. I *just* bought these bath towels, Janie. They're *brand* new."

"But I used them for something creative," Janie whined, daring to meet her mother's eyes. She'd once used her mother's only Chanel lipstick to write "Janie" over and over on the bathroom mirror, and just the word "creativity" got her off the hook.

Well, that, and the fact that she'd been five.

"Janie." Her mother tensed. "You think I'm upset because you did something creative? I'm upset because my daughter would do something like this without *asking* me first. It's basic courtesy. They're my *best* bath towels and they're *brand* new."

"Okay." Janie reddened with frustration. "I get it! All this drama over a towel from Bed, Bath & Beyond, I mean." A rueful little laugh escaped her lips. "Seriously!"

Mrs. Farrish took a small sip of air, but did not respond, choosing instead to look at her daughter with a dubious eye of an art dealer evaluating a painting for its authenticity. "Janie," she exhaled at last. "Why didn't you invite that girl inside?"

"Wh-what girl?" Janie stammered like an idiot.

"Janie . . ." Her mother had to smile, she was so damn exasperated. "I could see you outside my window."

Janie folded her arms across her chest, shifting her weight from one leg to the other. "I . . ."

"You know what?" Mrs. Farrish winced and briskly shook her head. "I don't want to hear it."

"Mom . . ." Janie wavered, queasy with guilt. "It's not that . . ."

"I don't want to hear it!" she exploded, throwing the dress in a white heap on the floor. "I'm *not* a fool, and I refuse to stand here while you treat me like one." She tipped to the floor, retrieving the dress in a single swipe, and looked up, her eyes glassy with irony and disappointment.

"And *not* that it matters," she concluded in a trembling tone, "but these towels are Ralph Lauren."

The Girl (sort of): Don John
The Getup: Classic pique extra-small white polo by
Lacoste, Ibiza plaid shorts by Juicy Couture, blue-
and-white Linea Rossa boat shoes by Prada.

He pulled up to "Farrish manor," sucking away on a See's latte lollipop and singing along to his freshest, self-entitled mix, "Sunday
Revolves Around Me!" What a joy it was — for the purring Jaguar and him both — to relieve the poor, abused stereo of that *depressing* French crap and put on something *fabulous.* He rolled down
the window, pumped up the volume, and gyrated in his luxurious
leather driver's seat.

"Under my um-ber-ella . . . ella . . . ella . . . oh . . . *uh-oh!*"
He straightened up in his seat, realizing he was not alone: there,
just some ten feet away on the front lawn of Ashley Tisdale's nose,
a girl in a *very* retro bob sat alone, her face huddled into her knees,
and her thin shoulders quaking in a way that suggested heightened
distress. Don John cringed, waiting for it to go away.

"Ah, hello!" he called at last, rolling the window all the down.
"Hello, there . . . crying girl on the lawn!"

Startled, she raised her tousled head and sniffed, her large gray
eyes teary and pathetic. "Charlotte's not here," she announced,
much to his surprise. *This* young urchin was the notorious Janie
Farrish? Huh. A lot *prettier* than Charlotte ever let on. "She got a
ride." She cleared her throat, wiping her blotchy cheeks.

"Well, of course she did," Don John clucked, spinning down the volume. "Girl's never alone for long." He returned to Janie, regarding her misery with a sudden, unwelcome wave of pity. He sighed. "*She* didn't do this to you, did she?"

"No, no." She attempted to smile, her pretty chin atremble. "I just have the worst life in the world, that's all!"

"Well, *that's relative*," he declared, propping his soft chin on his chiseled arm, his Elizabeth Arden–bronzered face framed by the Jaguar window. "I mean, you could be *me*," he dramatically sighed. "Unappreciated and alone. *Terribly* unloved."

Janie looked up at him, stunned, and he sympathized. It *was,* after all, pretty hard to believe.

"Here!" He brightened, digging into his pink and green "Rockit" print LeSportsac tote. He flailed his polo-clad arm out the window, and a glinting gold object arced through the air, landing with a bounce on the grass. "I keep them around to make me feel better," he explained as Janie got to her feet and padded across the lawn. "They totally work."

Janie plucked the squarish, brightly foiled lollipop from the ground, turned it around in her hand, and smiled. "Thanks." She looked up, smiling again. Don John shivered in his seat, genuinely moved by his small act of good will. "That's really sweet."

"Trick-or-Treat!" he cried, revving the engine.

And then he was gone.

The Girl: Blanca (last name unknown)
The Getup (by day): The loathed "maid's uniform."
The Getup (by night): Bright blue asymmetrical tank
by Bebe, black leather mini from Wasteland on
Melrose, knee-high lace-up black leather stiletto
boots by Pleaser Shoes, exotic purple orchid from Mrs.
Beverwil's greenhouse.

"Look at this," Nonna wavered at the foot of an ornately framed oil painting, blinking behind her black horn-rimmed glasses. In order to convince her granddaughter of the old adage, "There is more to life than Internets," she had arranged a visit to the Los Angeles County Museum of Art. *Of all places,* Nikki thought with a heavy sigh. After eight hours on her feet, she'd collapsed into a wrought-iron garden bench, the only one in the gallery, wedging herself into the far right-hand corner. Her bench companion, a grizzled old man in a wilted brown hat, hummed under his breath. Nikki held her breath.

He smelled like an unwashed fruit crisper.

"Nicoletta." Her grandmother rapped her pronged, aluminum cane against the floor. "Come here, please." She rose to her feet, and the old man's hum rose with her, swinging into a high, fevered pitch.

"Take a close look at this one," Nonna advised, indicating a painting with her crumblingly powdered chin. "What do you think of it?"

She'd asked that question at least thirty times that afternoon, and the answer was always the same:

"It's okay, I guess."

"You guess!" Her grandmother rasped with laughter. "If you *looked* at the painting, Nicoletta, you wouldn't have to *guess* all the time."

Indulging her, Nikki hooked a flaxen strand of hair behind her ear and really looked. The painting depicted a plate of cherries and a plate of peaches. It was called *Still Life with Cherries and Peaches*.

"Notice the redness of the cherries," Nonna crooned. "The way the bowl tilts forward, inviting you to take a bite. *Ach!* Wouldn't it be so delicious, to eat a cherry like that?"

"You know what we should do?" Nikki brightened. "Go to Whole Foods and get some *real* cherries." At the mere *thought* of Whole Foods, her heart rate elevated, because in addition to cherries, the grocery chain *happened* to offer free Wi-Fi. And true, she didn't have her laptop with her, but maybe — while Nonna enjoyed herself in the cheese aisle — she could beg one of the many aspiring screenwriters stationed at the tables for just five or so minutes? "I wouldn't ask except it's an emergency," she'd explain sweetly, and quickly log onto MySpace. Just to *check*.

"Nicoletta." Her grandmother clutched her arm, fracturing her glowing fantasy. "You cannot find such cherries at the market." She indicated the painting with her withered old hand. "These are cherries you must eat with your *mind*."

"Complete and utter caca," a clipped female voice interrupted from the right entrance, inducing the man in the brown hat's second fit of humming.

"What did you say?" Nikki's grandmother addressed their mystery intruder, wobbling forward on her cane.

"I said *caca*," she cawed like an angry crow. "As in, 'Oh! My mind just ate a pretty red cherry, and it tasted of *caca*.'"

"This painting is a Cézanne," Nikki the First informed the woman with a squint fierce enough to unstick her fake eyelashes. "An artist of *great* importance. A genius! Who are you to say he is what you say?"

"Who am *I*?" A spastic blue vein throbbed at the woman's temple. Black hair fell down her back in one snaking coil, and the sticker name tag on her leather mini–clad hip read BLANCA. "Has it occurred to you that I, too, am an artist? A *living* artist whose work remains unappreciated — unseen! — because fusty old ladies like *you* prefer the company of a dead man's *cherries*?"

"My grandmother is *not fusty*!" Nikki cried, shocking herself right down to her antique gold Nanette Lepore Hot & Bothered flats. She wasn't sure what fusty *meant,* exactly, but she could tell by the woman's *tone.* It wasn't nice. More like the kind of word she might scrawl across Nonna's locker in scarlet lip liner, assuming Nonna had a locker, which she didn't.

But *still.*

"I apologize," Blanca sighed, instantly contrite. "It's merely that I . . . I have an exhibit here. It's only a two-day thing, and well . . . nobody so far has come." She threw her elegant head back with a dry little laugh, gazing at the bleak expanse of ceiling. "Nobody!"

Nikki glanced at her grandmother. Her grandmother glanced back, pursing her bright orange mouth.

"Well . . ."

"Oh, thank you!" Blanca blurted, beckoning them both into an adjacent gallery. Nonna sighed her surrender, following the artist at a labored pace, but stopped at the archway, blocking her precious Nikki with a brusque, perpendicular sweep of her rubber-tipped steel cane.

"We do not want to see anything dead and floating in a jar," she warned. "Or anything inappropriate for my granddaughter."

"Oh, nothing to be concerned about," Blanca assured her.

Nonna lowered her cane and together, they stepped into the adjacent gallery. Instead of paintings on the wall, the entire *room* had been transformed, with garbage encrusting every spare square-inch of space. In one glance Nikki saw dented soda cans, rusted hubcaps, water-stained takeout fliers, crushed cardboard cups, and crumpled receipts.

"Wow," she murmured, looking all around.

"And what do you call this?" Nonna asked, sounding considerably less impressed than her teenage companion. She pushed her horn-rimmed glasses up the bridge of her nose, and sniffed. "Does it have a title?"

Blanca paused for effect. *"Rodeo Drive."*

"Really?" Nikki piped up. Like all red-blooded Winstonian girls, she *lived* for Rodeo. "Why?"

"Because," Blanca began slowly, testing her words like over-ripe cheese. "Even the most famous street in the world has its own special trash. Its own brand of litter. I call it — *the detritus of the privileged classes.* You find it tossed into waste bins. Strewn along the gutter. And why? Because it is worthless?" In her most impressively crow-like move to date, Blanca actually flapped, springing lightly from the floor. "Well, *not* to me. For three months, I roamed the streets and *picked up their garbage.* And now? I have created a thing more worthy, more *valuable,* than the contents of every luxury window display *combined* —"

"Yes, art is priceless," Nikki's grandmother interrupted, putting an end to the woman's very inappropriate rant. She gestured to an explosion of ketchup-stained burger wrappers on the wall. "But this? This is trash on a wall."

"Perhaps you should look closer," Blanca haughtily advised.

"Ah yes, forgive me." The old woman patted Nikki's elbow and amended her statement with a wry smile. "I meant to say it is *caca.*"

Obedient as ever, Nikki followed in her grandmother's wake, but not without a subversive backward glance for Blanca's benefit, a sweet, apologetic smile. Blanca returned the favor with a gracious, if imperious, nod. Satisfied, Nikki faced the small archway and quickened her step, but just as she swept beneath the glowing red EXIT sign, something caught her attention. She halted in her tracks, stunned to the base of her spine. Rooting the ball of her foot to the ground, she turned — her eyes as round as Cézanne dishes.

"Nikki?" her grandmother called. But her brittle voice sounded a million miles away. There — framed by a broken loop of dog leash and overlapping a empty matchbook — was a simple white clothes tag, a single word scrawled across its face. As Nikki drew near, the word blazed out, searing her mind like a branding-iron, until, at last, it was the only thing she could see.

POSEUR.

unwashed
chlorine-
scented
pony

Petra Greene

jagged
little
edges

CaR mechanic
cut-offs

Perfects the
"Cool Girl slouch"

$3.00 slippers
from Chinatown

Janie Parrish

The Girl: Isabel Greene
The Getup: "You're too young for getups!"

Petra breezed from her bedroom and trotted brightly downstairs, a tangled, chlorine-scented ponytail bouncing at her suntanned back. The Monday morning sun streamed through their enormous east-facing French windows, painting glowing runways along the polished hardwood floors. She sailed into the kitchen, tugging the end of her ponytail to her nose, and breathed in deep, surrendering to memories of last night. "Heya!" she sang, still smiling through her golden hair.

"Hiii, Miss Petra," Lola greeted her, a piece of yellow thread pulled taut between her teeth. "Hol' still," she instructed Sofia, whose tiny, bewildered face peeked out from a giant yellow felt orb.

"What are you supposed to be, Soph?" Petra smiled down at her four-year-old adopted sister, and quickly shielded her eyes. "Ooo . . . ouch! Are you the *sun?*"

"Nooooo . . . ," her little sister moaned in despair, and Lola grunted, straightening from her crouched position on the floor. She sent Petra a reproving look.

"No, the sun." She yanked an iron-on *M* from her apron pocket, pinching the lowercase letter at either corner. "She is M&M candy."

"Oh-oh-oh." Petra covered her face in a show of embarrassment. "Omigod, of *course*. What a good idea, Soph! M&M's are your favorite, right?"

But Sofia continued to look at Lola, her dark eyes glassy with disappointment. "B-but I do-don't want to-to be the *sun*," she whimpered.

"Hey." Petra grinned. She knew she had to act fast before all havoc broke loose. "Do you know who's coming over?"

To both Petra's and Lola's relief, Sofia loudly exhaled, and her breathing returned to normal. "Who?"

"My friend Charlotte," Petra announced. "Remember you met her? When we went to Melissa's house that time? Remember Melissa? You played with her cute little dog?"

Sofia responded to her older sister's cheerful interrogation with numb incomprehension, her small mouth slightly gaped.

"Anyway —" Petra smiled, sympathizing with Sofia's confusion — "she's coming over with a real-life ball gown for me to wear to school. Isn't that fancy? We're supposed to dress up as Oscar winners!"

"You are?!" Isabel's brassier, six-year-old voice interrupted. Petra glanced at the gaping archway entrance, got one eyeful of her sister, and promptly screamed.

"Why are you doing that?" Isabel frowned fiercely at her older sister as she clapped a hand to her mouth, staggered a small step backward, and leaned up against the kitchen wall. "Sto-op!" Isabel stamped her glittery purple platform-clad foot. "It's not supposed to be a *scary* costume."

"Yeah," Sofia echoed in agreement. A frowning Lola stuck the hem of her costume with a pin and got to her feet, raising her eyebrows at Petra.

"I no make it," she assured her, turning to Isabel with an appraising look. The six-year-old wore a purple mini-dress in body-molding vinyl. Neon-yellow piping coursed along the sides, curving in at the waist, flaring at the hips, and creating the disturbing illusion of a sexy silhouette. A synthetic wig hung to the back of her knees, drowning her small face and shoulders in a stiff cascade of gleaming brown hair.

"Izzie," Petra gasped. *"What* are you wearing?"

"My *Halloween* costume," she explained, with a defiant stamp of her purple platform. "I'm Yasmin!"

"What's a Yasmin?" Petra shook her head in amazement.

"Not *uh* Yasmin." Isabel rolled her eyes. *"Yasmin."* To Petra's dismay, she stuck a pair of candy-red wax lips into her mouth, and posed — hands on her hips, head at a perfect 30-degree tilt.

"See?" Sofia explained, handing Petra a plastic doll dressed exactly like her sister. "Yasmin is a Bratz."

"Isabel . . ." Petra gazed into the whorish doll in her hand in horror. "I'm sorry." She frowned. "But you can't go to school dressed like that."

"What?!" The red wax lips spilled from her open mouth and

fell to the floor on a broken string of drool. "But it's Halloween and it's the only time I don't have to wear a uniform!"

"I'm not saying you can't dress up at *all*," Petra clarified. "*I* know. Why don't you go as a *pink* M&M? Isn't pink your favorite color?"

"*No.*" Isabel gritted her teeth, puffing at the notion. "M&M's are *dumb*!"

At that, Sofia promptly dissolved into a fit of weeping, and half a second later Isabel joined in, gripping the kitchen island for balance. She howled and heaved, makeup-polluted tears streaming down her flushed cheeks.

"What the hell is going on in here?" Heather Greene, who hadn't emerged from her bedroom this early in weeks, shuffled into the kitchen, wearing her oversized black Armani sunglasses and a wrinkled ice blue Fernando Sanchez bathrobe. At the sound of their mother's voice, the little girls collapsed into complete hysteria. "Why is everybody crying?"

Petra covered her eyes in exasperation as Lola plucked the blubbering Sofia from the floor, planted her on her hip, and exited the kitchen. "Mom," she sighed, lowering her hand to her side. "Have you *looked* at Isabel?"

Heather yanked the refrigerator door toward her rail-thin body, an effort rewarded by a celebratory jingle of glass: bottled salad dressings, jars of mustard, marmalade, and mayonnaise. She gazed past the chilled shelves, appearing to fix her shielded eyes at a great distance — as if beyond the cartons of soy milk and soggy boxes of Zen Palate takeout there lay another, brighter world. She closed her eyes and inhaled.

"Mom," her older daughter gaped.

"Alright!" She shut the refrigerator and leaned up against it, a frosted bottle of Evian clutched to her plunging silk neckline. She pushed her sunglasses to the crown of her head, roosting them in a tangle of light ash blond hair. "Okay." She cleared her throat, wincing into the morning light. "What is it? What am I looking at?"

"You actually think it's okay for her to go outside dressed like that?" Petra dropped her jaw in shock.

"Oh, Petra." Her mother frowned, waving off her concern. "It's *Halloween.* And do you have any idea how much *time* I spent looking for that costume? They were sold out everywhere!"

Isabel flew to her mother's side, hugging her knees to her tear-streaked face. "See?" She glared at Petra, gaping her indignation. Somewhere in the distance a bell rang, but it took Petra a good twelve seconds to realize it was the door.

"Hi, everyone!" Charlotte sailed into the kitchen, dragging behind her the layered skirts of a gorgeous midnight blue silk Oscar gown. Whatever traumas Petra had unwittingly inflicted on her sisters evaporated in the instant.

"Wow . . . ," Isabel breathed. "You look so *pretty.*"

"As do *you,* you sweet thing," she lied through her teeth, leaning in to kiss Heather on the cheek. She dangled the black Barneys bag to Petra and smiled. "I brought you one of Mother's."

"Oh, how *is* your mother?" Heather oozed to her older daughter's instantaneous annoyance. Her mother *loved* to act as though she and Georgina were on the best friend-y terms, even though they barely knew each other. Last year, Georgina called the house to invite Heather to a charity benefit for Muscular Dystrophy — along with five hundred other people — and Heather acted as if she'd invited her to come over to paint toenails and braid each other's hair.

"She's wonderful, thank you," Charlotte oozed in return. "She's in New York, actually. Daddy's on location."

"I'm just going to change," Petra blurted, eager to escape this soul-crushing exchange of pleasantries. It killed her to see her mother act so sweet and polite for a perfect stranger. If only she could act that way around her own family once in a while.

"Oh wait!" Charlotte chirped, and with a reassuring pat on Heather's arm, kneeled to the floor, where a second Barneys bag sat at her feet. Reaching inside, she peeled apart the layers of tissue, extracted a small, delicious-looking object, and presented it with a flourish, rising to her size six feet.

"Le Trique or Treat-aire!" she announced with a merry laugh. Heather gasped.

"Isn't that *extraordinary*."

"Let me see! Let me see!" Isabel cried, jumping up and down.

"You're a master," Petra intoned, squeezing her tiny elbow, and wishing for one fleeting instant she'd learned how to sew. But of course she hadn't. Needles and thread had been permanently ruined for her by her father, who used them daily to turn human beings into creepy Hollywood clones. "Melissa and Janie are going to die."

"You think?" Charlotte grinned.

"Puh-lee-ea-ea-se!" Isabel reached for the exquisite couture bag, whimpering in despair.

As Charlotte presented the Trick-or-Treater to her little sister, *warning her to be gentle,* Petra bounded upstairs, her black Barneys bag in tow. She whisked into her bedroom, yanked off her pajamas in record time, and tipped the bag on its head, spilling the gossamer gold-embroidered white cotton dress to the floor. Kicking it apart, she stepped inside, tugging the light-as-breath fabric along her enviably lissome frame, located an invisible side zipper, and zipped. Quickly, she turned to the mirror and froze, flushing. Her family so strongly emphasized the importance of beauty, she rebelled by shirking it altogether. She hadn't dressed up in so long, her reflection blinked back like a stranger.

"Petra!" Charlotte called, knocking softly on her door. "Sorry, but . . . we're going to be late."

Petra pushed open her bedroom door, blushing at the sensation of Charlotte's appreciative gaze. "Petra," she gushed. "You look . . ."

"Thanks," she breathed, and beckoned Charlotte to follow her downstairs. She cut through the foyer, swinging open the heavy front door.

"Oh!" Charlotte gasped, stopping in her tracks. Turning on the blue silk heel of her Manolo Blahnik boutonnière pump, she bounded into the kitchen, returning moments later, the black Barneys bag clutched to her chest.

"Wouldn't want to forget this!" she nervously tittered, shaking her perfectly coiffed head.

"Omigod," Petra proclaimed, pressing a hand to her heart. "I can't even *think* about it."

The door shut behind them with a resolute thud.

The Girl: Charlotte Beverwil
The Getup: Restored ruffled silk and antique lace bow top, from Paris 1900, green silk petticoat skirt by Omo Norma Kamali, blue silk boutonnière stiletto pumps by Manolo Blahnik.

The Girl: Janie Farrish
The Getup: Multitiered lilac cotton petal dress by Lanvin, silver flip-flops by Haviannas.

The Girl: Petra Greene
The Getup: Long dress in white cotton with gold embroidered daisies by Charles Chang Lima, gold flip-flops by Haviannas.

The Girl: Melissa Moon
The Getup: Strapless black chain-link glitter gown with tulle overlay by Versace, silver satin stilettos by Dolce & Gabbana, and (coming soon!) the Trick-or-Treater by POSEUR.

"Omigawd-uh!" Deena teetered across the Showroom wearing too-small white kitten mules, a white satin corset, a bobbing pair of marabou-feathered angel wings and a tiny pink card in her hand. Melissa had arrived to school forty minutes early, sliding the paper inserts into locker vents, taping them to bathroom mirrors, classroom doors, and tree trunks, and scattering the rest along the Showroom floor (after Miss Paletsky's go-ahead, of course). She realized she could have asked Venice, but ultimately was glad she didn't. She wanted the satisfaction of doing the job herself. Not to mention the peace of mind Venice wouldn't screw it up.

" 'It's October first . . .' " Deena clattered at her side, reading the card in a dramatic voice. " 'Do you know where your candy is?' " She widened her purple-shadowed dark brown eyes in anticipation. "What is this?" she whinnied. "Where's my candy?"

"Read the back," Melissa laughed, watching Deena's face as she flipped the card on its head.

" 'POSEUR tells you where: Town Meeting, 8:00 a.m. Be there.' "

"And?" Melissa added, prompting her to read the tiny font.

"Can you read it?" She pouted, handing Melissa the card. She adjusted the glittering gold halo attached to her white headband. "I'd have to put on my reading glasses, and there are no glasses in heaven."

"It says —" Melissa slammed her gleaming platinum trunk, returning the card to her friend — "in five seconds this card will *Britney*? You know, like, self-destruct?"

"*Oh.*" Deena rolled her eyes, pinched the card between her

manicured finger and thumb, and fanned her somewhat horsey face. "Guess I'll take my chances."

Melissa unzipped her patent leather messenger bag, removed a rubber band–bound pack of index cards, and rolled the rubber band until it leaped free with a snap. In the Jungle, kids were already opening their lockers, jumping back in surprise as pink cards fluttered to their feet, and the Showroom thrummed with discussion: What was this about? Was this lame, or was this cool? And were they getting candy out of it? Melissa ignored their curious glances and shuffled through her index cards, knitting her perfectly gelled eyebrows in concentration.

"*AwrrrOOOooo!*" Marco howled from the other end of the parking lot, inviting the fawning attention and appreciative laughter of everyone within a thirty-foot radius. Everyone, that is, except his girlfriend. Undaunted, he pimp-walked his approach, swaggering his weight to one side, brushing his painted nose with the back of his hand. In addition to the standard T-shirt and track-pants combo, he wore an enormous white fox fur vest, plush brown slippers, and fuzzy tan ears to match.

"Holler," Melissa murmured urgently under her breath. Town Meeting was starting in less than ten minutes, and she had yet to commit her speech to memory. "This Halloween, the trick is our treat, and the treat? Is *tuh-ricked out!*"

"Melissa," a male voice hotly puffed against her neck.

"Ew!" She judo-smacked her boyfriend's chest, pushing him

off in disgust. "Tell me you did not just *lick* my ear." She frowned, checking her floor-length black Versace gown for drool.

"Who *me?*" Marco replied with a devilish grin. He hooked a finger to his blue Louis Vuitton rhinestone-studded dog collar, and slid it around his muscular neck. "Why would I do that?"

"Omigod." Melissa's eyes darted to the heart-shaped name tag on his neck. She clapped her hand to her mouth, and gasped. "You are *not* Emilio Poochie! *Ah-hahahah!*" She grabbed her best-friend's arm and squealed. "Deena, he's Emilio Poochie!"

"I heard." Deena shrugged, refusing to glance away from her black Bobbi Brown compact.

"Oh, Marco." Melissa threw her arms around her boyfriend's neck, peppering his face with butterfly kisses. "You are too cute!"

"I know." Marco grinned, pressed his hand to the small of her back, and pulled her in close. Maybe it was on the sick side, but he'd had a *feeling* dressing up as Melissa's dog might encourage a little bonus TLC. Now all he had to do was dress Emilio up as *him,* and he'd have Melissa all to himself.

"You know what you get," Melissa purred into his ear, "if you're a real good dog?"

"*Ho-kay,* this is giving me a bad case of bulimia." Deena gagged, flicking Marco's bicep as she passed. "Later, flea baiter."

"Yeah, in a while, duck-child," Marco muttered, still riveted to his flirtatious girlfriend. He put on his best puppy-dog face. "What do good dogs get?"

Melissa stood on her tiptoes and leaned in toward his ear —

so close that as she opened her lips, Marco heard a soft *pop*. "They get . . ."

"Melissa!" a shrill trio of female voices cried out in unison, and Melissa landed on her heels with a startled thump, twisting around. Charlotte, Janie, and Petra huddled together, dressed to the nines in floor-length gowns, a shimmering vision of gleaming satin, foamy taffetas, ruffled cottons, and glittering diamond-embellished appliqués. They couldn't resist a collectively smug look as they impatiently tapped their feet and reminded Melissa, Miss *Queen* of Punctuality, of . . .

"The time!" they cried in perfect unison, indicating their non-existent watches.

"Oh, baby." Melissa planted a distracted kiss on Marco's cheek. "I'll see you in Town Meeting, okay?"

"No problem," he croaked, mustering every ounce of will power to summon a smile. As Melissa and her pack made their swift departure, traversing the Showroom in a conspiratorial huddle, he even called out, "Save you a spot!"

And it wasn't until they were out of earshot that he tilted his head back, dropped his jaw, and yowled to the sky.

"*NoooOOOoooo!!!!*"

Charlotte Beverwil
looks to the side

Melissa Moon
looks straight ahead

what   are   we

Petra Greene looks down...

Janie "me" Farrish looks up...

janie farrish

looking FOR ?

"Okay," Melissa slammed the bathroom door. "Let me see it."

Charlotte crossed toward the mirror, the pearly-gray tiles echoing under the heels of her pale blue buckled brocade pumps, and lifted the black Barneys bag from the sink. "Shall I do the honors?"

Unable to handle the suspense, Melissa snatched the bag from her hand, tearing the white tissue out in tufts. The crinkled sheets floated to the tiled floor, and Charlotte and Petra shared a giddy moment of eye contact, anticipating her reaction. Melissa stared into the mouth of the bag.

"Is this . . . ?" Melissa looked up, darting her gaze from girl to girl, each of them grinning. "Is this some kind of *joke?*"

"Excuse me?" Charlotte ruffled, wounded to her Pilates core. She'd spent *forever* on that thing, pricking her fingertips so many times they were *bound* to callous, and for what? Another one of Melissa's childish tantrums?

"Petra told me she loves it!" she cried, stamping her tiny foot.

Melissa frowned, reaching into the bag. The stiff paper crackled around her bangled wrist as she lifted the object in one upward sweep, bobbing her perfectly gelled eyebrows.

Charlotte clapped her hand to her mouth.

"I don't get it." Janie, who had yet to see the new bag, winced in confusion. "What is that thing?"

"It appears to be a pumpkin bucket." Melissa frowned, hugging the grinning orange plastic jack-o-lantern to her chest. She bore into Charlotte with her sternest glare. "We do *not* have time for this."

"But I have no idea where that *came* from!" Charlotte insisted in her defense, removing her trembling hand from her open mouth. On her palm, a gaping red lipstick print appeared to gasp in surprise. "I swear to *God,*" she warbled, glancing at the stricken Petra. "I just *showed* it to you. At your house!"

"I know," Petra whispered, shaking her tangled head.

"So what are you saying?" Melissa crossed to the wall and frantically cranked a paper towel. "The handbag we just spent a *month* working on went up and *shape*-shifted into a *pumpkin* bucket?!"

"I don't know," Charlotte whimpered, leaning up against the sink as Melissa continued to madly crank. At last, Janie intervened, ripping the brown paper towel from the dispenser, and calmly handing it to her.

"This isn't happening." Melissa crushed the eight-foot-long paper towel into a crumpled ball, squeezed it between her hands, and dropped it to the floor. "First our contest is sabotaged. Now *this?* It's like we're cursed!"

"Do you think that girl Nikki's behind it?" Charlotte wrung her hands. She could just see Nikki skulking into the showroom and snatching the bag off of her trunk when Charlotte wasn't looking. But then how to explain the pumpkin bucket?

"No way." Janie shook her head. "She'd have to be some kind of diabolical mastermind. Which she's *not,*" she insisted, reading

Charlotte's mind. "She may have macked on Jake, but she got *caught,* okay?"

"Not really a mastermind move," Petra assisted her point. Nevertheless her mind continued to race. How the hell had this happened?

Melissa pushed her fingernails (appropriately manicured in Lancôme's Code Red) to her eye sockets. "Do you even know how hard I hyped this thing? The whole damn school is waiting for this big-ass reveal . . . what are we going to do?" She blinked, her dark brown eyes glossy with dread. "Go up to the podium and be like, *yo.* Just kidding?"

"I hate to say this," Janie whispered. "But TM's in three minutes."

"TM meaning *what?*" Charlotte buried her face in her hands. "Town Meeting? Or Total Mortification . . ."

"It'll be okay," Petra attempted a note of cheer, patting her tiny back. "We'll just go in there and *rip* off the Band-Aid."

"Yeah, I can never really do that," Janie confessed, gray eyes agleam. "I always just leave it on until it gets really gross and, like, falls off in the bath."

The four girls took her words to heart, staring at the floor in cowed silence. A moment later, the bell rang long loud and clear.

"Well," Charlotte sang, pushing off from the edge of the sink. She brushed her voluminous petticoats, squared her ribbon-festooned shoulders, and smiled. "Total Mortification it is!"

From their conception, Town Meetings never started on time. According to one of their many nonspoken agreements, Winstonians devoted the first two minutes to trickling in late and another three to four minutes either a) shrieking at pterodactyl frequencies, or b) launching into super-complicated high-five routines. Invariably, Glen Morrison danced about the perimeter, squeezing his hands together, and pantingly lobbing instructions for them to "Simmer down and face forward" or "Put on our paying-attention masks" or "When the hands goes up, the mouth goes . . ."

Very occasionally, someone responded, "Butt."

Jake weaved through the murmuring throng of seated Nomanlanders and beelined for his freshly re-earned and highly coveted West Wall spot, swinging his black canvas backpack from his shoulder. But before he could drop it to his feet, a streak of purple velvet swept across the floor, claiming his seat. Jake blinked in shock as Jules Maxwell-Whatever, imperious as ever in a powdered Louis XVI wig and royal blue satin sash, lay a bejeweled hand over the velvet garment.

"Um . . ." Jake lowered his backpack to the scuffed rubber edge of his black low-top Converse, scratching the back of his neck in mock confusion. "Sorry, but your *skirt* appears to be in my seat."

Jules tightened his jaw, flexing the expertly applied beauty mark on his cheek. "It is a cape."

"Are you protecting me from a mud puddle?" Jake grinned, pressing his hand to his heart. "What chivalry!"

"The chivalry is for Charlotte, not you," the humorless amber-eyed king informed him. "This is her seat."

"Ch'ello, stewdents!" Miss Paletsky's voice called from somewhere in the distance, striving to make itself heard. "Please take your seats so we can begin."

"Bronwyn, Amanda, Joaquin, Christina, *Jake* . . ." Glen Morrison listed the names of the defiantly non-seated, and pointed. "That means *you*."

"Jake!" A tiny voice cheeped behind him, and he turned to where an eager-eyed eighth-grade girl sat, her tiny moon-face shining up at him. She patted the patch of floor by her knee. "You can sit here."

"Uh, no thanks," Jake replied, his utter lack of enthusiasm inversely proportional to her twittering excitement. "Listen," he said, extending his hand to Jules. "Charlotte told me to sit here. I'm Jake?"

"Oh yes, of course!" Jules swept aside the cape, gesturing for him to sit. "Charlotte tells me we are to be great friends."

"Oh yeah?" Jake smiled, resisting the urge to flick the mole off Jules's unsuspecting, Frenchie-boy face. "That's cool."

"Alright!" Glen clapped his hands together, ignoring a mysterious burst of snickering at the Back Wall. "We have a very special

Town Meeting today. Instead of the usual round of announce-ments, POSEUR, the fashion label–slash–Winston special study, would like to treat us to a presentation of its first design! Let's go, Community Expression!" he cheered, swiveling his turquoise and black Navajo belt-bound hips.

"Actually . . ." Miss Paletsky tapped the back of his elbow. "So sorry," she murmured, tipping into a blushingly apologetic bow. "But . . ."

As she leaned into his ear, Joaquin Whitman crowed, "Way to go, *Glen!*" His Back Wall cronies tittered in amusement.

"Alright, that's *enough.*" Glen returned his attention to the hundreds of students gathered on the floor. "Small correction!" He cleared his throat and gripped the podium. "Instead of Community Expression, the young women of POSEUR prefer the term . . ." He cleared his throat again, closing his eyes.

"Chic Preview." Miss Paletsky leaped to his assistance.

Everyone cheered — everyone, that is, except the clearly crushed Glen. *What in the name of Tofu was a "Chic Preview"?* He attempted an enthusiastic grin, achieving only a bewildered half-smile. "After the presentation," he bravely pushed on, "we'll be conducting our usual bagel sale, along with an exciting new op-tion, the traditional Russian *bublik,* which are very similar to bagels except somewhat bigger, and with a wider hole."

"But let us return to POSEUR!" Miss Paletsky stepped sympa-thetically forward, relieving Glen of his duties. "Are we ready to see what all the buzz is about?" she asked, testing her latest American idiom.

"Yeah!!!" the crowd blasted in unison. Miss Paletsky beamed, her mascara-hardened eyelashes fluttering behind her octagonal eyeglasses. She knew she was expected to follow her question with the standard "Are you *sure*?" or the variant "I can't *hear* you," but she refused. She had enough volume to deal with at home, thank you — in Yuri's dismal apartment, with Yuri's equally dismal family. Always the yelling, yelling, *yelling*. Why she should drum these students into a crazed froth and invite *more* screaming into her life was beyond her.

"Without further adieu," she calmly announced, "we present the POSEUR *Chic Preview*."

Jumping into action, Venice shut the lights, cued the stereo to something Fergie, pumped the cool metal bar on the EXIT, and cracked the heavy glossy wood door open. A flood of semi-hysterical chanting pumped into the hallway — PO-*ZEUR*! PO-*ZEUR*! PO-*ZEUR*! PO-*ZEUR*! At last the door was all the way open, clicking to the wall with a hollow boom, and framed the four formally dressed girls like a prom picture. The crowd roared at the sight of them (literally, *roared*) like a sprawling six-hundred-eyed monster. Melissa was the first to break away, striding ahead, beaming, and waving, and one by one her three blushing colleagues followed in her wake. Underclassmen watched them with heart-wrenching awe. They were so beautiful. So *confident*. Who would have guessed how they *really* felt? Like pirate-ship captives walking the plank . . .

"Thank you so *much!*" Melissa cleared her throat as the monster calmed itself down, its six hundred eyes blinking in the dark. She cleared her throat again. "As you know, we're here to present our work. Thank you for showing so much support. The energy here is . . . yeah." She took a breath. "The thing is . . . POSEUR begins with *P*. Which stands for patience. And at this time . . ."

"Duuuudes!" a doofy-sounding backwaller wailed. "Let's get this *shizzle* on the *rizzle!*"

"Yeah!" his comrade warbled in mock despair. "I want my friggin' *bublik!*"

Melissa swallowed, growing pale. Then with all the courage she could muster, she clasped her hands, took a breath, and:

Boom!

On the opposite end of the expansive Assembly Hall, the emergency door swung open, smacking the adjacent wall, and emerging from the flood of daylight, a small figure staggered forward, hauling what looked like a garbage-encrusted wooden plank. For Melissa, the scene was familiar, and after a moment's bewilderment, her stomach heaved. *It was exactly like her dream.* The four Oscar dresses, the mysterious intruder . . . *Trick or Treat?*

They were doomed.

But then the door clapped shut, blocked the glare of sunlight, and revealed the figure's identity. "I didn't do it!" Nikki Pellegrini gasped as the plank slipped from her weakened grasp, crashing loudly to the floor. Two blue bottlecaps dislodged from the plank's jagged edge, briefly wheeled across the brushed concrete floor, and collapsed together with tiny clatters. She remained oblivious. She simply fixed her careworn cornflower gaze on Melissa. "Venice set me up!" she explained, sinking to her knees. "It's not my handwriting. I'm free!" Melissa, Janie, Petra, and Charlotte abandoned the podium and quickly crept forward, and the student body had swelled to near hysteria, nearly drowning the puny cries of Glen, vainly attempting to restore control. The members of POSEUR gathered around, following Nikki's pointed finger to a corner of the trash collage.

"I found it," Nikki whimpered, squeezing out a little laugh. "*I found the tag.*"

"There's only one word for this," Melissa gazed admiringly at the Dumpster artwork propped above the Greenes' fireplace, which blocked a good portion of their gargantuan, pastel painted family portrait. Turning to face the other three girls, she solemnly clasped her hands. "Providence."

"Like Rhode Island?" Janie frowned, plopping into a corner of the white brocade sofa and sifting through a bowl of candy bars.

"No," Melissa scoffed in a how-is-this-*not*-obvious way. "As in the divine and all-knowing."

"Oh." Janie tore into a mini Mounds bar. "Right."

"Seriously!" She shook her head in disbelief. "If Nikki hadn't burst into the gym today, do you even *know* what would have happened?"

"A nightmare?" Janie suggested.

"You have no idea." Melissa blew some air between her lips, gazing into middle-distance. "We would have been the laughingstock, of, like, the entire fashion world."

"Oh, don't be so *dramatique*," Charlotte sighed, her customary confidence fully restored. She turned from the fireplace and smiled, extending her elegant ballet arms on either side of the mantel. "We would have been the laughingstock of *Winston Prep*, I admit. But that's not the whole world."

"You think 'cause something *starts* with Winston, it *stops* at

Winston?" Melissa rasped. "I hate to break it to you, but laughter *spreads,* okay? It's like herpes."

"Well . . ." Charlotte bobbed her eyebrows. "Turns out Nikki's the laughingstock, not us. I don't see the point in brooding over *what might have been.*"

Janie chewed sadly on her chocolate cube and swallowed. "Poor Nikki."

"I know." Melissa frowned. "We should figure out some way to make it up to her."

"Make it up to her?" Charlotte scoffed, patting her piled-up curls into place. "*Excusé-moi,* but that girl deserves what she gets."

"Come on, Charlotte . . ." Petra turned around from the window facing the driveway. "So she kissed your ex-boyfriend. . . . Do you honestly think she deserves to be tortured by the entire school?"

"Jake was equally if not *more* responsible for what happened," Janie admitted on her brother's behalf.

"I second that," Melissa agreed.

"Okay, I think we're forgetting why we're here." Charlotte abruptly changed the subject, sweeping her rose silk-tiered skirt behind her with an impatient jerk of her wrist. "Shouldn't we be focusing on our magically disappearing bag?"

"We already searched the whole house," Janie sighed, ripping into a mini-Krackel. "We can relax for, like, a minute."

"For once, I agree with you," Melissa sighed as she plopped down next to her on the couch and lifted the bowl into her lap. "Girl, you take the last Krackel?"

"I just don't get it," a distracted Petra softly interrupted. She pressed her forehead to the glass, scanning the street for Lola and her sisters. "They said they'd be back by nine."

Melissa frowned, shaking her watch. "It's 9:08."

"Sweetie" — Charlotte rested a cool hand on her shoulder — "they're *fine*."

"I know." Petra nodded. But she was worried. Within the last hour the spastic mobs of trick-or-treaters who'd dominated her street, filling the darkness with their sugary howls and candy-corn cries, appeared less and less. The last bunch to visit their door (a grass-stained princess, a tiny pirate, and their nanny, the Grim Reaper) had accepted their peanut-butter cups and gummy fangs more than twenty minutes ago. According to Lola's note, which she'd left on the foyer side table, Mr. Greene was "staying late at the office" (i.e., with that woman), Mrs. Greene was "taking time off at the beach" (i.e., checking herself into the Promises rehab facility in Malibu), and Lola and the girls were "trick-or-treating until 9." *Meaning what?* Petra couldn't help but fret. How did she know "trick-or-treating," like everything else on that stupid slip of paper, wasn't a total and complete lie?

"Trick or treat!" a chorus of familiar voices giggled at the front door, wrenching her from her thoughts. Petra exhaled, woozy with relief.

"They're back," she announced, smiling to the room. According to a tradition she'd started, Isabel and Sofia always ended their night of trick-or-treating at their own house. Nabbing the candy bowl from Janie's lap, Petra ran down the glacial hallway in her stocking feet, skidded to a stop, and flung the door open, stunned to discover *not* her two young sisters, but a portly middle-aged man in a sand-colored linen seersucker suit. His hair sat on his head in a thick white crest, like toothpaste, and his blue eyes twinkled.

"Don't be alarmed," he greeted her with a mildly British lisp, holding up a deeply tanned and beautifully manicured hand. His other hand he kept hidden, valet-like, behind his back. Janie, Melissa, and Charlotte crept into the foyer, joining Petra at her side, and he bobbed his gray eyebrows, smiling. "I come in peace," he assured them.

"A piece of what?" Melissa crumpled her forehead, eyeing the man with unapologetic suspicion.

"I *heard* them." Petra turned to her friends in a sudden panic. "Didn't you hear them?"

"You must be referring to the ever-enchanting Sofia and *Isabel*," the man chuckled and, observing Petra's rapidly paling complexion, hurried to explain. "They went through the back entrance with their nanny. Dear Isabella was *quite* insistent on this point." He shielded the side of his mouth with his manicured hand, affecting a tone of confidence. "She seems to think you'll all be *très fâché*."

"And why would we be angry?" Charlotte inquired, pleased to have so fluidly translated his French. The man nodded, clearly impressed.

"I can assure you" — he held up one hand — "this is Isabel's impression, not mine. *My* feeling is that you'll be quite . . . *pleased*."

Dropping his hidden hand from behind his back, he revealed what he'd been hiding, presenting it to them with a gentle flourish.

"The Trick-or-Treater!" Melissa yelped, beside herself. Jumping forward, she swiped the beloved couture bag from the mystery man's grip, and cradled it in her arms. "Omigod," she burbled and gasped. "My little baby. You're more beautiful than I ever imagined!"

Janie smiled at the man, resolving to check out the bag sometime later, once Melissa had had her fill. "Where'd you *find* it?" she asked, completely unflummoxed.

"Well, I suppose you could say it found me!" The man chuckled, pressing his hands at his chin. "I live just a few blocks away, on Lexington and Crescent, and I was lucky to be visited by the *bewigged* Isabel and her candy-coated companion. You may imagine, after so many dreary pillowcases and perfectly *depressing* pumpkin buckets, my absolute *delight* upon espying her *terrifically* original little handbag."

"You mean she *took* it?" Melissa realized, turning to Janie and Charlotte in shock. Petra whipped around, just catching Isabel peeping from beneath the staircase. At the sight of her older sister, her shining black eyes widened with fright and she disappeared, quick as a ground squirrel.

"*Isabel!*" Petra cried.

"Now, before you get too upset," the man interrupted, holding up his soft hands. "*When* I noticed the handbag — which I could see was *far* too sophisticated for a little girl — I couldn't help but inquire: where did she *find* such a thing? And when she told me her *sister* designed it . . ."

"Her *sister?*" Melissa scoffed, fuming to life. "Excuse me, but . . ."

"Melissa," Janie stopped her in a soothing tone of voice. "He just meant . . ."

"We *all* designed it," Charlotte explained as Melissa pressed the Trick-or-Treater to her breast like a fragile newborn. She rolled her chlorine-green eyes and shook her head. "Despite appearances to the contrary."

"Is that so? *All* of you?" The man beamed, and then quickly collected himself, assuming a more professional tone. "Young ladies, are your parents home?"

"Not exactly." Petra frowned, shaking her head. "But they should be back . . . um . . . sometime."

"I see." The man nodded, thoughtfully remaining on the threshold. "Well, I'd prefer to talk this over with an adult, if you don't mind. Would you be so kind as to present to your parents my card?"

The girls watched with quiet fascination as he removed a platinum and olive green leather card case from his breast pocket, slipping free a gold embossed business card with his forefinger and thumb. Between these two fingers, the card flicked to attention, and he slowly lowered his seersucker-clad arm.

"Thanks," Melissa chirped, plucking the card from his fingers and tucking it into the folds of her black satin dress. Janie's mouth dropped. *She wasn't even going to look?*

"Ladies . . ." The man clasped his hands and tipped into a little bow, presenting them his toothpaste head. "It was a *pleasure*."

They watched him amble his exit along the moonlit crescent drive, transfixed by the peculiar motion of shortish legs. He clasped his hands behind his somewhat rounded back, crunching the gravel under his brown and cream Ferragamo wingtips, and occasionally stopped to flex his feet. When at last the crunching stopped, Janie, Charlotte, and Petra faced Melissa, their faces collectively agog.

"Okay," Petra ventured, tilting her bewildered head. "*Why* didn't you look at his card?"

"*Because,*" Melissa defensively huffed. "I don't want to act all giddy, like, hi! We're completely inexperienced."

"But we *are* completely inexperienced," Janie pointed out.

"Yeah, but as far as *he* knows, we accept business cards every day, and his card?" She pursed her lips, and shrugged. "Just another one to add to the collection."

"Savvy." Charlotte smirked, striking a match to the end of a slender, gold-tipped Gouloise.

"Well, *that's* the kind of impression we've got to make," Melissa declared, reaching into her back pocket. "The impression that we are *not* impressed."

And then, tilting the card into the light, she released a sudden shriek, clapping her hand to her mouth.

"What?" Charlotte leaned over, squinting beneath her knitted brow. Her just-lit cigarette dropped from her fingers. "*No.*"

"Omigod." Janie read the card and croaked, almost too excited to breathe. "Do you think it's really him?"

"Okay, who is it?" Petra snatched the card. "Ted Pelligan?" To her utter bewilderment, Janie, Charlotte, and Melissa clutched each other by the elbows and danced in a little circle, shrieking Holy Ice Water. "I don't get it." She frowned, lowering the card to her side. "Who's Ted Pelligan?"

"Petra. Ted Pelligan?" Charlotte's dark pupils expanded in their glittering blue-green pools. "As in *Welcome to Ted Pelligan?*"

"As in Ted Pelligan on *Broadway?*" Melissa added, clapping her hands.

"Or Ted Pelligan on *Melrose?*" Janie offered in a semi-hysterical squeak.

"Oh, I get it." Petra winced. "This is, like, a store, right?"

The three girls returned her understatement with individualized expressions of scandal: Janie gaped, Melissa gripped her head, and Charlotte pinched the bridge of her nose.

"Pet." Charlotte gripped her by the shoulders and swallowed. "I don't think you understand. Everything I'm wearing, down to the *underwear,* is from Ted Pelligan."

"My shoes!" Melissa affirmed in a strangled voice, gesticulating to her silvery satin-clad feet. "My shoes!"

"It's a celebrity watering hole." Charlotte remained calm. "Paparazzi are permanently installed. It's like they're *light* fixtures."

"It's like" — Melissa recovered, and held up a hand, fluttering her eyes shut — "a totally important store."

"An *institution*." Charlotte nodded.

"I bought a cookie there once!" Janie informed them with a squeal.

"Dudes," Petra sighed at last, "we don't know if this guy's *that* Ted Pelligan. For all we know, he might just, like, go around handing out business cards *as* Ted Pelligan."

"Why would he do that?" Janie asked, her voice tiny with dismay.

"I don't know." Petra shrugged. "To lure fashion-crazed teenage girls to his underground sex lair?"

At that the three girls were traumatized into silence.

"Ew," Charlotte uttered at last.

"But," Janie sputtered, attempting to brighten the gloom, "he wanted to talk to a parent, remember? Why would he do that if he wasn't legit?"

"I can't take this suspense," Melissa groaned, swiping the air like a cat chasing yarn. "Which one of us has a rental on the rental? My dad's in Tokyo, and if I don't make this phone call now, I am seriously going to die."

"Well, I can't help you," Petra reminded her, shaking her tousled head.

"My mother just left for New York," Charlotte whimpered in despair. "She won't be back for a week."

They turned their tragic, imploring eyes to Janie, their last hope, and clasped their hands to their chins. "Um . . ." She hesitated. "I don't know."

THE

TRICK

Color: "Atomic Turquoise"

gold chain/ribbon handle

gold zip closure

edges "stained" with diluted dye

Front Snap Pocket

purse profile – boardshort lace-up detail

STARBURST SHAPED!!

OR TREATER

Janie   Furrish

Materials: bamboo/soy/cotton blend "silk" shell pleather interior

"This Rolling Stones member is a graduate of the London School of Economics." Alex Trebek faced the camera, directly addressing the three members of the Farrish family sprawled about the living room: Mrs. Farrish lying on the slip-covered couch, her bare foot propped on Mr. Farrish's left leg, and Jake melted across the over-stuffed sofa chair. He looked up from his homework and rolled his eyes.

"Who is Mick Jagger?" he replied.

"Who is Robert Plant?" the blonde onscreen cringingly inquired.

"Robert Plant?!" Jake sputtered in indignation while his mother clucked her tongue, flipping through *Vanity Fair*.

"Don't yell," she reprimanded, wriggling her foot. Her husband gave it an automatic squeeze.

"But Robert Plant?!" Jake repeated, glancing from his mother to the screen. "Wrong band, you freakin' *moron*!"

"Don't call the idiot a moron," his father groused, getting to his feet. "Was that the doorbell?"

"Trick-or-treaters?" Mrs. Farrish checked her watch. "At this hour?"

Mr. Farrish swung the door open. "Jake," he called over his shoulder, "your entourage is here."

Jake and his mother got to their feet as Charlotte, Melissa, Petra, and Janie shyly rustled through the door, all but filling the room with their voluminous skirts, dramatically coiffed hair, and sparkling jewels. Janie humbly separated from the flock, allowing her three friends to smilingly introduce themselves: "Hey, I'm Petra . . . Charlotte, so nice to . . . Moon, yeah like the . . . finally meet you!"

From the corner, Jake saluted, his brown eyes resting on Charlotte. She smiled, hoping her Chantecaille "radiance" rouge concealed the more honest blush underneath. *We're just friends,* she scolded herself. (If only her damn, treacherous cheeks felt the same way.)

"Sorry, I forgot to call." Janie glanced apologetically between her parents.

"That's okay, sweetie," her father agreeably replied, blithely unaware of the tension between her and her mother. Janie glanced her way — she was chatting to Charlotte, smiling her friendly mom smile — and sighed. Now that her friends were actually here, it wasn't half as bad (aka they weren't half as judgmental) as she imagined. If only her mother would glance her way — give her a small sign she forgave her — but she wouldn't. Mrs. Farrish pretty much ignored her daughter like a thing rotting in the back of the fridge.

"So then" — Charlotte spread her tiny hands, drawing the focus of everyone present — "he handed Melissa his card."

"I didn't even look at first," Melissa proudly informed the room.

"And apparently" — Charlotte paused for effect — "he's Ted Pelligan."

"Oh?" Mrs. Farrish bobbed her eyebrows, vaguely impressed. "That's pretty cool."

"Or is it?" Petra drummed her fingertips together, releasing an evil laugh.

"Petra has this theory he's a pervert," Charlotte explained, rolling her pretty pool-green eyes. She linked arms with Melissa and patted her hand. "But *we* prefer to think of him as an *esteemed businessman.*"

"Well, chances are he's both," Mrs. Farrish wryly rejoined, glancing at her daughter. She smiled. "So you want me to call this guy, is that it?"

Janie nodded. "Can you?"

Her mother smiled. "Alright," she said, snapping her fingers. "I need a phone."

In an instant, four compact phones appeared in eager, outstretched hands, ready for her disposal.

"Okay," she laughed, perusing her choices: a rhinestone encrusted Sidekick, a purple Nokia, an iPhone, and a somewhat scuffed black Samsung. "I think this one." She accepted the Samsung, and smiled. Janie smiled back.

She'd chosen her phone.

Wedging into the corner of the slipcovered sofa, Mrs. Farrish smoothed the business card on her knee, squinted, and dialed. The four girls gathered around, cuticles between their teeth, anxious eyes fixed to her every move. She leaned back in her seat, looked up, and smiled.

"It's ringing."

November 1, 2:18 a.m.

Fellow Winstonians, Fashionistas, and Fabulazzi:

So sad we never got to reveal the Trick-or-Treater at TM, and also apologies for the drama yesterday—but no apologies for the drama right now! Hold up. Let me just get this out of my system. . . .

AHHHHHHHHHHHHH-HAHHAHHAHAHHAHAHAH!!!!!!!!

Ted Pelligan—yeah, you read that right!—wants to carry POSEUR's premier couture handbag, the Trick-or-Treater!!! *For real, for real.* This is a chance-of-a-lifetime opportunity to learn the *ins* and *ins* of the fashion world. And no, that was *not* a typo. This is Ted *Pelligan*, you hear me? Everything is in, in, in. . . .

Teddy (he totally told us to call him that ya'll) told us to keep our designs on the DL for now. But no worries. Before too long you'll be able to see the Treater—and buy it—at his flagship store on Melrose. *If* you can find a parking spot!!

I just want y'all to know that we at POSEUR are truly humbled, and be sure to check in on MoonWalksOnMan.com whenever you can for all the DLs and the TMIs! We are going to *tear* some shizzle *up*.

Yours with a cherry on top,

Melissa, Janie, Charlotte, Petra

P.S. Thanks to the *fantabulous* Nikki Pellegrini, our recently hired intern (Venice, thank you for your time), a vandalized tag has been discovered and is in the process of being analyzed *right now*. So, whoever you are (and you know who you are), we're a crucial step closer to the truth, and closing in fast.

Hope you got your black suede Salvatore Ferragamo Runway Sneakers on. . . .

In the words of Sylvia von Plath,
"Everything in life is wearable
if you have the outgoing guts to do it."

So what are you going to wear, anyway?

You can be a Janie, a Charlotte, a Petra, or a Melissa . . .
or even a crazy combination of all four. (Hm . . . are you
a Janetralissalotte?)

Whatever you decide, turn the page and make their
looks your own. New York City fashion label Compai
shows you how. It's easier than one, two, um . . . spree!

CHARLOTTE'S SLIP DRESS

1. Cut off shoulder straps from slip dress.
2. Stitch thin velvet ribbon around bottom trim of slip dress in two rows.

3. Cut wings from 1 butterfly and stitch them to the top of slip dress where shoulder straps were attached.
4. Replace shoulder straps with thin velvet ribbons; measure proper length using former shoulder straps.

You'll need:

1 simple silk slip dress
1 velvet ribbon 59 in. long and 1 in. wide in contrasting color
1 velvet ribbon 118 in. long and 0.3 in. wide in contrasting color
3 lace butterflies or 4 other "sew-on" appliqués of your own choice; sewing supply stores often have a broad selection.
Needle and thread

5. Put your dress on to figure out where your waist is; mark with a pin on each side about 3.9 in. from side seam.
6. Cut thick velvet ribbon in half and stitch one ribbon end to each side where marked with pins.
7. Stitch one butterfly to each ribbon end and tie in front with a bow.

PETRA'S GYPSY BELT

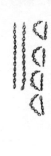

1. Carefully detach the pendants from necklace using cutting pliers.

2. Attach one of the pendants to a large hoop using needle nose pliers.

3. Attach a few inches of chain to the hoop, then a new hoop until you reach a desired length, about 2/3 of your hip measurements.

4. Cut a longer piece of chain and attach to the hoop closest to the pendant; attach the next hoop, creating a loop.

5. Continue until you reach the second pendant; finish off with a large hoop.

6. Cut a piece of chain 1/3 of your hip measurements; attach one end to pendant and the other to the watch.

7. Cut another piece of chain about 9 in. long. Attach one end to the remaining pendant and finish off with necklace clasp.

8. Your belt is ready. Feel free to attach more chains and pendants.

You'll need:

Thrift shop chain necklaces of
    various lengths
1 necklace with at least two
    larger pendants
An old pocket watch
Metal hoops of various sizes
    (hardware store)
1 necklace clasp
1 pair needle nose pliers
1 pair side cutting pliers

MELISSA'S TURBAN

1. If you have long hair, pull it back and wear it in a bun.
2. Fold your fabric in half lengthwise and drape it around your neck with each end hanging equally on each side in front.
3. Grab scarf ends and pull tight, from back of head, crossing over your forehead.

4. Bring scarf ends to the back, crossing the ends over your neck.

You'll need:
1 large rectangular scarf or a piece of fabric, measuring about 24 in. wide x 4 ft. 6 in. long

5. Bring back scarf ends to the front and cross them one last time over your forehead.
6. Tie ends in a simple knot.
7. Twist remaining ends and tuck them under turban.

JANIE'S TUBE DRESS

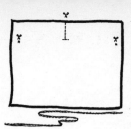

1. Cut a vertical slit at the top center of fabric about 7 in. deep.
2. Cut a 1/2 in. horizontal indent at bottom edge of slit.
3. Pierce fabric on each side of the short ends about 7 in. from top edge.

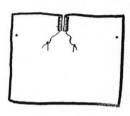

4. Fold slit edges as illustrated and stitch along the sides to create a "tunnel" on each side, wide enough for the rope to slide through.

5. Fold fabric in half lengthwise and sew sides together inside out.
6. Decide proper length of halter and tie rope with simple knot just above your bust.

7. Slip into the tube; make sure your tunnels are centered facing upward.
8. Thread rope ends through the tunnels.

9. Pull the rope ends tight, creating horizontal pleats, and tie in a simple knot.
10. Cross the rope ends and slip through holes in back, crossing once more and bring back to front; then tie a simple knot and let ends hang loose.

You'll need:

1 terry cloth wide enough to wrap around yourself and long enough to cover your knees and bust

1 thin long rope (look in interior stores—curtain string is perfect)

Needle and thread

Get ready to obsessorize over the next **POSEUR** novel.

Keep your eye out for the third book in this juicy new series, coming July 2009.

Feuds. Dudes. Attitudes.
You're not wearing that, are you?

poppy
www.pickapoppy.com

BETWIXT

A novel by Tara Bray Smith

FOR THREE SEVENTEEN-YEAR-OLDS, DARK MYSTERY HAS ALWAYS LURKED AT THE CORNER OF THE EYES AND THE EDGE OF SLEEP.

Beautiful Morgan D'Amici wakes in her meager home, with blood under her fingernails. Paintings come alive under Ondine Mason's violet-eyed gaze. Haunted runaway Nix Saint-Michael sees halos of light around people about to die. At a secret summer rave in the woods, the three teenagers learn of their true origins and their uncertain, intertwined destinies. Riveting, unflinching, and beautiful, *Betwixt* is as complex and compelling as any ordinary reality.

poppy

www.betwixtnovel.com
www.pickapoppy.com

Welcome to Poppy.

A poppy is a beautiful blooming red flower
(like the one on the spine of this book). It is also
the name of the new home of your favorite series.

Poppy takes the real world and makes it
a little funnier, a little more fabulous.

Poppy novels are wild, witty, and inspiring.
They were written just for you.

So sit back, get comfy, and pick a Poppy.

poppy

www.pickapoppy.com